DEAD AND IN PERSON!

DAVE BEAUCHAMP MYSTERY NOVELS

1. *Kill the Mother!: A Dave Beauchamp Mystery Novel*
2. *Eats to Die For!: A Dave Beauchamp Mystery Novel*
3. *Dead and in Person!: A Dave Beauchamp Mystery Novel*

ALSO BY MICHAEL MALLORY

The Mural: A Novel of Horror

DEAD AND IN PERSON!

MICHAEL MALLORY

WILDSIDE PRESS

PROLOGUE

Just because I've previously stared death in the face and watched it smile back at me doesn't mean I enjoy the experience.

As I felt the dull, metallic coldness of the gun barrel jammed into my head by someone who had already killed a half-dozen people, my thoughts turned to how my obituary in the papers would read. I realize that most normal people in a situation like this would be spending their final moments either pleading for their life or desperately trying to figure out some other way to keep from being killed.

Then again, I've rarely claimed to be normal.

In particular, I was thinking how nice it might be if my obituary described how I had uncovered the truth about L.A.'s most notorious unsolved murder spree, a serial-killer case that had spread a blanket of terror over the city more than thirty years ago. If I couldn't get the credit for that, then I hoped my obit would detail how I had cracked a contemporary string of murders so bizarre they belonged in Wonderland.

At least I *thought* I had the case cracked, but there were a few things I missed. Most notable of those was the actual identity of the killer, who was now denting my temple with a gun.

Some detective I am.

I wish I could help you, kid, Humphrey Bogart said. He wasn't really here, of course. He was a voice inside my head, one of many.

I never claimed to be on the Nobel short list for Sanity.

I wish you could help me, too, Bogie, I thought back.

But no one could help me now.

One of the world's biggest clichés is that bit about how one's entire life passes before their eyes as they are about to die. In my case, it wasn't my entire life, but rather the last week— seven short days, encompassing some of the best of times, and some of the worst—

Oh, for Christ's sake, kid, just get on with it! Bogie said. He could swear because the cameras weren't rolling.

Okay.

Well, the entire crazy affair began with the superhero in the bathroom…

1.

I recognized the guy walking into the bathroom as a man who in the mid-1960s had fought the wackiest villains imaginable every week on television, each time emerging from the serial-style fisticuffs without so much as a run in his lavender leotard.

He was "The Purple Shadow," a true superhero. He did things no ordinary man could do, chiefly maintain some shred of dignity while wearing a cape, a mask, and bright mauve tights.

"Hey, there," Tony Marsh said as he shuffled up to the urinal. "Having a good time at the show?"

"I am," I lied.

We were in the bathroom of the Renaissance Hotel, which was near LAX. It was the host site of the Hollywood Celebrity Expo, a yearly event that gathered scores of formerly famous actors together to meet their fans and sign autographs at twenty-five bucks a pop. For the most part, the fans in question were boomers who had grown up with these actors, watching them in movies or on TV back in the days when there was still a finite amount of entertainment options, which served to make each star just a little more special. Some of them were in the company of their children or grandchildren, who were more interested in their smartphones.

Then there was my crowd—millennials who were too young to see the stars the first time around, but who caught them on tape, disc or reruns.

One might think that the Hollywood Celebrity Expo would be Heaven for a total film nerd, and perhaps for some it is. But I find such events a little creepy, even depressing. While I had enormous respect and appreciation for these people, I felt that they still should be out there doing what they did best. Instead, some of them were mooching for their twenty-five bucks as unabashedly as the people one sees holding cardboard signs on freeway off-ramps.

But that was my problem. Tony Marsh didn't need to hear any discouraging words, hence my decision to lie about having a good time.

Finishing up at the urinal next to him, I said, "You know, under different circumstances, I'd shake your hand."

He laughed heartily. "Okay, son, I'll take a rain check," he replied. Then in a lower voice, he added: "As long as it's not yellow rain."

He still had a sense of humor. Anybody who appeared on national television each week wearing purple underwear had to be blessed with a sense of humor.

Tony Marsh seemed in pretty good shape for a man in his mideighties. His hair, once thick, brown, and studio-styled, was now white, wispy, and a little disheveled. His movements were certainly slower than they were back in his "Purple Shadow" days. What's more, I remembered reading somewhere that Marsh was six-foot-three, but the fellow next to me was no more than a hair above my five-eleven. Maybe he had shrunk with age, or maybe it was another example of the truism that everybody in Hollywood is two inches shorter than their press claims.

Even John Wayne was rumored to have worn lifts in his cowboy boots.

Those are fightin' words, pilgrim, Wayne drawled inside my head.

Yeah, well, sorry Duke.

To some, the fact that I hear the voices of old movie stars in my head would be an indication of schizophrenia, and maybe it is. But I've come to accept it. Sometimes the voices help me with my cases, sometimes they don't. A few chime in to wonder why on earth I ever became a private investigator in the first place; and to be perfectly honest, that's a question I've asked myself in the past.

But that was neither here nor there at the moment.

I stepped to the sink to wash my hands, and Tony Marsh joined me a moment later.

"Are you meeting a lot of fans?" I asked him.

"Oh, yeah," he replied. "But the thing that always gets me is that we made *The Purple Shadow* for kids. That was our audience. Now all these old people come up and tell me how much they enjoyed my character."

"Well, you know, Mr. Marsh, the kids you made *The Purple*

Shadow for are now about sixty."

He stared off for a moment, then shook his head and laughed.

"Judas K. Priest, how did that happen?" he asked. "But you're too young to have seen my show."

"Yes, but I'm a fan of long-gone Hollywood."

As soon as that was out of my mouth, I winced. *Long-gone* Hollywood was not the most tactful way to put it, but if Tony Marsh took offense, he didn't show it. To recover, I said, "Now that you're washed up, I can shake your hand."

Aw, *jeez*!

"Oh, no, Mr. Marsh, I didn't mean to imply that you were washed up in the Hollywood sense," I went on. "I just meant that you had washed your hands, and I…I…"

A brilliant recovery, the voice of Basil Rathbone sneered inside my head.

Tony Marsh chuckled. "I got your drift, son, don't worry yourself over it. I have no illusions about the state of my acting career. I had a pretty good run and I enjoyed it, but when it was time to move on, I moved on. What did you say your name was again?"

"I didn't, but it's Dave Beauchamp." I took his hand, surprised at the strength of his grip. "I'm here today with Palmer Hanley."

"Oh, good god, Palmer Hanley," Marsh said. "Now there's a guy who was smarter than all of us. I got into the real estate business and it was good to me, but Hanley had the brains to get out of acting and start a damned religion. He probably made more money than the rest of us put together. I see, though, where his outfit has gotten into trouble recently."

That was a mild way of putting it.

The pseudo-religion that Palmer Hanley had started in the late 1950s on a whim had over the decades become the cash-cow cult known as the Temple of Theotologics. It had been taken out of Palmer's hands decades ago, and in recent years, rumors of misdeeds and wrongdoings by Temple leadership were rampant. Not even the most outrageous of those rumors, however, could compare with the truth that finally came to light several months back.

I had a hand in bringing forth the revelations that crippled the Temple, though I took more personal satisfaction in having rescued Palmer Hanley from the Temple headquarters, where he had been held a virtual prisoner for thirty years.

Even though it was under investigation by every law enforcement entity from the LAPD to the DOJ, and even though its tax-exempt status had been pulled quicker than a rabbit from a magician's hat, somehow the Temple of Theotologics had defiantly remained open for business. It was operating in greatly reduced capacity, but it was still there.

Conversely, Palmer Hanley himself was thriving as never before. At the age of ninety-five he had finally become a star, more a testament to his notoriety than his talent—but a star nonetheless, and he was enjoying every second of it. A sign of his newfound prominence was that he had received special guest billing today at the expo.

"Palmer's just happy to have survived the Temple," I said. "He considers it his Frankenstein's Monster, something he created that nearly destroyed him."

"I can understand that," Tony Marsh said. "Hey, could I ask you to walk with me back to my table? I had a detached retina a few years ago and that eye is still a little out of focus. Makes it harder to navigate crowds now."

"I'd be glad to. Do you have anyone helping you today?"

"Oh, there are some people here who help you set up and all, but I didn't bring anyone. My granddaughter was talking about coming, but then something came up. I'll be fine once I'm seated again."

As we walked past the rows of former celebrities, I had to admit that some of the people here seemed to be having a great time interfacing with their public, and I was happy for them. But for others, the expressions of resignation and forced smiles told a different story.

Henry LeBlanc, one of the regular comic-relief bikers from the Frankie and Annette "Beach Party" movies, looked like he was awaiting a jury's verdict. He was sitting next to Shannon Freedlin, the leading lady of an early 1970s detective show called *Jim Luger* (and why TV detectives have to be named after guns I'll never understand: it's not like TV doctors are named *Ben Scalpel* or *Ivy Dripp*).

Tony Marsh's space was at the end of a row of tables at which sat Melody Britten, a Playboy centerfold from the late Eisenhower era, whose face showed more evidence of structural work than the Hollywood reservoir; Alex Johnson, the man who was inside the ape suit for the late 1980s sitcom *Gorilla My Dreams*; Mitchy Salens, a former child actor who had co-starred in *Captain Orbit*, television's first science fiction show from 1948; and Geneva Merrill, a one-time MGM specialty-number dancer who in the 1980s became an anti-drug activist.

As Tony settled into his chair, a loud, shrill voice cut through the hall: "No, no you don't! Don't you *dare* do that!"

Marsh shook his head and muttered, "Mount St. Hellcat is erupting again."

I turned around and saw a woman with salmon-colored hair sitting at a table across the aisle from us. A large banner behind her proclaimed *Cinema Legend Miranda Love*.

Not only was her billing an exaggeration, so was her name. As Miranda Shawlee—the name by which Palmer Hanley had known her—she had been a starlet in the 1950s. By the sixties she had become a minor movie star, but never achieved the success or acclaim of such contemporaries as Anne Bancroft or Lee Grant.

Miranda Love was actually the reason I was at the Celebrity Expo. Palmer had asked me to come because he feared there might be a problem if Miranda spotted him, though *problem* might be an understatement. His exact words were, *If the two of us ever get together again, someone is gonna die.*

"Why are you still *down* there?" she screamed at a fleshy man with a scraggly beard. He was kneeling on the floor of the ballroom in front of her table, angling a Smartphone in his hands. "Did you not *hear* me?"

I would have thought they could have heard her in Portland but the guy with the camera remained on the floor.

"I'm trying to get your sign in the shot," he said.

"A fucking *sign*?" she shouted back. "Is that your reason for shoving the camera up my nose? I am so *sick* of *you people* taking pictures from the worst angle possible! You always do it, too! If you really must *steal* a photo of me instead of *buying* one like a *decent* human being, get your fat ass up off of the floor!"

Duly chastised, Miranda's fan stood up and raised his phone high, pointing it down. Miranda Love responded by turning on her sweetest former movie-star smile while he snapped the photo.

"Would you like to see it?" he asked her.

"I *know* what I *look* like, moron!" she cried, her smile having disappeared like a ghost in a *Topper* movie. "And it's all *real*, too! Some of the other elephant seals here have had so many facelifts they're sporting goatees, but not me!"

"Um, well, thank you, Miss Lo—"

"*Thank you Miss Love*," she mimicked, rather accurately. "You've *stolen* your picture, *robbed* me of my livelihood, taken the *food* out of my *mouth*, now *be gone*, you freeloading cheese hog!"

The poor guy ran off and disappeared into the crowds.

"God, I *hate* these people!" Miranda Love spat to no one. Her photographs on the table showed a very young Miranda. At least the photos seemed to affirm her claim that she had not had her face altered. Her bone structure was the same, and what wrinkles she possessed were small and fine, and not noticeable from a distance.

Aside from hair color, the biggest difference between the pictures and the real Miranda was that a smile was fixed permanently on her face in the photos; whereas, without a camera present, smiling seemed to be as painful to her as passing a kidney stone.

I confess that I had accompanied Palmer here more as a way of humoring him than because I genuinely thought he might be in danger. But now having experienced Miranda Love in person, I realized what he meant.

Miranda caught sight of me examining her photos. "No window shopping allowed!" she barked. "Either buy one or go away."

I should have turned around and gone away. I know that now.

Instead I attempted to be polite.

"I watched *The Man From Tucson* with you and James Stewart recently," I said. "I really enjoyed it."

"Oh, god, I *loathe* Westerns!" she said. "Hip deep in horseshit on some godforsaken location for weeks on end, and playing opposite drawling shitkickers like Jimmy Stewart! He just stammered like a village idiot and everybody was fooled into thinking he was giving a performance."

"Um, well, he did win an Oscar."

The glare she trained on me would have cut through the door of a bank vault.

"Don't you *dare* contradict me," she said in a low and menacing voice. "You're nothing but an infant. You know nothing. Now either buy a photo or go away and stop wasting my time."

"Maybe I'll buy one on the way out," I said, then rushed back to Tony Marsh's table.

He was laughing over the top of a water bottle. "Congratulations, son, you just got a Miranda warning," he said, then took a swig of water.

"You heard?"

"How can you not hear Miranda Love? People driving on the freeway probably heard her. I've been sitting here watching her go off on people all morning."

"It takes all kinds, I guess," I said. "But it was a real pleasure to meet you, Mr. Marsh."

"Same here…Dave, right?"

"Right, Dave Beauchamp."

"If you have a card, I'm assembling a mailing list to let people know when I'm doing these things. If you don't want to be bothered, that's all right, too."

"No, I'd be happy to hear from you." I fished out a card and handed it to him.

Tony Marsh looked at it and raised his eyebrows. "You're a private investigator?"

I prepared myself for what would inevitably follow: *You don't look old enough to be a private in the army.*

I'm thirty-three years old, but most people think I'm studying for my SATs.

But Tony Marsh didn't comment on my appearance. Instead he asked: "Would it be all right if I called you sometime on a professional basis?"

"Absolutely," I said. "Do you have a problem?"

"I don't know, exactly. I've been getting some puzzling mail."

"Is it threatening?"

"No, just puzzling. Oh, it's likely nothing at all, but I'll give you a call and we'll talk about it."

He suddenly began coughing convulsively.

"Are you all right, Mr. Marsh?"

After regaining control, he reached for his water bottle and took a large swallow. "Yeah, I'm okay. I've been talking a lot more than usual today so that's most likely the problem. Either I'm wearing out my throat or I had a windpipe accident. That's what we'd call it when my granddaughter was little and something would go down the wrong way. We'd tell her she had a windpipe accident."

"I won't take up any more of your time then," I said.

As I stepped back from the table, Tony Marsh gave a little waving salute—a gesture I recognized from *The Purple Shadow*—and a gray-haired man with a tote filled with photos and books came up to speak to him. I made my way back to Palmer's table where at least a dozen people were lined up for him.

Palmer appeared to be having a good time chatting with people and signing newly-taken headshots, but I could see he was getting tired. The man was, after all, ninety-five years old.

Hannah Skaal dragged me over. She was a sweet woman of twenty-six who somehow still got away with wearing her coarse red hair in pigtails. Hannah had been Palmer's nurse and caretaker while he was imprisoned within the Temple of Theotologics compound. She escaped from the organization along with him and continued to look after him on the outside, quite capably. But the years she had spent in the clutches of the Temple, which came after a period of drug dependency and rough living, had eroded the idea that she could be responsible for her own life and decisions. In short, Hannah needed to be needed by Palmer as much as he needed her to get through the day.

"Dave, he hasn't stopped for a break all day," she said, leaning over the table to talk to me. "I'm afraid he's going to wear himself to a frazzle."

"Let me see if I can make a break in the line of people waiting for him," I said, adding that we should let through the people who were already in line. Reluctantly, she agreed.

I walked to the rear of the line and when more people showed up, said: "Hi, folks, I'm sorry but Mr. Hanley has to go on lunch break in a few minutes. Please come back at..." I looked at my watch. "... one o'clock."

That would give Palmer a solid hour to rest and eat.

Most were understanding, though one man groused about how I must think his time meant nothing.

I directed him to Miranda Love's table.

Once the last person in front of me had met Palmer and gotten his signature, Hannah helped him into the wheelchair that he didn't really need, but which made it much easier to get him through crowds. While the two of them headed for the green room, I sat at Palmer's table and answered whatever questions I could for the people who wandered by. I even signed an autograph for someone who recognized me from the news reports of the Temple's downfall, though I felt a little strange doing so.

Then without warning, the crowd of people milling about in front of the table started to part like the Red Sea, and I heard a voice shout, "Get out of my way, you swine!"

It wasn't Moses charging toward me like a runaway train.

It was Miranda Love.

2.

"*You!*" Miranda Love screamed. "I should have known! Don't you *dare* try to cover for him!"

"What?" I said, which, at the moment, in this context, I thought was pretty insightful.

"Where is that cockroach? Hiding under the table?"

"What are you talking about?"

"Don't try to be cute," Miranda Love snapped. "Where is that shitbag?"

Now a crowd was beginning to form to see the show.

"Look, lady, I don't—"

"Don't *lady* me! I'm no lady!"

"Okay, fine, you're not a lady. I still don't know what you're talking about, old-man-in-drag."

I heard a high-pitched laugh inside my head, followed by the sarcastic comment, *Always know how to make a bad situation better, don't you?*

It was Robert Mitchum.

Of all my brain voices, Robert Mitchum's had, for some reason, become my perennial nemesis. I don't know why. I can't remember ever saying anything to provoke his ghost. But if any of the stars populating my consciousness was going to poke a stick in a tender spot, it would be Mitchum. This time, though, he had a point. Insulting Miranda Love was probably not the wisest course of action.

Miranda's eyes bugged out and her face began to redden. With a violent swing of her arm, she swept all of the photos of Palmer Hanley off of his table, sending them flying everywhere. Several were caught by the fans encircling us, some of whom rushed away with their free twenty-five dollar prize.

"Hey, that's vandalism!" I shouted back.

"I'll tell you what vandalism is, you miserable dung beetle! Stealing one's livelihood, *that's* vandalism!"

I bolted up from the chair. "No it isn't! As a former lawyer I can tell you that vandalism is the deliberate destruction of property, like what you've done here."

Now a man I had not previously seen huffed and puffed his way toward us. He was extremely overweight and wearing a red blazer and a clownish, yellow bowtie. His too-black hair was crammed under a maroon fez and his too-small nose was so sharp and shiny he could have cut bread with it. While it was clearly the product of a surgeon's art rather than nature, his Cary Grant cleft chin appeared to be real. Capping his contradictory appearance was an Ernie Kovacs mustache that looked even more ridiculous on him than the fez.

"What is the problem here?" he asked, and I noticed a badge clipped to the breast pocket of his blazer that read, *Event Organizer*. "You there, why are you at Mr. Hanley's table?"

"I'm waiting for him to return from lunch," I said.

"You are not allowed to be there."

"Look, I'm in Mr. Hanley's party—"

"No you're not or I'd have seen you before," the man said. "He arrived with a young woman in attendance."

"Yes, I know, but he asked me to be here, too."

"I'm not sure I believe you. You could simply be someone who is infiltrating to get close to him."

"Well, let's go ask him then."

"He's crazy!" Miranda Love suddenly shouted. "Look at all these pictures all over the floor. He threw them at me!"

"*I* threw them?"

I pointed to the crowd around us. "Any one of these people can tell you what really happened."

"And now he's going to hit me!" Miranda shrieked, and then theatrically shielded her face with her hands. Several of the bystanders applauded her performance.

Or maybe they were encouraging me to hit her.

"Somebody here is crazy, but it's not me," I told the organizer. "She is the reason the photos are on the floor. She ran up and became abusive and destructive."

"I've heard enough," the man said. "Sir, I am going to ask you to leave the premises. I do not allow the visitors to annoy the guests. You will either leave at once or I will summon a hotel security guard."

I threw my arms up in the air and Miranda reacted as though I had slapped her.

"Did you see that?" she cried. "Did all of you see that? He struck me!"

Oohhh, you're such a liar, the voice of Joe Besser squealed inside my head.

You remember Joe Besser, right? Funny little bald man who specialized in playing infantile brats.

Since I was still on the other side of the table, and my reach was not that of a pro basketball player's, there is no way my hand could have made contact with her face, but that hardly mattered to the crowd, which was beginning to rumble ominously.

"Fine, I'll go," I told the organizer. "But at least give me a chance to say goodbye to Mr. Hanley."

"No sir, I insist that you leave immediately and—"

I didn't wait to hear the rest of the man's insistence. Marching out of the ballroom I went to the event's green room, which was down the corridor. Palmer was there, sipping a Dr. Pepper. A half-eaten chicken salad sandwich, which I knew must have been made by Hannah, sat forlornly on a plate in front of him.

He waved me over, and then got a concerned look on his face. "You okay?" he asked.

"Why?"

"Your fists are clenched, and your head's stuck down into your shoulders like a turtle's."

I pulled up a chair and sat down. "Miranda Love," I said. "I mean, Shawlee."

"Uh oh. I told you, that woman is Lady Macbeth without the compassion. What'd she do to you?"

"I was manning the table for you when she came over and knocked all your photos to the floor. Some of them got bent up."

"Well, they're only pictures," Palmer said philosophically. "What did you say to set her off?"

"Well, I probably shouldn't have intimated that she looked like George Burns in drag."

Palmer nearly passed his soda through his nose, which alarmed Hannah, who shot me a dirty look.

"Oh, lord," he said, chuckling. "I wish I'd been there to watch."

"I don't think that would have been good," I told him. "She really does harbor a lot of animosity toward you. I'm assuming she had some experience with the Temple."

Hannah involuntarily flinched upon hearing the word *Temple*.

The old man set down the soda can. "No, that's not it," he said. "I know what the trouble is. It's something that took place probably sixty-five years ago. She still can't let it drop."

"What happened between you two?"

Before he could answer a screeching voice came from the hallway: "So *this* is where you've hidden that bastard!"

Looking over, I saw Miranda Love coming toward us like a heat-seeking missile. I don't mind admitting that my first impulse was to leap up, run and hide, but I was not her intended victim. Palmer Hanley was.

"You miserable piece of excrement!" she screamed, literally looming over him in his wheelchair. "I should kill you!"

To his credit, Palmer didn't cower. "More dangerous people than you have tried and failed, Ms. Shawlee," he said.

"Love!" she screamed. "I am *Love*, and don't you forget it!"

Her words were nearly drowned out by the sounds of that new wing being built in the Irony Hall of Fame.

Hannah now rushed over and wedged herself between them. "Back off, madam," she said, firmly.

Now the obese event manager waddled red-faced into the green room. "I thought I told you to leave the premises," he panted.

"And I told you I would as soon as I said goodbye to Mr. Hanley," I said.

"Let's *all* say goodbye to *Mister* Hanley," Miranda shouted. "Permanently!"

"Perhaps you should try to calm down, Ms. Love," the organizer said, his voice an octave higher than normal.

"You stay out of this, you mustached Macy's balloon!" she screamed. "This is between Hanley and me!"

"Okay, for god's sake!" Palmer Hanley said in a surprisingly loud and commanding voice, quieting the room. "If my presence here is the problem, it's easily fixable. I'll leave. I probably never should have come in the first place. It's not like my little voice didn't tell me there'd be trouble."

"No, no, sir, I don't want you to leave," the organizer said quickly. "You're our special guest."

"Special guest!" Miranda cried. "*That* mummy?"

"Ma'am, you are really beginning to annoy me," Hannah said, reaching out as though she wanted to pinch the older woman.

The man in the fez, whose red face was now turning an unhealthy shade of gray, pointed to me. "You are the one who must leave," he said, almost pleadingly. "I can't have the guests annoyed like this."

Since my leaving seemed like the easiest pathway to a truce, I threw my hands into the air once more and told Palmer that I would see him later.

"Now wait just a second, Dave Beauchamp," he replied, then turned his gaze to the organizer. "This man is my special guest. If he leaves, so do I."

"It's about time!" Miranda Love crowed.

"No, no, Mr. Hanley, you can't do that," the man in the fez croaked. "A lot of our customers came here today specifically to meet you. I cannot allow you to walk out."

Turning to Miranda, the man said: "Why don't you take a short break, Ms. Love, and then go back to your table…and everything will be fine."

"I shall go back when *he* is gone," she replied, imperiously.

"Please don't put me in this position."

"And what position is that?"

For a moment I was afraid the obese man was going to cry.

"I think what he's saying, Miranda," I began, "is that if the choice is between Palmer and you, Palmer stays and you don't. See, he's a *special* guest. He outranks you."

At that moment, Miranda Love gave a brilliant audition for *Who Wants to Turn the Color of Grapes*? Her eyes bulged and she started to shake so violently that trained-nurse Hannah Skaal looked alarmed.

Then the explosion came.

"*Nobody outranks Miranda Love!*" she bellowed, and I envisioned the pens on the Cal Tech seismometers moving back and forth.

Mirror, Mirror on the wall, who's the rankest of them all? the voice of Judith Anderson said inside my head. At least I think it was Judith Anderson.

"I will not stand here in this palace of *amateurs* and be insulted!" she went on. "I *refuse* to stay here a moment longer! Rest assured, you will be hearing from my lawyer!"

With that, Miranda Love marched out of the green room, and disappeared, trailing repeated shouts of *"Get out of my way!"* The organizer remained huddled behind the chair, until Hannah went over and helped him up and into it.

"Are you all right?" she asked. "Do you need me to call 911?"

The man shook his head. "After last year I said I would never invite Miranda Love back, but she was so insistent. She promised she would behave." He looked up at me with million-year-old eyes. "My abject apologies, sir. I know you weren't the one who caused the commotion. But I have to cater to my celebrities. Do you have any idea what it's like dealing with fifty of them at once? Sometimes I just have to go with the path of least resistance. Who are you, anyway?"

I introduced myself and stuck out a hand, which the guy shook wetly.

"My name is Boris Verdugo," he said.

"Boris?" I asked, unable to stop myself.

"He sighed. "Yes, and I don't have a brother named Bela, so don't bother asking. Mr. Hanley, my apologies to you as well. If there is anything I can do to make it up to you, please let me know."

"Oh, I'll be okay, young fellow," Palmer said. "Don't worry. Matter of fact, I think it's time to get back to work, if the people are coming here to see me."

"Mr. Hanley, you should eat some more of your sandwich," Hannah said.

"I'm not all that hungry, and the soda pop pepped me up pretty well. So let's go. Wheel away, my dear."

For the first time I realized just how big a charge Palmer Hanley was getting out of appearing at the Hollywood Celebrity Expo. Even if he was overextending his energy level a little, I wasn't going to ruin it for him. Stepping closer to Hannah, I whispered: "With the two of us looking after him, he'll be fine."

"Okay, I can't fight both of you," she sighed, getting behind Palmer's wheelchair and starting to push.

We hadn't even made it to the door of the green room when a young blonde woman raced in. "We have a problem," she cried.

"I know, Amber, I know," Verdugo said. "Miranda Love has

stormed out."

"No, it's not Miranda Love, it's Tony Marsh!"

"Tony Marsh? He's one of the easy ones. Don't tell me *he's* giving us trouble now."

The young woman swallowed hard.

"No, Mr. Verdugo. He's dead."

3.

Everybody in the green room froze in place.

It was Palmer Hanley who finally broke the silence.

"Good god a'mighty," he said. "I always joked that if Miranda and I ever got together again someone would die, but I didn't figure it would be someone else."

"I tried to find a pulse and I couldn't," Amber said.

"Hannah, could you go check Mr. Marsh and make certain?" I asked.

She nodded and followed Amber out of the room.

"God...Tony Marsh...dead." Boris Verdugo uttered.

It was a tragedy, no doubt, but like many of the guests here at the expo, Tony Marsh was old, and sometimes old people simply die. Of course, I was not going to articulate that in front of Palmer.

The room fell back into silence until Hannah and Amber returned.

"The man's dead all right," Hannah confirmed.

"What do we do, Mr. Verdugo?" Amber asked.

"I...I...I don't know," he wheezed. "This has never happened before."

"Well, I think the first thing to do is call the police," I offered.

"Yes...all right. Amber, call the police."

The young woman pulled out a cell phone and ran to a corner to make the call.

"I don't know if I can deal with this right now," Verdugo said.

"Dave is a detective," Hannah said. "He's used to dealing with the police. Why not let him handle it for you?"

I started to protest, but Verdugo cut me off. "Would you?" he begged.

The man who wanted to throw me off the premises minutes earlier was now asking me to take charge of the situation.

Maybe Hannah thought she was returning the favor for my bringing up her nursing skills a few moments ago, but I really did not want to get lured into handling damage control for an event I had not wanted to attend in the first place.

"This hotel must have personnel who can take charge," I argued. "A house detective, or a manager."

Both Verdugo and Hannah looked at me imploringly.

Inside my head I heard a voice say: *Help us, Obeauchamp Kenobi, you're our only hope*!

"Okay, okay," I sighed, "I'll talk to the police. Hannah, you take Palmer back to his table, and if anyone should ask what's going on, say you're not sure."

She nodded and wheeled him out of the green room.

By now Boris Verdugo's color was so bad and his breathing so labored that I wondered if he was suffering from congestive heart failure.

"Should I get Hannah back in here to examine you, Boris?" I asked.

"No, I just need another minute to rest," he whispered. "This has been such a shock. If you really want to help, find someplace to take Marsh's body."

"I think we need to wait for the authorities before we move him."

"We can't leave him where he is."

"I'll think of something," I said.

On the way back to the ballroom housing the expo I passed a smaller conference room, which was being set for some kind of dinner. Rushing in, I begged one of the waiters for a tablecloth. Since he didn't seem to speak English, I grabbed a folded cloth and ran back out. I planned to cover Tony up with the cloth until the police arrived.

When I got to his table, though, the cloth dropped from my hands.

I stood there in shock.

Someone had propped Tony Marsh's body back up in his chair and was taking a selfie with him.

"Oh, for god's sake," I yelled. "What kind of person are you?"

The man with the cell phone smirked. "The kind who's going to sell this photo to the highest bidder. *TMZ* should pay a year's wages for this."

"Get away from him, you idiot!"

The man left the body of Tony Marsh walked around the table and up to me, pushing his face into mine. He was about four inches taller than me and a good thirty pounds heavier. "What if I don't?" he challenged.

I've been in only one actual fight in my life, many years ago in school, and I lost. But right now I was angry enough to rip this guy's phone out of his hand and ram it down his throat.

My face must have reflected that, too, since another man stepped in and took him by the arm.

"C'mon, Phil, don't make a scene," he said. "You've got the shot you wanted. That's all that matters."

"This guy's an asshole," Phil said. "He thinks he can tell me what to do!"

"I may be an asshole but at least I'm not a ghoul," I told him.

"Phil, forget it, man," his friend said, finally succeeding in pulling the idiot away.

Fueled by rage, my body remained rigidly tense until the two disappeared into the crowd, and I became aware that a few of the fans around me were applauding. Then the act of unclenching my fists caused me to become so dizzy that I nearly fell down, as the tension gushed out of me like air from an opened balloon. Pulling myself together, I reached down for the tablecloth and draped it over Tony Marsh.

Then Amber appeared and stated that the police were on their way.

"Why do you think he died?" she asked.

"I have no idea."

"I thought you were supposed to be a detective."

"A detective is not a medical examiner. He was coughing earlier. Maybe something was coming on and he didn't realize it. Do you have any family contact information for him?"

"There's a space for an emergency contact on the paperwork the guests fill out, but Mr. Verdugo is the only one who would have access to it."

I would have to check with him later. I did not want to leave Tony's body unguarded.

It was another ten minutes before the first wave of police arrived, followed by a group of EMTs from a rescue unit. Tony's body was uncovered and examined for signs of trauma, after which it was hefted onto a gurney. Suddenly a flurry of phone camera flashes came from all directions.

"Oh, come on, people, stop that!!" I cried. "Show some respect."

"He's not complaining," someone shouted back.

Somebody oughta belt you in the mouth, John Wayne said inside my head.

People started to form a circle around the gurney so as to get better pictures. I tried yelling at them, but it was clearly a lost cause.

Then the Voice of God sounded: "That is *enough* people!"

I don't mind admitting that I was among the many who instinctively cowered. At once, all sound in the ballroom ceased. Even the EMT's froze in place.

Looking over, I saw that the bellow had come from Wilbur Constable, a powerful African American actor who specialized in big-screen Westerns until big-screen Westerns faded out. He had also played God in a 1990s comedy called *You Can't Hide*, which became controversial in some parts of the country because a black man was cast as the Almighty.

This was years before Morgan Freeman put a lock on the role.

"Have you no decency?" Constable continued, his bullhorn baritone supported by a powerful frame and towering height that was unbowed with age. "A man has died. He deserves respect. I do not want to see another camera or cell phone, is that clear?"

While a low, muttered rumble of complaint from the crowd followed, the phones began to disappear from view. Only a handful of truly tacky people continued to snap shots, but once Tony's body had been re-covered by the EMT's, they backed off as well.

As normal sound in the hall was starting to return, I walked up to Wilbur Constable and said, "Thank you for that."

"People can be so lousy sometimes," he rumbled. "Tony deserves better than that. Hell, we all do. Are you a friend of Tony's?"

"It was a very brief friendship, unfortunately. I only met him today."

"He was a good man. One time back in the seventies I was having a rough patch and was about to lose my union insurance. Tony found out about it and made sure I got a week on a film he was doing at the time. That kept me going."

Wilbur Constable sized me up and down.

"You can't be one of us unless you were a child actor in something," he said.

"No, I'm here with Palmer Hanley."

"Oh, man, Palmer Hanley. I haven't had a chance to say hello to him yet. The first film I ever did was with him and Mantan Moreland. Something about zombies."

"*Zombie Castle?*"

"That sounds right. But how would a kid like you know about it?"

"I'm a classic film buff."

"*Zombie Castle* was no classic," Wilbur Constable said. "I was all of sixteen and in high school, and they cast me because of my height. I was six-four even then. Pretty much all I did was stand around and stare off at nothing, or shuffle around like I was dead, but it got me my guild card and enough money to buy an old junker car and take my gal out to dinner. The hardest part of that film was keeping a straight face around Mantan, who could make a cat laugh."

"I've always enjoyed his work," I said.

"He was a hero to a lot of us because he was headlining in movies way before Sidney. Then he ran afoul of the NAACP, which didn't much care for the old eye-rolling, running from the spooks stuff."

I could see Amber, across the ballroom, pointing me out to a uniformed officer, so I said, "Mr. Constable, I'm afraid I have to go talk to the police now. But it's been wonderful to talk to you."

He shook my hand with a grip that could have broken rock. "Same here, though I never got your name."

"Dave Beauchamp."

There was a flicker of recognition in his face. "Oh, sure, now I know where I've seen you. I kept up with the news of that mess regarding the Temple. That's why you're here with Palmer Hanley."

How ironic is that? I'm standing amidst dozens of old, genuine celebrities, and I'm the one getting recognized.

"I'm going to go say hi to the old guy, see if he remembers me," Constable said, turning and striding to Palmer's table, as the first policeman arrived.

"Your name Beauchamp?" he asked. "I was told you can fill us in as to what's going on here."

As I was giving the officer all the information I had, the EMTs wheeled the gurney away. When I was finished I suggested we go see if Boris Verdugo had next-of-kin information, providing he was in any condition to reply.

I was glad to see that Verdugo's color had returned and he was once more on his feet. I would have hated to give the EMT's a two-for-one offer.

Verdugo said he kept his paperwork in his car, so he lumberingly led the policeman and me out of the hotel and to the parking lot. The gurney containing Tony Marsh's body had yet to be loaded into the ambulance, whose lights were flashing even though it was not moving.

Verdugo's Lexus was parked nearby. After opening the trunk, he looked across the lot, and then dropped his head and muttered: "Oh, god, here they come."

Glancing over, I watched a television news van speed into the parking lot, the first of what would most likely be a fleet of them, each from a different station. After quickly going through a stack of papers in a leather briefcase, Verdugo pulled the one for Tony Marsh out and handed it to the officer, who looked at it, nodded and went back inside. Verdugo slammed the car trunk shut and said, "I just can't deal with this. Would you talk to the press, too, Mr. Beauchamp?"

"Boris, our agreement was that I'd talk to the police, not the media," I told him.

"I know, but I...I can't. I just can't. Please help me out."

"All right, I'll do what I can."

A young female reporter from Channel 4 who might have been Asian or Latina or African American or Armenian, or any combination of the above, was running up with her crew, a guy with a camera and another young woman with a smartphone. "Can anyone tell me anything?" she asked to the wind.

"I'll try," I said.

"Good. You are...?"

"Dave Beauchamp." I dug out a card and handed it to her.

"Private investigator?" she asked, looking puzzled.

"I'm not here professionally. I came with one of the guests."

"So you're an attendee, not a representative of the expo?"

"I've been asked by the organizer to speak to the press."

"Good enough for me," she said. "Rafael, let's do this."

Her cameraman turned on the light, which indicated to me that they were rolling. The reporter whispered, "Beauchamp, Beauchamp," for practice, and then looked into the camera and said: "I'm standing in the parking lot of the Renaissance Hotel, where—"

Suddenly an agonized wail drowned out the reporter's voice.

Turning around, I saw Miranda Love drape herself across the bagged-up body of Tony Marsh, making a spectacle of herself like the grief-consumed Pola Negri howling over Valentino's coffin in 1926.

Nobody said anything inside my head. Films in 1926 were silent.

"Is that Miranda Love?" the reporter asked.

"Yep," I said.

"Good. Rafael, refocus and start rolling over there."

As I stood forgotten, the reporter and her crew dashed toward Miranda, who was now so hysterically distraught over the death of Tony Marsh that she cried off one of her false eyelashes, making it look like a spider was crawling down her nose.

A thought struck me: the news van had shown up in no time at all, not long after the police and EMTs. How had they found out about it so quickly? Sure, news stations habitually tune in to police band radio, but the reporter already knew about Miranda Love and knew she was going to be here. She did not recognize Miranda by sight, because she had to ask me, but she knew the name.

There was only one logical conclusion: it had to have been Miranda who called the station and reported Tony's death. Instead of leaving the event, she must have heard about the tragedy and realized that she could use it as an opportunity for publicity. Now she was playing it out.

Make that overplaying it out.

I sidled up behind the news crew.

"Can you tell us what you're feeling right now, Ms. Love?" the reporter was asking her.

Miranda took her moment and then declared, wetly: "My heart is broken. One of my dearest, dearest chums in the industry, and a brilliant colleague, passed to the other side before my very eyes. I saw his spirit leaving his body, and then..." She collapsed into the kind of projected-to-the-back-row grief that would have given Gloria Swanson pause, and moaned: "I don't know if I can go on."

The reporter turned to the camera and said, "Obviously, you can see the effect that the death of actor Tony Marsh is having on his friends, like former actress Miranda Love."

Miranda dropped the grieving act like a stripper dropping her robe.

"Former, nothing!" she shouted into the camera. "I am still available for work!"

I turned and started to go back inside, but the reporter caught up with me.

"Wait a minute, we're not finished," she said. "How well did you know Tony Marsh?"

"Not well at all, except by reputation," I said, unaware as to whether I was being recorded or not. "I met him today, though I can say that from our brief encounter I found him to be a very fine gentleman."

"Okay, hold that thought. Rafael, let's get this."

Suddenly there was a light in my face, so I knew we were rolling.

"Um, are you sure this is—" I started to say, but the reporter interrupted.

"What did Tony Marsh mean to you?" she asked.

There seemed to be no way out, so I gave a brief rundown of what I knew of his career, mostly his years as the Purple Shadow, pointing out that it was not an easy task for an actor to wear garish tights and a cape and still maintain his dignity.

"Was he still acting?" she asked.

"I don't believe so. I think he went into real estate and became successful at that."

"What do you think happened to him today?"

"Um...he died."

"Yes, we all know that, but what do you think was the cause?"

Now I was getting uncomfortable.

"Mr. Marsh was in his eighties, I believe, so death from natural causes cannot be considered out of the question. Aside from that, I really have no idea."

"You don't know exactly how old he was?"

"No, I don't, not exactly."

The crewwoman was frantically working her smartphone. "Eighty-six," she called out, having gotten the information online.

"Is there anything else you can tell us about Tony Marsh?" the reported asked.

"Well, all I can say, for any actor, there is probably no better way to go than to be surrounded by friends and fans, knowing that you are still loved and appreciated."

After a beat, the reporter turned to the camera and said: "A fitting tribute to a fine actor, Tony Marsh, dead today at eighty-six, surrounded by the people who loved him. From the Renaissance Hotel in Los Angeles, this is Carina Akoti." A few more seconds passed before she added: "Okay, cut it. Are we good, Rafael?"

"We're good," the cameraman said.

"That last quote was platinum, Dave," she told me.

"I don't mean to tell you your business, Carina," I said, "but how can you be on the air with this already? I mean, I doubt Tony's next of kin has even been contacted yet."

The reporter smiled. "We weren't on live. I'll embargo everything until we get official confirmation, but by then we'll have this tape and that great quote of yours, and my close. The only thing that matters is that Channel 4 was the first on the scene."

Not by much, since the second wave of news teams were now arriving.

"Ha ha, sloppy seconds!" Carina shouted to the oncoming vans. "Do me a favor, would you, Dave?"

"What kind of favor?"

"If you talk to any of the other stations, don't give them the same exact quote. I want an exclusive."

"I'll do my best not to repeat myself," I said, and she seemed satisfied. Then she and the crew raced to beat their competitors flooding into the ballroom. I strolled in to see the various celebrities being interviewed. I was pretty sure most of them had no idea what had actually transpired, but were happy to talk to the press.

I retreated to the green room, where Boris Verdugo was fending off a young woman who was firing questions at him, while another fellow with a Mohawk was filming it for posterity on his phone.

"You are not allowed in here!" Verdugo protested, holding his hands in front of his face. Then he saw me. "You! You said you would deal with the press!"

"I can't deal with everybody at the same time," I replied.

"We are *not* the press!" the young woman said, with great indignation. "The press is fake news! We are *Hollywoodsucks-dot-com*, the premiere blog for show business truth!"

"Well, here's some truth of the inconvenient kind," I said to the woman. "He's right, you can't be in here. Let's move on."

I gently took her arm and tried to steer her out, but she broke away from me.

"Get your hands off me!" she screamed. "That's assault, and I've got it on camera!"

"Is there a problem in here?" a voice behind me asked, and I turned to see a uniformed policeman, complete with a pot belly and a droopy moustache that would not have been out of place on *Police Woman* forty years ago.

"Please escort these two out," Verdugo demanded.

"Don't bother, we're going," the woman said, "but just wait until you read my blog!"

"Looking forward to it," I said as they left the green room.

I looked for the big policeman's nametag so I could thank him personally for showing up, and I realized something was wrong. His nametag, which read *Brucker*, looked regulation, but his badge did not.

It was not from the LAPD. It was from Hollywood Toys and Costume.

"Oh, jeez, you're not a real cop, are you?"

"I'm here with a friend of mine, Mr. Gayne Prescott," the guy said, puffing up ludicrously. "I take mugshots of people who want to pose with him."

Gayne Prescott, for those who don't remember, was an actor whose dulcet, deep voice made him a natural for crime drama...on radio. But on television, his round, doughy face and short stature proved at odds with the voice. He starred in a mid-sixties cop show called *Arrest Squad*, but came off looking more like a local Three Stooges host. The show did not even make it through one season, after which Prescott regularly turned up in small parts on TV for a while, then went back into radio, this time as a deejay, carving out a niche at oldies stations.

"Mr. Prescott asked me to find out what was going on," Brucker said. "Is there a problem?"

"You could say that. Tony Marsh died."

"Which one is he?"

"Star of *The Purple Shadow*."

The uniformed guy shrugged. Apparently his knowledge of baby-boomer entertainment expertise went no further than *Arrest Squad*.

"Do you dress up like a cop often?" I asked.

"I got the outfit after doing some extra work as a policeman on a TV show. See, I'm Mr. Prescott's next door neighbor, and after I got laid off I thought I might try to get into acting. I've been asking Mr. Prescott for advice. He suggested I come along today and take pictures of him, and maybe in the process I'd meet someone and make a contact that could help me in my career."

Yes, and maybe I'm the mother superior, David Niven said inside my head.

"Are you in the business?" *faux*-Officer Brucker asked me.

"No, I'm a private investigator."

"A real one?"

"Yes, a real one. See?" I pulled a card out of my pocket and handed it to him, but it was not even out of my grip before I started wondering if I was making a mistake. "But, look, Mr. Brucker, if that's your real name—"

"It is, Terry Brucker."

"Okay, Terry, here's the thing. There are real policemen around here, and impersonating an officer is an actual offense."

"But I'm not impersonating an officer," he argued. "I'm an actor in wardrobe."

"The cops don't always acknowledge semantics."

Brucker frowned. "You mean they don't like Jews? I thought it was only blacks."

Oh, boy.

"I mean you should take the hat and badge off," I said.

Brucker did so, but he looked miffed as he left the green room.

Too bad.

Before long a real policeman, the one to whom Verdugo had given the contact sheet for Tony Marsh, entered with a distraught-looking woman. She was thirty-something, offbeat-attractive in a Virginia Christine kind of way (you remember Virginia Christine; the reincarnated Princess Ananka in *The Mummy's Curse*?), and had flame-orange hair. Unless her mother was Jessica Rabbit, it had to be a dye job. She was wearing a large pair of tinted glasses, which were not able to fully obscure her puffy eyes, red from crying.

"Who am I supposed to talk to?" she asked the policeman, who then pointed me out. Walking up, she said, "I'm Karen Robinson, Tony Marsh's granddaughter. You are…?"

"My name is Dave Beauchamp, Ms. Robinson. I'm very sorry for your loss."

"I didn't want Granddad to do this show. He's been in and out of the doctor's office the past couple months. He's on heart medication, and has been a little bit down about suddenly not being in perfect health. His doctor thought that being here might be good for him, perk him up a little, but I was afraid it was going to be too much. Looks like I was right. As I was driving him to the hotel this morning I had to fight the impulse to simply turn around and go back, but I didn't, because he seemed so eager to come and meet his fans. Now I wish I had."

"None of this is your fault," I said.

"I never said it was. I said I wish I had put my foot down and prevented him from attending. Do you have any idea what happened to him?"

"I don't, I'm sorry. I met him shortly before he…"

"Died. You can say it, Mr. Beauchamp. Hearing the truth makes what I'm feeling now neither better nor worse."

"I'm sorry. In the brief time I knew him, I really liked him."

"He had that effect on people.

"You are the next of kin, though, right?" I asked.

"I am. My mother died two years ago. Look, is there a reason I was asked to come and talk to you?"

"Well, Mr. Verdugo, the guy who organizes this event, is a little overwhelmed at present, and he asked if I could help out. They seem to be sending everybody my way now. But since you're here, may I ask a question?"

"I suppose."

"Your grandfather mentioned to me that he was having some sort of problem. He said he wanted to speak with me about it."

"Why you?"

"I'm a private investigator." I fished out my last business card and handed it to her. "He said he was getting some puzzling mail. Would you know anything about that?"

"To my knowledge, the biggest problem my grandfather had was that his garden was dying because of the drought restrictions. Other than that, he was fine. I don't know anything about any mail."

"All right. And again, I'm very sorry."

She nodded and walked away.

That was the last I saw of Karen Robinson that day. Meanwhile, the expo, incredibly, went on. The only two empty tables were the ones vacated by Miranda Love and Tony Marsh—for different reasons.

By the end of the day, Palmer Hanley was clearly exhausted, but looked as happy as I'd ever seen him.

"Whew!" he cried. "That was really something! How much did we make, Hannah?"

"About nineteen-hundred dollars," she said. "In one day!"

"Guess it was worth it, then," I said, helping to pack up his remaining photos, some of which were permanently creased as a result of Miranda Love's tantrum.

"For all of us," Palmer replied. "Well, maybe not for Tony Marsh."

As Hannah wheeled Palmer out, several of the other guests, including Wilbur Constable, made a point of saying goodbye to him. Palmer stood up out of the wheelchair so he could give Constable a proper handshake.

One parting conversation, however, was not so convivial.

A woman that I barely recognized as Edie Gogos stood in front of Palmer and glared. In the late 1960s she had been one of the versatile young musical comedians from the mod series *Tune In, Turn On, Laugh Out!*, popularly known as *TiToLo*. Then she was blonde, bubbly and energetic. Now her face was bloated and overly made-up, and her once lithe figure was now tented by a shapeless dress.

"Don't you forget what I said, you prick," Edie spat at Palmer. "I hope you die, and soon!" Then she spun around and stormed away.

"What was that all about?" I asked.

"Her daughter was another victim of the Temple," Palmer said, sadly. "She got sucked into it and it ruined her life, and now the mom's blaming me for it. I tried to tell her I was as much a victim of the place as her daughter was, but she wasn't in the mood to hear it. Hell, I can't blame her. That damned phony religion I started as a prank is going to be the albatross around my neck until the day I die. Nothing I can do about it now." Turning to Hannah, he added, "Let's just go on home, honey. I'm getting kind of peckish. Can we take some of that cash I earned today and get some good fried chicken?"

"Of course we can," Hannah said. "And you know, I wouldn't even worry about that woman. I think she was just venting. I don't think she really meant any of it."

Palmer Hanley closed his eyes. "She meant it," he whispered.

I could only pray he was wrong.

4.

The next week started out normally enough, meaning that I had no pending cases.

I still had enough in the bank to get me through, but the bump in activity I'd received after the Temple business had gone back down.

I was midway through a rented DVD of *Route Thirteen to Hell*, which I was watching on my laptop—a new and improved one, since my previous computer had been a casualty of my last case—when the phone rang. I was surprised to hear the voice of Karen Robinson.

"I hope I'm not bothering you," she said.

"No, no, not at all. What can I do for you?"

There was a long sigh.

"Ms. Robinson, is everything all right?"

"No, everything isn't all right. The results of my grandfather's autopsy came back. It revealed that he had ingested a large quantity of peanuts in some form or other on the day of his death."

"Well, maybe he snacked on a Payday bar at the hotel."

"Granddad was deathly allergic to peanuts, Mr. Beauchamp, and I don't use the word deathly in a casual way. When I was a little girl he accidentally consumed some peanut oil in Chinese food and nearly died. After that, he wouldn't go near Chinese food, just in case."

"He might have eaten them by accident."

"He was too careful for that. Trust me, I knew him. He always asked about any food he did not prepare himself."

"He cooked, too?"

"He was quite good at it."

I was jotting notes down on a pad that I kept by my phone, but it was really more of a habit rather than the desire to maintain information. Some people doodle; I make notes.

"So, Ms. Robinson, what is it you are asking me to do here?"

"Isn't it obvious?"

"Um…no."

"I want you to find out why my grandfather was murdered and

by whom."

"Murdered?"

"He would *not* have eaten peanuts in any form, which means they had to be administered forcefully. I call that murder."

Coming soon to this theatre: Murder by Peanuts, *starring Jumbo the Elephant.*

"Ms. Robinson, I only met your grandfather that one time, but my impression is that everybody liked him. Why would someone want to take his life?"

"That's what I want you to find out. You said you were a private eye."

"Have you called the police?"

"Yes, and I talked to someone who just said 'uh-huh, uh-huh' over and over again, and then laughed at my suspicions. They are more than suspicions, Mr. Beauchamp."

"All right." I recommended that she come to my office where we could talk more about it. I hoped that I might be able to convince her deliberate murder seemed like a long shot. But she professed to be too busy to make the drive, instead asking asked if I could come to her home.

I jotted down the directions and left right away. The thrilling conclusion of *Route Thirteen to Hell* would have to wait.

Karen Robinson lived in a large apartment complex in Woodland Hills, which is the further-most civilized point of the San Fernando Valley. Her apartment, however, did not look very lived-in. Unpacked boxes lined the walls of the living room and kitchen, and the furniture was sparse.

"Moving in or moving out?" I asked.

"In," she replied. "I'm going through a divorce."

"I'm sorry."

"Don't be. It's been dragging on for quite a while. But that's neither here nor there. I asked you over here to talk about my grandfather."

"Um, Ms. Robinson—"

"Technically it's Mrs., but I'm planning to go back to my maiden name when the divorce is final. Just call me Karen, okay? I'll call you Dave."

You should hear the things his past clients call him, Robert Mitchum said inside my head.

Very funny, Mitch, very witty.

"All right, Karen, but I have to be brutally honest with you. Murder is going to be a pretty hefty charge to prove, given the circumstances."

"So you don't believe me either?"

"Let's just say I've never heard of anyone dying from being force-fed peanuts."

"Then why did you bother coming out here?"

"I guess it's because I liked your grandfather."

And you don't have any better offers, a voice said in my head... and it was mine.

"But you don't believe what I'm telling you," Karen challenged.

"Look, let's say I take the case. There's not a lot to go on, which means it will be an open-ended investigation and that might get expensive. I charge fifty dollars an hour."

"This apartment might not indicate it, but I'm really pretty well off."

"Mind if I ask what you do?"

"I write songs. One song I co-wrote ten years ago was recently covered by Adele and money's coming in like I've never seen before. I have other songs that get placed in film or TV soundtracks, or commercials, but this is a new experience for me. So the thought of paying you does not frighten me. Now, will you take the case?"

"All right. I'll email you the paperwork tomorrow to make it official. But I need to point out in the interests of fairness that you're asking me to go on a fishing expedition, which means I just can't guarantee any results. Either way, though, I'll have to bill you."

"I understand."

"I'm also going to need some additional information from you. Who else knew of your grandfather's peanut allergy."

"His doctor and somebody at the Celebrity Expo, obviously," she said.

"Did the hotel provide food to the guests?"

"For the others, I don't know, but I'm certain Granddad packed himself a lunch to take. Like I said, he was mistrustful of strange food. He liked to go to this one market that had incredible deli meats, and he'd make these unbelievable sandwiches. Any time I'd come to visit, he'd have one waiting for me."

A tear leaked from her right eye and she quickly wiped it away. "Sorry," she said.

"Not a problem," I said. "Well, I suppose I'd better get started. I'll go talk to Boris Verdugo and see where that leads."

"Before you do, there's something else," Karen Robinson said. "You told me Granddad had a problem he wanted to talk over with you, right? I might have discovered what it is."

She went to the counter that separated the small kitchen from the smaller dining area and picked up a manila folder, handing it to me.

"These were at Granddad's house. Take a look for yourself."

The envelope contained five handwritten letters, all signed Michael Baroni. The name sounded familiar but I couldn't place it. "Is Michael Baroni someone you know?" I asked.

"No, but the names of his parents might ring a bell, Leonard and Rosemary Baroni."

Just like the postman, the bell rang twice.

Leonard and Rosemary Baroni had been murdered by a serial killer in the early 1980s, a killer who had been dubbed the Valley Slasher, since his victims all resided in the San Fernando Valley.

"I can see from your expression that you know who I'm talking about," she said.

"We studied the case when I was in law school," I replied, "but I don't remember all the details."

"You went to law school too?"

"I was a lawyer before getting my investigator's license."

"If you don't mind my saying, you don't look old enough to be either."

I sighed. "So I've been told. A lot. But I'm thirty-three, honest."

"Really? I'm thirty-six."

"I guess you win, then."

That made her smile.

"Since you don't remember the details of the Baroni case, they were the first victims of the Valley Slasher, in 1982. There were nine more murders over the next two years, though no connection between the victims was ever established, outside of the fact that each had his or her throat slashed. After 1984, the murders stopped. Nobody knows why, though the police assumed the killer either died or moved away."

She rattled off the facts like she was writing a book about the murders. "How do you know so much about the case?" I asked.

"I've known about the Baroni family since I was a little girl because Granddad was the real estate agent who sold them their house. The same house in which they were killed by the Valley Slasher."

"Oh," I muttered. "But he would have had nothing to do with the killings."

"Of course he had nothing to do with them. But he could never shake the feeling of guilt at having sold the place to them. Maybe guilt is too strong a word. It was more like regret. We were watching television together one time when the case was mentioned, and he lowered his head and said, 'I should never have worked so hard to convince them to buy that place.' He felt Leonard and Rosemary would still be alive if he hadn't. My mom used to try and convince him that the murderer was after the people, not the address, but he couldn't be assuaged."

I looked at the letters again. "Is that what these are about? Michael Baroni also blamed your grandfather?"

"He never says that. He says that he has to meet Granddad because he's realized the truth about the murders, and gets a little more insistent with each letter about receiving a reply."

I could see why Tony Marsh might think this could turn into a problem. If anything, he had been overly casual about it.

"Karen, do you think Michael Baroni is the one who killed your grandfather?"

"Honestly, I don't know, but I need to find out. I need you to help me. You said fifty dollars an hour, right? Do you need a retainer?"

Taking a deep breath, and expecting to have it punched back out of me, I said: "How about one week's worth, up front, forty hours? Two-thousand dollars."

"Fine," she said, going to her purse, which was also on the counter, and pulling out a checkbook. Writing out the check, she handed it over without batting an eyelash.

"Thank you," I said, pocketing the check without looking at it.

It felt good in my pants.

"May I take these with me?" I said, holding up the letters.

"Yes."

"I don't suppose your grandfather saved the envelopes, did he?"

"Not that I've found, which is a little surprising since he saved everything. And just so you know, the house in question was torn down years ago, so I know Michael Baroni is not living there."

"If he's still around, Karen, I'll find him," I said, confidently.

Don't make promises you can't guarantee, junior, Bogie said in my head, but this time I ignored him.

After pledging to keep her apprised of any progress that I made, I took my leave.

On the drive to my bank to cash Karen Robinson's check, I started thinking about how to proceed. Talking to Boris Verdugo and obtaining any contact information regarding the guests at the Celebrity Expo was Step One. There were also sheets at the front table on which the paying attendees left their names and emails, too, which might prove helpful as well.

Then my thoughts turned to the Valley Slasher case.

I knew that it was one of L.A.s legendary murder sprees, like the Manson family killings and the Hillside Strangler case, but unlike those it remained unsolved to this day. Some crackpot author a few years back claimed that the killer had been O.J. Simpson, but nobody took that seriously.

My gut feeling was that I was looking at two separate cases: the death of Tony Marsh, which may or may not have been murder, and the reason for the mysterious letters from Michael Baroni.

Well, three cases, if whatever information I turned up finally solved the Valley Slasher case.

Oh, suuuurrre, Robert Mitchum sneered in my head.

Okay, fine; I'd accept solving two out of three.

5.

After depositing the majority of the money in my account and keeping out just enough to maintain my primary vices—renting DVDs and eating—for another week, I headed back to my office. Figuring that I might as well do something to earn my retainer, I read over the letters Karen had given me, which revealed little other than the fact that Michael Baroni really wanted to talk to Tony Marsh. Then I powered up my laptop and entered the name "Michael Baroni."

Predictably, the list of sites that popped up was topped by two ad-based ones that promised to find Michael Baroni in seconds, for a price. Since they would have claimed the same had I typed in Jimmy Hoffa or Judge Crater, I ignored them.

The next dozen sites were dedicated to the Valley Slasher murders in general, but contained nothing specific about the deceased couple's son, except that he was a school kid at the time.

From there I checked a professional database, a tool that most private investigators had been using for years, but one I could only recently afford. Nine different Michael Baronis popped up for California. A further scan of the information revealed that none of them could be my Michael Baroni, given that they were all either too young or old to be a school kid in 1982.

Expanding the search nationwide still failed to reveal a Michael Baroni of the right age, which today would be somewhere around forty-eight. The Baroni for whom I was searching had dropped under the radar.

After writing *Baroni—Nada* on my note pad, I reached for the phone to call Boris Verdugo, only to realize that I did not have his number.

Assuming that there couldn't be a wealth of guys named Boris Verdugo in the world, I typed the name into the computer, feeling grateful when only two matches popped up, both for Verdugo & Associates Realty in Glendale. Apparently Boris was a realtor by day who organized the Celebrity Expo as a side business.

Maybe the real estate connection was how he met Tony Marsh, and because of that he went on to develop the expo.

First things first, kid, Bogie said in my head. *Just dial the number.*

Right.

The call picked up on the second ring.

"Good morning, Verdugo and Associates, Amber speaking."

"Oh, hi Amber, this is Dave Beauchamp," I said. "I was the guy who was with Palmer Hanley at the Celebrity Expo, the one who helped out after the unfortunate situation with Tony Marsh."

"Oh, right. What do you want?"

"Is Boris in?"

"No, he's at lunch. Are you interested in buying a house?"

"Not at the moment. I wanted to talk to him about the information that is required from each of the guests at the expo."

"Why?"

The question was so tersely direct it took me back for a moment.

Finally I replied: "As part of an investigation into Tony Marsh's death."

There was silence on the other end of the line.

"Amber, all I want is a little information about the kinds of paperwork filled out by the Expo guests. I'd be happy to talk to Boris when he gets in."

"You mean like their contracts? That kind of paperwork?"

"That would be helpful, yes, as well as contact information."

I heard another phone ringing. Amber said, "Hold on," and then put me into temporary limbo. She came back about two minutes later.

"Verdugo and Associates, Amber speaking," she said.

"Amber, it's still me, Dave Beauchamp."

"Oh." Her tone sounded like she was hoping I'd have hung up. "Okay, what is it you want, *contact* or *contract* info?"

"Both, ideally, but what I really need to know is whether any of the paperwork specifies health matters, like whether the guests have food allergies."

"Food allergies? Why would we ask that?"

"Well, you do provide food while they're there, don't you?"

"Some bagels in the green room. If someone has celiac disease, I can't imagine they'd eat them."

"I think I really need to speak to Boris. Do you know when he'll be back from lunch?"

"It's hard to say. He eats a lot."

Was she deliberately obfuscating?

I can obfuscate a little! Sonja Henie said inside my head, and I wished she hadn't.

I heard another line ringing in the background.

"Shit," Amber muttered. "Look, I have to answer the phones. Try calling back around two. He should be here then. I hope he's back, anyway, because I'd like to get lunch myself."

I started to thank her, but she had already hung up.

While waiting for Boris Verdugo to return to the office I Googled peanut allergy, finding out little except that if one is allergic to peanuts they shouldn't consume them.

Why, even I coulda told you that, the voice of Lon Chaney, Jr., as Lennie, said inside my head.

Giving up on the research for a while, I resumed watching *Route Thirteen to Hell*.

John Ireland had just gotten gunned down by the state police when the phone rang.

"Hello, Mr. Beauchamp, this is Boris Verdugo," I heard. "I understand you called while I was out."

"Yes, and thank you for getting back to me," I said, going on to explain what I wanted.

"The police still have the sheet the unfortunate Mr. Marsh turned into me, so I cannot check it for you, but in general we have no questions specifically pertaining to food allergies. If someone wants to write it in, that's their business."

"But you don't remember anything like that on Tony Marsh's paperwork?"

"What, if I may ask, is your interest in this?"

"I'm investigating his death at the request of Tony's daughter."

After a long silence, Verdugo asked: "Is this something about which I need to be concerned?"

"How do you mean?"

"Am I about to be sued?"

"Not to my knowledge—unless you force-fed Tony Marsh peanuts."

"Our guests may earn nothing but peanuts from these events, Mr. Beauchamp, but I do not force anyone to eat them. I suggest you contact the police and ask to see the form."

"Speaking of contact, I wonder if I might be able to obtain copies of the paperwork for the other guests."

"*All of them?*" he cried.

"I know it's asking a lot, but—"

"It's asking for the impossible. The records for our guests contain their addresses and home phone numbers. They give me this information under the assumption that I will protect their privacy, which I have always scrupulously done in the past. I cannot give it out to you or anyone else."

"You know, I did help you out a little bit at the Expo, didn't I? Maybe you can think of this as returning the favor?"

There was a silence.

"How about just a list of names with no addresses or phone numbers, and I'll try to find them on my own?"

Another silence, followed by a sigh so heavy I could almost smell the lunch on his breath through the phone. "Very well," Verdugo said. "I'll transfer you to my assistant and she can get you a list."

"Thanks. Oh, and a list of the attendees would be good, too."

"Oh, good god!"

"I saw people signing up on a mailing list. Can I get that list?"

"Not everyone provided their information."

"Right, but those who did would be helpful."

Another sigh. "Fine, I will have Amber photocopy the pages of address labels for you, but on the same basis as the guests. No addresses, simply names."

"How about names and cities, no street addresses?"

"Sir, I have sold million-dollar houses with less negotiation than this! Fine, names and cities, but the street addresses redacted."

"Thank you. Can I drop by this afternoon and get them?"

"We do have other work to do here, you know. Tomorrow afternoon is the earliest we can do this, and that *is* returning your favor. Come by at three."

"All right, I'll see you then," I said. "And thank you, Mr. Verdugo."

"If you really wish to thank me, buy a house. A big one."

The line went dead.

Since there was not much I could do until I got all those names (and the question of what, exactly, I would do once I had them all began to dawn on me), I did what everyone with too much time to kill at their job does: I checked my home page on the laptop.

There were no new emails…well, no new *real* emails, just a few from spammers offering to tell me how to jumpstart my career, improve my brain through pills allegedly endorsed by Donald Trump, protect my loved ones in case of death, and augment my breast size.…but then a headline in the news section caught my eye: *Former Western actor dies at 84.* Clicking on it, the full article appeared, and my body temperature dropped to the gooseflesh zone as I read:

> *Wilbur Constable, an actor whose formidable presence and booming voice was lent to the role of God in the 1991 comedy* You Can't Hide, *has died in Los Angeles. Constable's agent reported that his death Monday was the result of complications from diabetes. He was 84 years old. Constable's imposing six-foot-four height and resonant voice made him stand out in an era when African American actors were often cast in subservient roles. He gave a commanding performance as abolitionist Frederick Douglass in the 1953 film* Two Brothers, *with Charlton Heston, but his size could also trap him in inferior roles such as the giant alien in the 1957 sci-fi cult classic* Flying Saucer from Venus.

The article went on to include a few more credits, but I was only reading words, not information. My comprehension had stopped at the mention of a complication from diabetes. Wilbur Constable had looked in fine shape when I saw and spoke to him a few days ago, and not like someone debilitated from the disease.

What's diabetes look like on the outside, smart guy? Broderick Crawford barked inside my head.

What I meant was that Wilbur Constable looked strong and healthy, and if he had the disease, he was obviously managing it. Yet only two or three days after that he was dead from "complications."

As in ingesting sugar, or some other substance harmful to his condition.

Just like Tony Marsh ingested peanuts after managing his condition for years.

Was I being swayed by the suspicions of a woman who was paying me to investigate what she believed to be the murder of her grandfather? Or was there a killer out there who had specialized knowledge about his victims, particularly what their dietary weaknesses were? Even if that was the case, how did the murderer get Tony and Wilbur to ingest the dangerous substances?

I doubted someone simply walked up and said, "Hey, hi, eat this, would you?"

The killer, if indeed there was one, had to be someone that each victim knew and was comfortable enough around that the offer of food or drink from them would not be unusual.

Like a family member? the raspy voice of William Tallman insinuated inside my head. *And by that, of course, I mean like Karen Robinson?*

No, sorry Bill, but I'm not buying that one. Karen had been genuinely distraught over her grandfather's death. Even if she did nurse a secret grudge against Tony Marsh and want him dead, what would that have to do with the death of Wilbur Constable?

Even if she what? Lauren Bacall asked inside my head.

"Nursed a grudge," I said aloud.

That's what I thought you said.

"Okay, Angel Face, what are you trying to tell me?"

Then I got it.

Nursed a grudge.

Took you long enough, kid, Bogie said. *By the way, don't get so familiar with the missus.*

Who would know the specific afflictions of any number of older people and be trusted to dispense medication to them? Who might visit a senior's home periodically to offer dietary advice as well as medicine, and do so without arousing any kind of suspicion?

A nurse.

All well and good, but what connection did that have with Michael Baroni and the Valley Slasher case?

I had no answer for that one.

6.

Any hopes that calling Karen Robinson would result in a quick answer regarding the employment of a home nurse crashed and burned in my ear. I got no further than her voicemail.

After the beep, I framed my message more from the standpoint of having started the investigation—to give her the impression that she was not wasting her money, if nothing else—and then broached the subject of nursing. Since I wanted to talk to her as soon as possible, I left my office, cell, and home numbers.

By six o'clock she had not called back, so I locked up the office and headed for home, where I knew a frozen turkey pot pie cried out to be nuked.

I noodled around the internet for the rest of the evening, all the while trying not to obsess over the problems of this case, the biggest of which was that I didn't have the faintest idea what any of it meant. Tomorrow, after I received the information from Boris Verdugo, I hoped I would be able to start connecting enough dots to come up with a rough sketch of a solution, but of course there was no guarantee of that.

Which was why I was so restless tonight.

I tried to stop obsessing after brushing my teeth and changing for bed, but it didn't work. After tossing and turning for most of the night I finally gave up on the thought of meaningful sleep about 1:30 in the morning.

Then I promptly fell asleep.

The insistent ringing sound at 6:40 the next morning caused me to lurch out of bed and stumble to the phone.

"Hi, I hope I didn't get you up," Karen Robinson said when I answered.

"Hmm? Oh, no, I was asleep anyway," I drawled through a yawn, which drew a laugh from her.

"Sorry. But I wanted to get back to you about the nurse question. Do you mean someone who lived in and took care of him?"

"Yeah, like a regular nurse who came into the house."

"Then the answer is no. Granddad was capable of taking care of himself. He saw doctors, but nobody came over on a regular basis. Why is this important?"

"I'm just covering all the bases," I said.

"Anything else?"

"Not yet." I yawned again. I couldn't help it.

"Sorry again for calling so early," she said. "There's just so much to do, and no one else to help, that I'm trying to get a jump on things."

"I should probably let you go about your business then."

"And go back to bed?"

"Oh, now that I'm up, I doubt it."

"Keep me posted."

"I will, and good luck with all your stuff."

"Thanks. I have an appointment to talk to the casket salesman this afternoon," she said. "I'm looking forward to that like a scheduled amputation."

She rang off.

I scratched "nurse" off of the list inside my head and got in the shower.

Since I often do my best thinking standing under the water, I was hoping maybe I'd get an inspiration. But, no. The best I could claim was the washing away of the notion that the deaths of Tony Marsh and Wilbur Constable were tied together. Both, after all, were in their mid-eighties, and even though they had been together in a hotel ballroom a few days ago did not mean their fates were connected.

And let's be completely honest: there was no real, actual proof that Tony Marsh was murdered.

After dressing, I started to fire up the coffeepot, but then had a better idea. Since I had risen earlier than usual and had money in my pocket, I decided to take myself out for breakfast. It had been a dog's age since I'd had a professionally prepared plate of sausage, eggs and hash browns.

Bindy's Coffee Shop was halfway between my apartment and my office. It was one of the last original post-war diners in L.A. boasting Googie architecture, complete with a ski-jump roof and sculpted neon signage.

You've seen the place in films and on TV dozens of times.

I was offered a booth but opted instead for the counter and gave my order. Someone had left a copy of the *Times* there, so I picked it up and started perusing. I usually get my news from the radio, TV or computer, but actually holding a newspaper is nice every now and then.

I started with the most intelligent and meaningful section first. Upon finishing the comics page my food arrived, delivered by the perky waitress.

The eggs were perfectly cooked, the hash browns tasted like potatoes instead of plastic strips that had been soaked in oil, and the sausage was so fresh it might have been oinking yesterday afternoon. Even the toast was done perfectly. I savored every bite, knowing that eating such a large breakfast would probably mean I didn't have to worry about lunch that day.

It was only after my third cup of coffee that my stomach began to turn, and it wasn't because of the food.

It was because of the article in the *Times*.

Television comedienne Edie Gogos dies at age 72, I read.

She had been found dead in her Torrance, California home. Authorities were still investigating, but her death appeared to be due to a freak accident: she had apparently died from the stings of wasps, several dozen of which were found inside her house.

It was Edie Gogos who had wished Palmer Hanley a quick death at the Celebrity Expo because her daughter had been a victim of the Temple. While the deaths of Tony and Wilbur, one right after the other, might be chalked up to coincidence, what were the odds of a third? Astronomical, I'm sure.

Just like I was pretty sure that research would show Edie Gogos was allergic to wasp venom.

But what proof did I have of anything?

After settling up with the waitress I headed back for the office, forcing myself to keep my attention on the traffic lights and the other cars, many of which were apparently being driven by graduates of the Braille Institute, rather than trancing out and obsessing about what appeared to be a diabolically clever string of murders.

Back at my building, which was a rare commercial example of 1950s "Dingbat" architecture—

How fitting, Robert Mitchum zinged inside my head.

—I stowed my car in the carport and went up to my office. Once there I noticed the blue light on my phone
had a message. I hoped it was Boris Verdugo telling me not to wait until early afternoon to pick up the contact sheets from the expo, but to come on by right away.

It wasn't.

Mr. Beauchamp, the voice said, pronouncing it buh-SHAWM, *my name is Jay Leach, esquire, and I am calling you on behalf of my client Ms. Miranda Love. Ms. Love has instructed me to file suit against you for public defamation of character in regards to an incident that occurred on Saturday, May 21st, at the Renaissance Hotel in Los Angeles. I am certain you remember the incident in question, and may I say, you should be ashamed of your rude and reckless behavior against a woman who never did you any harm.*

Like Godzilla never did any harm to Tokyo, the voice of Cary Grant said inside my head. It took a second to figure out why Cary Grant was talking about Godzilla. Then I got it: *Destination Tokyo*, 1943.

My particular brand of insanity may work in strange and mysterious ways, but it is often logical.

Leach's voice went on: *You will, of course, want to consult with your own attorney, and for your sake I hope he is good. We will be sending you an official summons in short order, and don't even think about trying to avoid it because our servers are the best in the business. This call is merely a courtesy, to let you know of Ms. Love's intent. Have a nice day.*

I'd be the first to admit that I was no great shakes as a lawyer—

(*And I'd be the second*, Gregory Peck said inside my head; thanks, Atticus)

—but even I had never heard of an attorney tipping off a defendant that a summons was coming. Either Jay Leach, esquire, was attempting to intimidate me, or he did not expect me to take the call seriously. Whichever it was, I made a mental note to ask Boris Verdugo when I saw him if I could use him as a witness to the incident with Miranda Love, just in case.

My next mental note was to wonder why, if someone really had to kill off old actors, they couldn't have started with her.

So much had already happened this morning and it was only

9:53. How was I going to occupy myself until it was time to go see Verdugo?

I decided to go see Palmer Hanley.

The reasoning was three-fold. One, Palmer liked to talk, so any visit with him required a lot of time, which at the moment I had to spare; two, I could also line up him and Hannah Skaal, who lived with him, as witnesses if Miranda's suit actually went to trial; and three, I could find out if he had any allergic weaknesses.

Palmer had moved into the Los Feliz Parkview Apartments, a striking art deco edifice in a neighborhood just north of Hollywood that had once been home to the likes of Cecil B. DeMille, W.C. Fields, and Basil Rathbone. While the neighborhood has lost some of its sheen since the 1930s, it had proven to be blessedly resistant to modern demolition and development.

Parking was a problem, but I was finally able to scavenge a spot on the street right as someone in a mini-van was vacating it.

At the front door I punched in Palmer's code and waited for Hannah Skaal to reply. After she buzzed me in, I checked in with the security guard at the lobby desk. He then walked me to the elevator and used a card to program it to go to the ninth floor.

Unlike my building, the Los Feliz Parkview had security.

Hannah was waiting for me when I got off.

"Hi, Dave," she said. "Is anything wrong?"

"No," I fibbed. "I just came by to see how Palmer was doing."

"He'll be happy to see you."

After ushering me into the apartment, she called: "Mr. Hanley, Dave Beauchamp's here."

Palmer Hanley emerged from his bedroom. He was upright and walking, instead of seated in a wheelchair, but was still in his pajamas.

"Hey, there, young fellow," he said, cheerfully, extending his hand. "What brings you here? Is it Take A Broken Down Old Man To Lunch Day already?"

I shook his hand and said: "If it was, I'd be calling on Gayne Prescott instead."

"Oh, Mother of Mary!" he laughed. "Don't let him hear you say that! Well, whyever you're here, it's always good to see you."

"Thanks. I was in the neighborhood and thought I'd pop in to see how life was treating you."

"Life? Who knows? But Hannah's treating me like royalty."

Behind him, Hannah smiled.

Framed by her cascading red hair, it was a nice smile.

Palmer walked toward the white sofa and half-fell onto it. "Sit down, son," he bade.

I seated myself in a chair across from the sofa and accepted Hannah's offer of an iced tea.

"You think you could bring me a Pop Tart, too?" Palmer asked her. Then turning to me he added: "I dang near got addicted to those things in captivity, and you know why? Because eating Pop Tarts was the only thing I had control over. I couldn't leave the place, I couldn't even move very far, and I didn't have many people to talk to. But whenever I wanted a Pop Tart, they ran and got one for me. Sometimes I'd set my alarm for three in the morning, just so I could get up and request a Pop Tart, 'cause I knew it made someone get out of bed and run for it."

When Hannah returned from the kitchen she had my tea in one hand and an unwrapped strawberry Pop Tart in the other, which she handed to Palmer.

"So, Dave Beauchamp," he said, having never lost the habit of calling me by my full name by way of a nickname, "what else can I do for you?"

"Well, maybe something in a matter regarding Miranda Love."

"Oh, murder."

First things first, Peter Lorre said inside my head.

"Remember that little altercation we had with Miranda at the Celebrity Expo?" I went on.

"Hard to forget," Palmer said. "You know how some people mellow as they get older? I think Miranda has gotten sharper, like cheese. How someone can stay so angry for so long is beyond me. What's she doing to you?"

"She's suing me."

"For what?"

"Defamation of character."

"Oh, that's plain silly."

He took a big bite out of the Pop Tart, in the process dropping crumbs all over himself.

"Yes, I know," I said, "but a lot of silly lawsuits get filed these days. I was wondering if I could ask you and Hannah to back me up as to what really happened between Miranda and me at the Celebrity Expo, if this goes to deposition."

"Fine with me," Palmer Hanley said. "I'm sure it's fine with Hannah, too."

But Hannah Skaal's expression did not reflect that it was fine. She had suddenly gone pale.

"Dave, you didn't get a phone call from someone named Leach, did you?" she asked.

"Yes, Jay Leach, attorney-at-law," I replied. "How did you know?"

"He called here, too."

"What?" Palmer asked. "What are you talking about?"

Hannah went to the old man's side. "I didn't want to bother you with it, Mr. Hanley, but a lawyer called here yesterday and threatened to sue you, too. He said it had something to do with that actor show. I'm worried."

"Oh, now, honey, after everything we've been through together, a lawsuit'd be a walk in the park."

"Hannah, have you received any kind of document giving instructions for a court appearance?" I asked.

"No, nothing like that."

"Good. Let's hope this is all bluster."

Now Hannah began to look like a puppy whose owner just came home to find the living room under a snow drift that had once been a box of tissues.

"I may have gotten us in trouble," she said. "Something I said."

"What did you say?"

She looked at the floor. "I told this Mr. Leach what I thought of Miranda Love and then slammed the phone down."

"Is that all?"

She nodded.

I glanced over at Palmer Hanley, who merely shrugged.

"Tell me exactly what you said."

"I said Miranda Love was something that rhymes with *witch*. I still think she is, too."

"Did you actually say that she was a bitch?"

Hannah looked shocked. "No!"

"Then I don't think you have anything to worry about," I told her. "As far Leach or as anyone could prove, all you did was call Miranda Love *rich*."

Upon hearing that Hannah visibly relaxed, but now it was my turn to frown.

"But I just realized something," I said. "If all three of us are being named as codefendants in the same suit, I don't think we can't be witnesses for each other. Hannah, let me know if any paperwork about this comes in, okay?"

"Sure," she said.

"Since we're on the subject of the Wicked Witch of the West Coast, though, do you mind if I ask, Palmer, what caused the rift between you and Miranda?"

"Oh, heavens," he sighed, wiping the Pop Tart sprinkles from his fingers. "Make yourself comfortable, Dave Beauchamp. This might take a while."

7.

"Okay, then," Palmer Hanley began. "It was back in the fifties, '52, '53, somewhere around there. You know about live television, right, Dave Beauchamp?"

"Yes, I know."

"'Course you do. What was I thinking? Anyway, back then Miranda used the name Shawlee. She was just starting out, I think. But despite her youth she was savvy enough to know how to get backing from a producer, if you know what I mean."

"I'm not sure I do."

Palmer Hanley leaned in and whispered: "Spent a lot of time in the producer's office, on her back."

"Ah."

"I can't remember the producer's name anymore, but he was a big one in town, and Miranda was his protégée. A lot of producers had young female protégées back then. The saying was they're still protégées because they haven't turned pro yet, if you know what I mean."

"Yes, that one I got."

I was starting to wonder if I should hook Palmer up with my friend Jack Daniels, who happened to be a bestselling author, so the two of them could write a book called *The Golden Age Hollywood Glossary*.

"The point is," Palmer went on, "Miranda's patron of the arts kept dangling a studio deal over her head. Probably something else, too but we won't go into that. But it was just to keep her within reach. The scuttlebutt was the guy wasn't sold enough on her acting ability to actually put her under contract."

"Did it really matter? Her acting talent, I mean?"

"Yeah, some. I mean, in a lot of films from that era, you see, the leading lady is given the full star promo treatment, like they did with Lauren Bacall in the forties. And Betty…that was her real name, Betty Perske…just got better and better after she married Bogie. But some of those gals that got the same build-up, you never saw again. The movie magazines might have said it was because they wanted to retire and get married and start a family, and all that. But a lot of times it was because when the actress finally earned her big break, it turned out she couldn't hack it on camera. Boy, I can relate to that."

I knew Palmer's story well. He had been fine on stage, but for some reason, the motion picture camera proved to be a cruel mistress, robbing him of any semblance of life. Whatever photographic alchemy it was that turned Marilyn Monroe into a goddess, it had the opposite effect on Palmer Hanley. His failure as a film actor was what led him to create a pseudo-religion for quick money.

"So Miranda's benefactor didn't think she could act," I said, hoping to bring him back on point.

"Hmm? Oh, right. He didn't, but that wasn't really what he was grooming her for, either. So it was up to her to prove that she could carry a role. She landed a job on a live television show, one of the better programs. Might have been *Studio One*, I don't recall. The part was a good one and she was pulling it off. But then a day or so before airtime, the leading man on the show got subpoenaed by the committee. I presume you've heard of the McCarthy witch-hunting committee?"

"Oh, yes."

"Well this actor's name was in that book, the one that listed all the would-be Commies. Oh, what the hell was it called?"

"*Red Channels*?"

"Yeah, that's it, *Red Channels*. God, what a mess that damn little pamphlet made of things."

He paused, seeming to be deep in thought. Then he said: "What was I talking about?"

"The actor in the live TV show was pulled before HUAC," I prompted.

"Yeah, HUAC. Damned committee. There were maybe only four or five actual Communists in town during those years, and they were waiting for their paychecks like everybody else. Anyway, this actor was subpoenaed right before the broadcast and that scared the network to death. To make sure the sponsors didn't back out, they dropped the guy like he was covered in worms. He had to be replaced in a hurry. So, Dave Beauchamp, guess who got the job?"

"You did?"

"Yep," Palmer Hanley said, grinning. "Everybody else was working or blacklisted, and since I wasn't working enough to get blacklisted, I got the gig. They needed someone and there I was, and I needed a job, so I took it."

"Seems reasonable."

"Yeah, well, the problem was, during the last dress rehearsal on the day of the show, everything fell to pieces. It became clear to everyone else what I knew from the git-go, which was that I was dead-bang wrong for the part. It called for a John Derek type, handsome as hell, and that wasn't me. The producer was yelling at the writer, the writer was yelling at the director, the director was yelling at me, and Miranda was yelling to everyone that they should never have dropped the original actor, or if they really had to, they should have found a suitable one to replace him. Everything fell into such a shambles that the network decided to pull the plug on the whole damned show."

"Cancelling a live television show seems a bit risky," I said. "How did they fill the time slot?"

"Well now, Dave Beauchamp, that was the interesting part. You're right. The network suddenly had ninety minutes to fill up and only a few hours to figure out how. Someone said, 'Oh, let's just run the kinescope of last week's show, but they didn't want to do that because the television critics, who were all pretty vicious back then, wouldn't have stood for it. But time was running out and the options were running...outer, I guess. Then I had a brainstorm."

He requested another Pop Tart and a glass of ice tea from Hannah, and in the pause I asked: "What did you suggest?"

Hannah brought him his pastry and tea, and he took a bite, chewed it, swallowed it, then washed it down.

I suspected he was enjoying leaving me hanging with his tale.

"What did I suggest, you ask?" he said, finally. "Well, once I got the director to stop yelling at me, I suggested they go down the street and see if there was any Broadway show that could play in front of the cameras. It was a Monday, so all the theatres would be dark, but the actors would already be rehearsed, and all you had to do was bring them into the studio and point a camera at them. Even if you just got a handful of them to sing the songs from their show in front of a curtain, like they did later on the Sullivan show, it would fill up the time. So someone started checking up on the legit shows and they found one that was perfect. It was some English actor...I can't remember his name now...but he was doing a one-man show on Charles Dickens, with almost no sets and only a few props. They tracked him down and made a deal for him to do the show live on TV, right then and there. All the studio had to do was turn on the lights and follow the guy around with the cameras. So in the course of about forty-five minutes I went from being the saboteur of the network to the guy who saved everyone's cans. The network was so happy they gave me five hundred bucks, which I needed. The actor playing Dickens...he had an odd first name, that's all I remember about him...he was thrilled to do it, too, since it was one long commercial for his play. When he found out it had all been my idea, he slipped me another fifty. He and the show wound up winning Emmy awards."

He finished off his Pop Tart and took a swig of his ice tea.

"But there was one person who wasn't happy at all," Palmer continued. "Miranda Shawlee. Or Love, I guess. Not only was she robbed of the chance to prove she could act, but her producer found out that she and the show's director had been engaging in some private rehearsal sessions at night, if you know what I mean. So he banished her from the movie studio, and she had to wait a few more years to get her big break. She didn't chalk it up to bad luck, or even the fact that she did herself in because her legs were like the wings of an eagle...ready to spread at moment's notice."

Hannah gasped, but also smiled.

"Miranda blamed me for all of that," Palmer said. "Still does, even though she later changed her name and got her career back on track. But that, young fellow, is why Miranda wants to kill me, because of something that happened a lifetime ago. Now, then, Dave Beauchamp, since I'm all wound up, is there anything else you want to know?" he asked.

"Well, one thing, Palmer," I said. "Are you allergic to anything?"

"Allergic?"

"Yeah, you know, do you have an intolerance to food or drink or medicine? Anything?"

"I had a doctor one time ask me that, and I told him I was allergic to only two things, horses and pain."

"Horses?"

"Yeah. I was cast in a Western once, just a bit part, like usual, but I had to leave the set 'cause the damn horses made me sick. Stayed away from them after that."

"I don't blame you."

"Why are you asking about allergies?"

"Oh, no reason, really," I lied. "I just heard something on the radio on the way over is all. The incidence of peanut allergy is growing and nobody knows why."

"Well, I never cared for peanuts all that much, and since I don't plan on doing any steeple chasing any time soon, I guess I'm safe."

That was my assessment of the situation as well, since it would be a lot harder to slip somebody a horse without being detected than it was a bit of dangerous food.

I could see that despite the sugar rush from the Pop Tarts, and the high from having a captive audience, Palmer was beginning to crash. Ever vigilant, Hannah asked if he wanted to go back to bed.

"I don't want to be a bad host," he said.

"Oh, that's not a problem, Palmer," I said. "I have to be on my way anyway."

After we said our goodbyes, Hannah escorted him to his bedroom, returning just a minute later.

Walking up close to me, she whispered: "He didn't sleep very well last night."

"That's all right," I whispered back. "I really do have to go."

"It was nice seeing you, Dave."

"Nice seeing you, too, Hannah. He's really lucky to have you."

She beamed, and stepped closer.

Not having been this close to her since the time we were both struggling to escape from the Temple of Theotologics compound, I'd forgotten how good she smelled.

I took my leave.

Glendale was not that far away—in fact, Los Feliz Boulevard could be thought of as the bar of a weight set with Glendale on one end and Hollywood on the other—but it was still too early for me to descend upon Verdugo & Associates.

To kill time I drove around the residential foothills of Griffith

Park, taking in all the houses, which were not quite mansions, but still impressive.

Not only could I *not* afford one of those houses, I probably couldn't even afford a good oil painting of one.

Ordinarily I would have stopped to grab a bite of lunch, but I was still full from breakfast. Instead I parked on Vermont Avenue—a challenge in itself—and strolled up and down the street, poking into Skylight Books, and wandering through the many antique stores that now dotted the neighborhood. In one I almost bought a vintage gray fedora, but decided it was too expensive. I don't know how Bogie afforded them.

They were cheaper than the shag carpets Warners plastered on my dome, he responded in my head.

After wasting enough time on Vermont, I headed toward Glendale.

Early or not, here I come.

Traffic was a mess all the way to the Mulholland Fountain, which was across from the entrance to Griffith Park, and then it lightened.

Who knows why?

I stopped to top off the gas tank and, leaving the station, managed to get lost.

It probably takes talent to get lost in Glendale, but I'll take anything I can get.

By the time I managed to find the street address for Verdugo & Associates, I was no longer all that early. It was a sub-address located behind a medical building, across the street from the Glendale Galleria. Unfortunately, I missed the nearly hidden driveway that led to its parking lot and ended up a block south, where I parked on the street. That wasn't the bad part, though. The bad part was that there was no access to the lot from that street, so I had to clamber over a concrete wall. Clambering was not my strong suit.

You're out of shape, son, go get yourself fit, Burt Lancaster admonished in my head.

Like Scarlett, I'd worry about that tomorrow. Right now I hoped no one inside any one of the small offices lined up next to each other was watching me scale the wall with all the *élan* of Oliver Hardy.

Crossing the parking lot, I walked into the tiny office, which was cramped and decorated with what looked like thrift store artwork.

Seated at a desk, Amber was barely visible behind a large and not particularly new computer monitor.

"Can I help you?" she asked, without looking up.

"It's Dave Beauchamp. I know I'm a little early, but I was hoping—"

Now she glanced up at me. "Oh, yeah, you," she said. "I got the stuff for you. The boss hasn't come in yet, which is weird, so I didn't have anything else to do."

She got up and thrust a stack of papers at me. A quick glance revealed copies of the address labels, written in hundreds of different handwritings, and a list of the celebrities. The labels were indeed redacted.

"I was up half the night crossing out the street names," she said.

"Thank you. This will help a lot."

"Good. And now that you've got them, I can finally go get something to eat."

"Before you go, there's one other thing that might be helpful. Do you have a prepared general information sheet for the guests, letting them know what to expect on the day of the show?"

"Yeah."

"Could I get a copy?"

"You want the one for general guests or special guests?"

"Both."

Amber opened a drawer, pulled out two sheets of paper, and then handed them to me.

"I really hate these expos," she grumbled. "I don't get paid any extra for working on them. Now, is there *anything else*? Wash your car, maybe?"

"Uh, no, that's it. Thank you again."

I started to leave, but at the door turned back. "Out of curiosity, you said it was weird that Mr. Verdugo hasn't come in yet. What did you mean by that?" I asked.

"Like I said. He's usually here by now. This is the first time he's not shown up at all."

"Have you tried calling him?"

"Of course I've tried calling him. I hate being left here alone. I'm not supposed to leave unless he's here, but it's after two."

"There was no answer at his house?" I asked.

"No answer."

"Doesn't that worry you?"

"I'm not paid enough to worry," she said. "Now, if you don't mind, I'm starving."

"He's never left you on your own before," I thought out loud.

"Am I going to have a problem with you?" she asked, reaching into her purse.

"No, no, I'm just having some troubling thoughts."

She pulled a can of pepper spray from her bag. "They better not involve me."

"They involve your boss."

"Eeuwww," she uttered.

"I don't mean it that way! Look, Amber, do you remember when I asked if the forms you send out to your celebrities had a section covering food or drug allergies?"

"Sure, and I still think it's dumb."

"Does Boris have any such allergy?"

"To food? Are you kidding? No, he doesn't...oh, wait."

"What?"

"One time I was cleaning the office toilet, which is part of my exalted duties here, and I put on some rubber gloves, and Mr. Verdugo nearly had a cow. He told me to get rid of them immediately. He said he'd nearly died once when he came into contact with latex rubber. Isn't that weird? Of all things to be allergic to."

"Do you know where Boris lives?"

"Yeah, but I can't give out his address. He's insistent on that."

"Will you take me there, then?"

"That's kind of the same thing, isn't it?"

"It might be important," I argued. "We can go in my car. I'll bring you back."

"But I'm hungry."

"We'll stop somewhere and I'll buy you lunch."

She regarded me with an expression of concern for the first time.

"Shit, you really think something might have happened to him, don't you?"

"I have reasons to worry, Amber, though I pray they're wrong. I really do. Now, will you take me to Boris's house?"

She held the pepper spray can in front of my face.

"Okay, but you try anything funny and they'll be dishing up your eyeballs at Chipotle."

Amber was in no mood to clamber over the wall to get to my car, so I had to do it (the sight of which seemed to make her day), get the car, and drive around to the front to pick her up. Fortunately, she was still there. Maybe in her own way she was worried about the fat man, too.

At her insistence we stopped at a nearby fast-food joint where she ordered a rice bowl with some sort of fish on top. As bad as it smelled in the restaurant it was even worse inside the car. I doubted Bruce, the Shark from *Jaws*, would willingly eat whatever topped the bowl, but Amber said she patronized the place all the time.

Maybe it was an acquired taste.

Like cheap rye, or getting hit on the head with a sap, Bogie said, helpfully.

I was heading toward Glenoaks Boulevard, per Amber's directions, when she said through a mouthful of rice: "You know, we're probably being dumb."

"How so?"

"I just remembered Mr. Verdugo had an appointment to show a house somewhere in the valley this afternoon, so he might be out there prepping the place."

"Wouldn't he call the office to let you know where he was?"

"He always has in the past, but..." She shrugged.

"Better dumb than sorry, Amber."

The home of Boris Verdugo was less than five miles away from his office, on the border of Glendale and Burbank. It was a tiny guest house in back of a vintage Craftsman-style home. You would think a realtor would have a fancier place of his own, but maybe this is why he didn't want Amber giving out his address.

That, however, was a minor surprise compared to the main attraction: the body of a very large man, naked except for an exceedingly overtaxed Speedo, lying face-up at the bottom of the swimming pool that separated the two houses.

Anyone else might have questioned the identity of the body, given that the face was covered.

But since it was covered by an over-the-head, latex Halloween clown mask, I had no doubt that it was Boris Verdugo.

8.

Amber sunk to her knees at the edge of the pool, not crying, but gasping.

"Oh my god, I'm going numb," she panted.

"You're hyperventilating," I told her. "Cup your hands over your mouth and try to control your breathing."

She did so, and after a couple minutes showed signs of recovery.

"What are we going to do?" she asked.

"Call 911 for starters." I pulled out my phone, only to discover that the battery had gone dead. "Aw, jeez...do you have a phone, Amber?"

"Yeah," she said, pulling one of the smart variety out of her purse and handing it to me.

"I don't know how to work these things," I confessed. "I still have a geezer phone."

"You're kidding."

After negotiating a deal whereby she dialed and then I talked, we managed to call in the emergency, after which I handed the device back and checked the main house to see if anyone was home.

If anyone was, they were sleeping, hiding, or dead themselves.

Now why did you have to say that? Myrna Loy's voice said inside my head.

Returning to Amber, who had finally managed to gain full control over her respiration, I asked: "Do you know if Boris was in any kind of a relationship?"

"Not with me, if that's what you're thinking."

"I mean with anyone, any other person who might have access to his house."

"To my knowledge there was nobody. I'm not even sure if he was gay or straight. Maybe he was nothing. God, I've gone my whole life without seeing a dead body, and then I get two in one week. You knew he'd be dead, didn't you?"

The sound of a siren could be heard, wailing in the distance.

"No, I didn't know, but I thought he might be in danger."

"Why?"

"It's a long story. I'm going to go to the street and wait for the police. Will you be all right here?"

She nodded, and I took her at her word.

"I need to sit down, though," she said, moving to a wrought iron patio chair.

The first police vehicle arrived on the scene at the same time as the EMTs, giving me the sensation that I'd been in this movie before. I led them toward the pool.

Soon more police arrived and now people were emerging from the houses up and down the street to see what was going on. One of the officers, a plainclothes detective,
me to come back to the scene, where Amber was still huddled in the patio chair.

The man flashed a shield, which identified him as Detective Harve Morgan. "You the one who called?" he asked.

"Yes."

"You discovered the body?"

"Along with the young lady over there. She worked for the vic."

"The vic? Do you have some knowledge that this guy met with foul play?"

"Um, no, I meant the deceased."

Turning to another detective, Morgan instructed him to see what Amber had to say, then turned back to me. "All right, sir, who are you?"

I introduced myself and told him what I knew, which wasn't much really, except that we had come over to find Verdugo because he had not shown up for work, and found him doing a great impression of the Titanic.

"What's with the mask?"

"Your guess is as good as mine," I said, unwilling to reveal mine.

Morgan went over to talk to Amber, who shuddered as she answered his questions. I couldn't hear what she was saying, but I had to assume that she was mentioning the part about Verdugo's allergy, an assumption that was confirmed when the detective returned to me, a sneer on his face.

"The girl says the DB was allergic to rubber," he said.

"Dee-bee?"

"Dead body. It's related to being a vic. So tell me, Mr. Beauchamp, how are you involved in this?"

"I told you, I went to see Verdugo, and—"

"But you didn't tell me why. The girl's got a connection to him, she worked for him. What were you to him?"

"Nothing, personally. I mean, I met him at the Hollywood Celebrity Expo, which he organized."

"Hollywood Celebrity Expo?"

"A gathering of old actors who meet their fans and sign autographs. A couple of its attendees died within the last few days as well."

"Oh, right. One guy that played the Purple Something."

"The Purple Shadow."

Detective Morgan was now scrutinizing me. Then he said: "Okay, right, now I know where I've seen you."

"The Temple of Theotologics case."

"The what? No, I thought you were on TV a few days ago talking about the Purple guy."

"Oh, yes, I did that."

"So you knew that DB, too?"

"I'd only just met him."

"Just met him right before he died?"

"Um, yes, that's right."

"And you met the guy in the pool for the first time at this expo, and then a few days later he's dead?"

I cleared my throat. "Yes."

"Have you just met anyone else I should know about for future reference?"

"Look, I only met Amber over there at the expo, too, and she's still alive."

"So far," the detective said.

"You can't seriously believe I had anything to do with this," I protested. "Why would I call for the police if I was the killer? Why wouldn't I simply leave?"

Morgan shrugged. "You tell me."

"Look, I wanted to speak with Verdugo, but he didn't come into work today or even call the office, which Ms...."

For the first time, I realized I didn't even know Amber's last name.

"…which Amber thought was unusual, so we came out to check up on him and we found him in the pool. That's all, detective."

"And no theory as to the trick-or-treat mask?"

"Maybe he was a kink who was into creepy clown sightings," I offered.

"All right. We might need to speak with you again. How do I contact you?"

I pulled out my wallet to fish out a business card, but I had none left. I had forgotten to restock after the Celebrity Expo. So I rattled off my phone number. "I'm also in the Yellow Pages."

"Who uses the Yellow Pages anymore?"

"May I quote you the next time they hit me up for an ad?"

Detective Morgan actually smiled. "All right, thanks," he said, walking away.

I waited for Amber who was still being interviewed by the other detective. I could see her nodding and answering questions, even though she kept her eyes firmly on the ground. She looked up just in time to see the body of Boris Verdugo being pulled to the side of the pool with pikes and then laboriously hoisted out and laid onto the tile edge. One of the policemen pulled the mask off, revealing the puffy, bloated, red and bumpy face of the realtor, broken out from the latex contact.

Amber was asked to identify the body and she did, nodding.

Then she nearly fainted. A policeman caught her and set her back down in the chair.

When she was able to rise and walk, she came towards me. I held out a hand for her, which she ignored. Instead she punched me in the shoulder, hard.

"What was that for?" I demanded, rubbing what I was pretty sure was going to be a heavy bruise.

"Because every time I see you someone dies and I have to talk to the police," she replied. "Since it was my boss this time, I don't even have a job now."

"It's not my fault, you know."

"Then why does it only happen when you're around?"

That sounds like a reasonable question, Jack Webb commented inside in my head.

I threw my hands up in the air. "Are the police finished with you?"

Amber nodded. "They figure he might have fallen in accidentally because he couldn't see through the mask, but that doesn't explain why he was wearing it. They're scheduling an autopsy to see if he was drunk or on anything."

"Did you know him to be a drinker?"

"I'm tired of being asked questions. Can't we just get out of here?"

I walked her down the driveway, past the big house, to my car, which fortunately had not been blocked in by emergency vehicles. Since she seemed to be having trouble buckling her own seatbelt, I tried to help her, accidentally brushing my hand across her breasts. For a second I was afraid the mace can would come out, but she seemed not even to notice.

"Are you all right now?" I asked.

"There was always something wrong," she said, softly.

"About what?"

"About Mr. Verdugo. I always…oh, never mind."

"No, no, Amber, whatever you have to say, go ahead and say it."

"Well, I always got the idea that there was another side to him he never revealed at the office, like he was living a double life. Sometimes it seemed like he was acting a part, putting on that extreme personality, with strange clothes, and that stupid Shriner's hat, and the kind of moustache nobody wears anymore."

"Anyone who puts together the kinds of events that he did must have been interested in acting on some level."

"Yeah, but it was more than that."

I started up my trusty Toyota and pulled away from the curb.

"You ever watch soap operas?" Amber asked, out of the blue.

"Not really my cup of entertainment," I said.

"I used to watch them all the time. For a while I thought I might be interested in going into acting, but I got over it. It's not a very wholesome business."

"Why did you ask me about them?"

"Well, if you watch soaps you can always tell when an actor forgets his line. They get a certain look, their eyes go vacant, and you know they're not sure what to say next. Sometimes Mr. Verdugo would get that look in everyday conversation. He'd be talking, and it would be like he'd rehearsed what he was going to say, and then I'd ask him a question and he wouldn't know how to answer it for a moment, like he was unprepared or was playing a role and suddenly forgot his lines." She fell silent for a moment, and then added: "Why was he wearing that stupid mask? It makes no sense."

"It might if it was someone who knew of his allergy and wanted to get rid of him," I said.

"You mean *murder* him?"

"Think, Amber. Do you know of anyone who might want to see Boris dead?"

"He wasn't what I'd call a people-person, but I don't know of anyone out to get him. Except…"

I didn't even have to think before saying *Miranda Love* along with her.

But I didn't really see Miranda as an actual murderer. She was far too much of a victim herself.

"Were there any problems with the realty business?" I asked. "Unhappy clients, anything like that?"

She shook her head, which I could only detect peripherally from her swinging blonde hair. "This client Mr. Verdugo was supposed to meet today was his first in several weeks. Things have been a little slow lately."

"When I called yesterday it sounded like you were busy on the phones."

"I was, but not with clients. People from that stupid show were calling to find out when they were going to get their honorium."

"You mean their honorarium?"

"Whatever. Their money. We give each one two hundred bucks just for showing up. You'd think it was the difference between life or death for some of these losers."

"What's going to happen to the Celebrity Expo now?" I asked.

"It goes away, I guess," she replied. "I hope it does, anyway. I really hate those things. Some of those actors are such pains. I've never heard of most of them, but that doesn't stop them from behaving like they're still hot. I mean, if it was Ryan Gosling or Kristen Stewart, someone like that, I could see waiting on them. But those people are just washed-up nobodies who still demand this kind of bottled water, or that kind of yogurt, or a taller chair than everybody else, or refuse to sit next to so-and-so. Have you ever heard of somebody named John Vanson?"

John Vanson played the patriarch of a large family who took in foster kids in the 1980s sitcom *Yours, Mine, and Theirs.* He was handsome, affable, and was able to zing out a line. For a while at least, he was America's dad.

"I've heard of him."

"Yeah, well he walked out when he discovered his deal didn't include a supply of cocaine."

"Ah. But they're not all like that, are they?"

"Well, no, not everyone, but enough. Too many."

We drove on a little further in silence, then Amber said: "So, are you going to figure out who killed Mr. Verdugo?"

"I have to be hired by someone before I can take a case. Are you willing to pay my rates to investigate?"

"No. I just thought you'd be interested, is all."

"Tell you what," I said. "I'll keep my ear to the ground and let you know what I hear. How does that sound?"

"Like a good way to get an earful of dirt."

When we were nearing Verdugo's office, I asked: "What are you going to do now?"

She shrugged. "Try and contact the people he was going to show the house to today and tell them it's off, then go home, I guess. I'll worry about tomorrow when it's tomorrow."

"All right. Do me a favor, though, okay? Tell me your last name."

"My last name?"

"I've never heard it."

"Holmes."

"Like Sherlock?"

"No, like Katie."

This time having successfully made my way into the parking lot of the small complex housing Verdugo & Associates, I pulled into a spot and Amber got out of the car.

"Thanks for lunch," she said, "though back at Mr. V's house I was afraid I might lose it."

That would probably not have made much difference in its quality.

"Would you mind taking the empty with you?" I asked, and with a slight sigh she picked up the soy-stained styrofoam container and took it with her into the office. I hoped the smell inside the car would go away in time.

There was nothing waiting for me back at the office, which was fine with me. In particular, I was happy to see that Miranda Love's attorney had not phoned back.

Speaking of phone, I plugged mine into the charger.

Pulling out the file that Amber Holmes had given me, I started looking through the list of guests at the Celebrity Expo. Many of them I recalled seeing, but several I had not, and there were a few names even I couldn't recognize.

As opposed to the sixty or so celebrities in attendance, more than four hundred paying customers had filled out address labels, though that was likely only a fraction of the people who attended. Looking at the first several pages of photocopies, I quickly realized that this was going to get me nowhere. Even if I did research and contact all seven-hundred-plus people, what would I say? *Hi, you don't know me, but, um, are you by any chance killing off old actors? Just asking.*

So, where did that leave me?

Running around in circles with a burgeoning headache.

I decided to try looking for Michael Baroni again. Surely he had to be *somewhere* on the internet.

Typing in his name I hit on everything that came up, even the ones I was pretty sure had to be for a different Michael Baroni. After twenty minutes of searching, I was about ready to give up.

Then I found the "I Want to Be A Murder Victim Just Like Mom and Dad" website.

As tasteless as the name was, the site was even worse. It was hackneyed fan-fiction written by someone hiding behind the avatar "Deathmaster," who fantasized that the children of various murder victims met equally gruesome ends as adults.

One of the sections was dedicated to the Valley Slasher case and after pulling it up and scanning down the page, I stopped on a photograph. It showed a family at Disneyland, a smiling mom, a grinning dad, and a chubby boy of about twelve in front, who was scowling at the camera despite his mouse ears and some guy in a Goofy suit posing next to him—or maybe because of them. The caption read: *The Baroni family in happier times.* The quality of the photo indicated it had been cut out of a newspaper and scanned. But this was my first actual look at the elusive Michael Baroni, and only a few seconds after I began studying the face, I went cold.

"Oh, no," I uttered, copying the photo on a new page and enlarging it. Plugging the laptop into my small office printer, I made a copy, which reduced the quality, but not so much that I could not see the kid in the Mickey Mouse ears. Grabbing a pencil, I carefully erased, or at least diminished, the mouse ears (the up-side of buying cheap toner cartridges) and the sides of the face. Then I drew in new lines that made the face fatter, rounder, erased the tip of the nose and sketched in a smaller, sharper version. After that I added in a little bit of aging with the pencil tip, finishing by drawing on a straight moustache with a gap over the philtrum. Then I sat back and looked at my handiwork, and got cold all over again.

There are facets of people's faces that don't change from their youth to their middle-age. Usually it's their eyes, their expression, or an attitude that never goes away despite thinning hair, age lines, weight change, even a nose job.

With this kid it was the deeply cleft chin.

While I doubted any court in the country would accept this as evidence, I had just produced a police sketch-quality likeness of Boris Verdugo.

9.

Are you sure *this is a good idea*? the smoky voice of Lizabeth Scott asked inside my head, as I drove back to the home of the man I knew as Boris Verdugo.

It was a legitimate question, and I would have loved to have been able to answer "yes," just like I would love to discover irrefutable proof inside the guest house that Verdugo and Baroni had been the same person.

Because if I did, then breaking into his house, which at present was also being treated as a crime scene, might be a chance worth taking.

It was twilight when I got to Verdugo's street, not quite dark enough for breaking and entering without risk of being seen. The absence of police cars on the street was a good sign. A better sign was the fact that the front house on the street was dark, indicating that no one was present.

It would probably be too much to ask that there were no motion sensors anywhere on the property; regarding that, I would have to take my chances.

I turned my car onto the side street at the end of the block and parked, then sat and waited for it to get completely dark. I spent the time listening to the closing arguments inside my head as to whether breaking and entering was really a risk that would pay off, or an incredibly stupid and dangerous act committed by someone who tended to make up plans as he went along.

James Cagney argued for taking the risk, while Henry Fonda countered that I was asking for trouble.

Then my old friend Robert Mitchum chimed in: *I don't care one way or the other, junior, I'm dead. It's your ass.*

No one could put things into perspective quite like Mitch.

Hedging my bets, I hunted under the seat until I found the old bucket hat I kept in the car, which would offer a modicum of disguise, should anyone be looking.

When the streetlights came on, I got out of the car and walked to the house that faced the street. The dark house. Even though I was convinced it was empty, I stepped up onto the porch, rang the doorbell, and waited. If anyone answered, I was ready with a pretense about how I'd just moved into the neighborhood and was walking my dog, which had slipped its collar and run away.

If a policeman happened to answer, I was ready to say that I had been questioned that afternoon and had just remembered a pertinent bit of information that I had not divulged.

But after a sixty-count, no one had come to the door.

Just to make certain, I rang again. Then I knocked. Then I shrugged (for the benefit of any neighbor who might have been watching) and went down into the yard calling, "Malcolm, here boy!"

Malcolm is my nonexistent lost dog.

I made my way into the back, around the pool, and into the shadows of the guest house. There was some yellow crime tape around the pool, but nothing around the house. After slipping on a pair of thin leather driving gloves, I tried the doorknob. It was locked, which was no surprise. Taking out my professional lock-pick, the detective's best friend, I had it open within fifteen seconds.

Stepping into the bungalow, I quickly closed the door behind me and pulled out a tiny but powerful directional flashlight. Since I didn't know exactly what I was looking for, I headed to my favorite starting place: the refrigerator.

My belief is that you can tell a lot about somebody by what you find in their fridge. It can be a chilled insight into one's life.

Boris's contained three opened jars of pasta sauce, two containers of Miracle Whip, a half-bottle of Bailey's, a brick of Velveeta, and more packages of bacon than I've ever seen in one place outside of a grocery store's meat counter. This argued that he might indeed have suffered a heart attack and had fallen into the pool—but it didn't explain the clown mask.

I was about to close the fridge when I noticed something.

While the Miracle Whip jars were identical in size and labeling, one of them was a slightly different color than the other. Opening one jar, I found Miracle Whip. The other one, however, revealed a surprise.

That jar had been washed out and painted on the inside, which made it look like it still held dressing, at least at first glance. But it was really a makeshift safe. There was something inside that was rattling around. Adjusting the light, I could see what it was…a drive.

"Bingo," I uttered. There had to be something of value contained on the drive; why else would it be hidden in the refrigerator, the last place most normal people would look?

Every now and then, not being like normal people proved to be an asset.

Even so, I was hesitant to take the device home and plug it into my computer. It wasn't so much the concern over invasion of privacy, since Boris Verdugo was dead, as the fact that I'd had a very bad experience recently sticking an unknown drive into my laptop. It had proven to be a diabolical weapon, and the images it loaded onto my computer could have sent me to prison.

Verdugo must have a computer of his own; if I could find it and get it powered up, I could see what was on the drive right here and now.

Snooping through the rest of the tiny house, I could see nothing that looked like a computer or a laptop, though Verdugo had apparently believed that the laundry fairy would soon arrive and take care of the mountain of dirty clothes on the floor of the bedroom, which reeked of sweat.

Once again I wondered why a realtor would live in a place like this, with no space, few amenities, and such thin walls.

That last part I had become aware of through hearing voices coming from outside.

Someone was approaching the house.

Logic dictated that there had to be a back door somewhere in this little crackerbox, but a very quick search failed to reveal one.

Neither was there was any place to hide.

I heard someone say: "Hey, the door's unlocked."

Another voice, a woman's, said: "Well, go in then!"

Turning my mini-light off and sticking it in my pocket, along with the flash drive, I backed into a corner, hoping against reason that I might be rendered invisible.

As I watched a much more powerful flashlight beam than mine probe the darkness of the bungalow, I desperately tried to think of something to do.

Well, the best defense is offense, the voice of Ronald Reagan said in my head.

Whether it was Gipper Ronnie or President Ronnie I couldn't tell, but at the moment I was not in a position to split hairs, dyed or otherwise.

Feeling around the wall for a light switch, I finally found it and flipped it on.

The man holding the flashlight jumped so violently from the sudden, shocking illumination that he dropped it on the floor. "Christ!" he shouted. "Who's there?"

The guy was probably in his fifties, balding, and with a gin-blossom nose. His clothes looked like they were off-the-rack from Goodwill. Squinting from the light, he held up his hands defensively in front of his face.

"Who are you?" he asked as I stepped out from the corner.

"Who wants to know?" I said in my best Bogart, which was none too good.

"You a cop?"

"What if I am?"

"Shit! Look this wasn't my idea."

"Whose was it, then?"

Now I heard a woman's voice call: "Jay, who are you talking to?"

Jay?

Oh, jeez.

"Mr. Leach, esquire, I presume?" I said, remembering the name of the lawyer who had left that threatening message on my answering machine.

The woman came through the door. "Jay, what in holy hell—" She stopped upon seeing me, and then said: "Oh, my god, it's *you!*"

"Hello, Miranda," I sighed.

"What is this?" Leach asked. "Who are you?"

"My name is Dave Beauchamp," I said. "That's the way it's pronounced, by the way, not *buhshawm*, like you left on my machine."

"Buhshawm," Leach muttered. "Oh, you're one of the people we're—"

"Threatening with trumped up charges that Judge Roy Bean would have laughed out of court," I finished for him.

"Mr. Beauchamp, I have to do what my client says."

"You think you can intimidate us?" Miranda Love asked.

"I'd say I'm already halfway there," I replied.

Leach winced. "You gonna call the cops?"

"I don't know. Maybe if I find out why you're here, I won't have to."

"We should be asking you the same," Miranda said, icily. "And take off that idiotic hat. Were you never taught how to behave before a lady?"

I considered questioning her self-description, but quickly decided there was no point. Whipping off the bucket hat (which probably did look stupid), I shoved it into my back pocket.

"I'm a private investigator," I said. "I'm here investigating. Now it's your turn."

"I don't have to answer your questions!" she declared. "You are not the police."

"You're right, I'm not. So let's go ahead and bring them in."

I pulled out my cell phone, which had gotten charged up only halfway before I grabbed it and ran out of the office, and started dialing. It was my office number, since this was a bluff.

"No! Don't do that!" Leach wailed. "I'm only here on account of my client."

"You *cockroach*," Miranda sneered. "You're fired, immediately!" Then turning to me, she added: "And as for you, you…you… *ohh*! I have no words for you!"

With that Miranda Love pivoted around and stormed out of the bungalow.

I was hoping for the sound of a scream and a splash, but no such luck.

"Christ," Leach said, "I tried to tell her this was a bad idea. That woman never listens. Ha. Like *any* woman ever listens."

He sat down on a love seat and put his face in his hands.

Through the bungalow's open door I could hear the *bleep bleep* of a car being unlocked by a keyless entry remote, followed by the sound of a car door being slammed, and then the squeal of tires as it took off.

"There she goes," Leach commented, "leaving me to take the rap again. I don't believe it. No, that's a lie. I do believe it. Is there any liquor around here?"

I decided to keep the knowledge of the Bailey's in the fridge to myself.

"Okay, look, Leach," I said instead, making a show of putting my cell phone back into my pocket, "if you tell me why you came here, maybe we won't need to involve the police."

"I already told you, Miranda made me come. Christ, this place gives me the creeps. Let's go somewhere else, and then I'll tell you."

"Where?"

"That's up to you. I came with Miranda, and she ditched me. You have a car, don't you?"

"It's around the corner," I said. "Let's go. Oh, and pick up your flashlight. No sense leaving your prints here."

"Shit, they're on the front doorknob, too," he said, reaching down for the light with a shaking hand.

After switching off the room light, I ushered Leach out of the house. I decided to leave the door unlocked, but wiped the knob clean of prints with a handkerchief. Then I headed for my car, telling Leach: "If we run into anyone, we're looking for a lost dog."

"I am a lost dog," he muttered.

Having long ago misplaced the keyless entry remote that came with my pre-owned 2001 Corolla, I had to open the doors the old-fashioned way. After unlocking the passenger door for Leach, I got in on the other side, pulled off my gloves, and tossed them into the back seat. I pulled the hat out of my back pocket, too, which made sitting a lot more comfortable.

I had not even started the engine before Leach reached into his pocket and pulled out a pack of cigarettes.

"Sorry," I said, "but I don't smoke and I'd really rather you didn't, too."

"Christ. You nonsmokers think you run the whole fucking world."

"No, just this car. You can always get out and walk if you want a cigarette that much."

"Okay, fine, I won't smoke. But I do need a drink. Do you know where Club 38 is?"

"Not a clue."

"It's mid-Wilshire, not far from the Wiltern."

The Wiltern I knew. It was a theatre located inside one of the most stunning art deco buildings in Los Angeles, one that had so far escaped the fate of so many other historic buildings in Los Angeles, which was to be torn down and replaced with a strip mall. That had been the fate of the legendary Brown Derby, once located only a few blocks away from the Wiltern.

Getting from this part of Glendale to mid-Wilshire was going to take a little time, so I decided to occupy it by quizzing Jay Leach about his role in this bizarre drama, unwitting or otherwise.

"I'm telling you, it was all Miranda's idea," he maintained. "She showed up at the door of my house tonight and demanded I come with her right then and there. I'd just sat down to dinner, but she didn't care. When that bitch wants something, you have to do it. You've got no choice."

"What about refusing?"

"Maybe some could refuse her, but I can't."

Ohhhhhhhhh, Humphrey Bogart sang meaningfully inside my head.

"What's she got on you, Leach?"

"What's that supposed to mean?"

"What does she know about you that allows her to force you into service?"

At first I thought he was going to become all lawyerly indignant over the very thought, but then he seemed to deflate. "It's a long story," he sighed.

"We're going to be in the car for a while," I said.

"Yeah, without a goddamned cigarette."

"At least tell me how you got tied up with Miranda Love in the first place."

"Well, this is probably before your time," he said, "but there used to be a show on television about father and son attorneys. The *Brady Bunch* dad played the son."

"Right, Robert Reed, and E.G. Marshall was the father. The show was called *The Defenders*. Miranda wasn't on that show, was she?"

"I don't know and I don't care. The point I'm making is that I had a situation like that with my own father. We were partners, me the junior partner, obviously. Dad was Miranda's lawyer for decades, and after he died, I inherited her. Until then, I never realized how much my old man disliked me."

"All right. Now, as to my first question—"

"What's she holding over me, I remember. Okay. Miranda has this granddaughter who's a real piece of work."

"I didn't realize she had any family at all."

"She pretends she doesn't. She even pretends she was never married, but she conned some poor schmuck into putting a ring on it in the sixties. The marriage lasted just long enough for her to get pregnant and drop a kid, a daughter, who, naturally, Miranda blames for the downturn in her career. Melissa is her daughter's name, and I don't think she even speaks to the old bat any more. She lives back east, which is where her own daughter Tiffany, was born and raised. Melissa turned out to be a decent person, but Tiffany…it's like the bitch gene skipped a generation and landed in her."

"What did she do?"

"Well, once the little snot figured out her dear gran-gran was a one-time movie star, she showed up out here and started causing all sorts of problems. Tiffany was arrested on shoplifting charges a few years ago, and Miranda wanted me to represent her."

"Did you?"

"Yeah, I took the case. It wasn't long after my father died, and I was just starting to get sucked into the hellhole that is Miranda Love's universe. I was actually trying to get on her good side back then, impress her with my skill. Prove to her I was as good as my old man. Christ, if only I'd told her that the kid was guilty as sin and should plead out and do her time, everything would be so much different. But I didn't."

"You're sure Tiffany was guilty?"

"They had an eyewitness, a clerk at the store in Beverly Hills, who saw Tiffany try to walk out with a Gucci handbag worth a grand-and-a-half. Believe me, it was a slam-dunk for the prosecution. My only hope of getting the stupid little bitch off was if the eyewitness suddenly got unsure about what she had seen. So I made sure she got a little sketchy."

"How?"

"How do you think? I paid her off. It wasn't like Tiffany had murdered someone. She stole a purse, big whoop. Even though the witness worked in a high-end store, the pay wasn't all that good, so she was happy to get a little bonus by unrecognizing Tiffany Love.

That's what the brat was calling herself, because she wanted people to know of her connection to Miranda. Tiffany Love. Christ, sounds like a porn star, doesn't it?"

"So she managed to beat the rap?"

"Yeah, little Tiffany went free. Then about a year later, she broke into Miranda's house and stole some money. That was it for Miranda. Having coerced me into breaking the law to get the little snot acquitted, Miranda now wanted Tiffany out of her life for good. Then she got it into her head that if I hadn't bribed the witness, Tiffany would already be in prison and out of her dyed hair. So everything is my fault, see? In Miranda-logic, it's all my fault. Look, Beauchamp, I'm dying for a smoke. If I stick my head out the window, can I have a cigarette?"

I sighed. "Okay, open the window, keep the cigarette out there, and blow the smoke out."

Jay Leach had the cigarette fired up within five seconds. He did his best to blow the smoke outward.

"Better?" I asked.

"Oh, yeah. It'll be better still when we get to the club," he said.

"Going back to your story, I'm still not sure how Miranda got her claws into you because her granddaughter robbed her."

He took a long drag, blew out the smoke (some of which blew back in), and continued his sad tale.

"The deputy D.A. prosecuting Tiffany for shoplifting knew damn well she did it, and it really pissed him off that the witness changed her story. But there was nothing he could do about it. He couldn't prove I'd bribed her. But as we were leaving the courtroom he told me that he would be keeping his eye on me, and that if it even looked like I was stepping over the line in the future, he would personally take me down. The prick. I didn't plan on giving him either the opportunity or the satisfaction. But then Miranda turned on me. So now, if I don't carry out her every wish, no matter how idiotic, she'll leak it to the D.A.'s office that I paid off the witness to get her granddaughter off, and I go up the river."

Leach fell silent again and stayed that way until I passed the Club 38 about fifteen minutes later. From the outside it looked like a bigger dive than the one Esther Williams made in *Million Dollar Mermaid*.

I found a parking spot a couple blocks away and as soon as Leach was out of the car, he lit up another cigarette, reducing it to ash in three draws.

Entering Club 38 gave me the most extreme case of *déjà vu* I've ever had. It was like I had been here not simply once before, but a hundred times. Then I realized that every bar in every film and every TV show of the 1950s and '60s looked like this place.

Maybe a few of them were even filmed here.

It was also smoke-filled, even though that was supposed to be illegal in Los Angeles. Now I understood why Leach patronized the place.

The bartender blended in perfectly with the décor. He was completely bald, looked like he could pick up a tractor, and had eyes that would have frightened Boris Karloff. Leach ordered a double scotch and lit up another cigarette. I had intended on getting a ginger ale, but then wondered if Leach was one of those guys for whom not drinking alcohol was a sign of suspicion. Since I didn't want to close the door I had already opened with him, I changed my order to a lite beer.

"Got some I.D?" the bartender asked.

After I produced my driver's license, the guy nodded and went to pour the drinks.

When they came, I said, "Now that Miranda has fired you, are you afraid she will leak the information to the D.A.?"

Leach laughed and tossed down his entire drink in one gulp, slamming the empty glass onto the bar.

"She hasn't really fired me," he said. "She only ditched me at that house. At least once a week she screams 'You're fired immediately!' over something or other, and then she calls back with the next thing she wants me to do. My wife yells at me all the time to tell the old bat where to go and what to do once she's there, but Leslie doesn't understand what's at stake."

"Leslie's your wife?"

"Yeah. She's out of town this week, so at least I didn't have to deal with her screaming at me for leaving the dinner table."

"I'm sorry," I offered, coughing from the smoke.

"It's not your fault. Haven't you been listening? It's my fault. Everything's my fault."

"You want another drink?"

He laughed again, grimly.

"One's too many and a thousand's not enough."

I recognized the quote.

"Ray Milland in *The Lost Weekend*," I said.

"How the hell do you know this shit? Like *The Defenders*. You don't look old enough."

"I'm a film buff."

"Yeah, well, with me and booze, one's too many and eight-million's not enough, so sure, keep 'em comin'."

When his fresh drink arrived he took a gulp, but this time left some.

"So, I'll bet you still want to know why Miranda and I were at that house tonight, right?" he asked.

"Right."

"Okay. Miranda wanted to find some incriminating evidence that whatshisname… Verdugo…was a flame, so she could use it to blackmail him."

"Proof that he was gay? In this day and age, that's not really blackmail material."

"Yeah, well, you know that and I know that, but like I said, I do what I'm told. But look, it doesn't even matter. Even if I'd found a photo of the guy in a hot tub with Elton John, Miranda would have forgotten about it in a few days. She likes hurting people, and she likes making me help her hurt people, because she knows that hurts me, but she never follows through."

"So is your threat of a lawsuit against me just so much smoke?" I asked, coughing again.

He finished his drink and signaled the bartender for a refill.

"What did I threaten you with?"

"Defamation of character."

He snorted out a laugh. "Oh, that's a good one!"

The bartender returned with a filled glass, which Leach tossed back.

"Don't worry," he said. "Even if she does remember it, I'll tell her it's taking forever because of a black…backlog in the courts. Eventually she'll forget."

I could tell that the scotches were beginning to have an effect.

"Can I assure Palmer Hanley that the suit with which you threatened him is likewise not going to happen?"

"Yeah, sure. S'long as you tell me why the hell you were at that creep's house t'night."

"I was looking for some clues to his murder."

Jay Leach dropped his glass, prompting the bartender to rush over with a towel to clean up the spill.

"Fuck!" Leach screamed. "Jesus Christ! Aw, shit! We broke into the house of a guy who was *murdered*?"

"Can you keep your voice down?" I said, looking around at the other patrons of Club 38, most of whom were pretty hard cases and not paying much attention to us.

"You want another, mac?" the bartender asked.

"Yeah, make it a double," Leach groaned. "A triple, if you do those."

The bartender glanced at me, and I said: "I'm driving." He nodded and went to make the drink.

"Goddamn," Leach said, "Miranda must have known he was dead."

"Why do you say that?"

"Because she assumed he wasn't going to be there when we arrived. Why would she assume that if she didn't already know he wasn't going to be there?"

"But if she knew he was dead, why look for blackmail material?" I asked. "What would be the point?"

"I dunno…"

The triple scotch arrived and Leach gulped half of it down. I wondered how much longer he would be able to converse coherently.

The answer arrived quickly.

"That bitch," Leach moaned.

Then at the top of his lungs he yelled: "*Fuckin' bitch!*"

The bartender came back. "I'm gonna have to cut him off," he said.

"Yes, I think so," I coughed. "I doubt he could hold any more anyway."

"Oh, he could. I've seen him do it. He can hold enough to kill a horse."

"Horse!" Leach cried. "That's right! That mare'll…she'll be the death of me!" Then he began laughing.

"Usually he stays quiet," the bartender said. "I don't like commotion in my bar."

"I'll take him out," I said, pulling out my wallet. "What do I owe you?"

The tab came to thirty-eight dollars, which made me wonder if that was why the place was called Club 38.

"Come on, Jay," I said, "we have to go."

"God," he drawled. "I hope she goes to hell. Some days I wish I could just murder the bitch and send her there."

"You shouldn't say things like that, even about Miranda."

He looked at me with bleary eyes and laughed, though he no longer had enough control over his mouth muscles to frame it inside a smile.

"How d'you know I meant M'randa?" he asked.

Somehow I got him out and into my car, though it took four tries to get his address out of him.

I kept my window open as I drove, savoring the fresh air.

Jay Leach's home was a small Craftsman house on La Jolla Street in West Hollywood, which was a pretty pricey neighborhood for someone who looked like he wasn't making all that much money, unless he spent his money on something other than clothes.

"Thanks, Beeshum," he said, getting out of the car and leaning back in to offer his hand. "I hope we see each other again."

Yeah, if I'm picking up the tab, I'll bet you do.

"One last question, if you don't mind," I said.

"What now?"

"Where is Miranda's granddaughter at present?"

"Tiffany? Hell, I dunno. I gave the li'l bitch five g's and told her to get lost, and that if she ever came around again I'd have her 'rested for bugglery. I think she believed me, too, though the money's prob'ly long since gone up her nose or in her veins. I don' really care. See ya later, pal."

Closing the car door, he managed to light up a cigarette and staggered to the house, which had large front windows. So large, in fact, that I could see someone inside.

It was a woman.

Since Mrs. Leach was, by her husband's account, away, it could not have been her, unless she had returned unexpectedly. That might have been the case, since Leach seemed clearly startled by her presence. So startled he almost fell down.

Even at that, though, he wasn't half as startled as I was upon finally recognizing the woman when she stepped closer to a lamp. Her bright orange hair gave her away.

Either I was completely insane, or the woman in Leach's house was Karen Robinson.

10.

I continued to watch the show through the window.

After a lot of agitated gestures, Karen Robinson threw her arms up in the air in frustration and stormed past Leach and out of the house. I crouched down in my car as she went by, got into her vehicle, pulled away from the curb and disappeared into the night.

Peeking up again, I saw Leach guzzle straight from a liquor bottle, then lurch to the window that served as the proscenium for this drama, and pull the drapes closed.

What in heaven's name had I just witnessed?

Part of me wanted to go home and call Karen and ask what the heck she was doing at Jay Leach's house, but if I did that I would have to explain how I knew she was there without sounding like a peeping tom.

I had a better idea. It was time to call on Jack Daniels.

Jack was a British ex-pat living in Santa Monica, a city that had a high concentration of Brits and enough English pubs to remind them all of home. He was also the bestselling author of the "Tory Poacher" series of thriller novels, written under a pseudonym that you would recognize. I had met him some years back through a writers convention at which I had been asked to speak about the private detective trade (the event coordinator apparently having assumed I knew what I was talking about; there, Mitchum, I beat you!), and had kept in touch with Jack ever since. He asks me for tips on PI procedure and technique, and I call on him any time I am totally stuck on a case because of his ability to see problems from a half-dozen different points of view simultaneously and come up with the most outlandish insights imaginable.

Often they prove invaluable.

It was about 10:30 when I got home, but that was of little consequence. Like Allan Pinkerton used to say, we never sleep.

Unless there's nothing else to do.

On my landline (yes, I still have one at home) I punched in the number for Jack.

At first I thought he might still be out at the pub, since it went to five rings, but then a woman answered.

"Daniels residence," she said.

"Hi, is this Kim?"

Kim was Jack's wife.

"Yes, who is this?"

"It's Dave Beauchamp. I'm calling for Jack."

"Oh, Mr. Beauchamp, I remember you. Well, Jack's on deadline right now. His editor insisted on changes in his new book that he's not very happy about."

"Okay, I can call back some other time."

In the background I heard Jack's voice call out: "If that is Christina Kemp, tell her to go play with her Barbies! She'll get the book when it's ready!"

"It's Mr. Beauchamp," Kim called back, then to me said: "Hold on, he's coming."

"David, my boy!" Jack said when he took the receiver. "Has anyone ever encouraged you to become a writer?"

"Um, no."

"Good. Don't let them. It's horrible."

"I thought you loved writing."

"I do. It's editing I hate. What can I do for you?"

"You sure you have time now?"

"Yes, I need to take a break from attacking this paginated windmill before I go barking."

"Well, there's something I'd like to run past you."

"A new case?"

"Yes."

"Very well, but you know I cannot talk on a dry throat." Turning away from the phone, he said, "Luv, would you be so good as to fetch a Bombardier?"

"Bombardier? Who do you have in your sights?"

"My copy editor, a charming young lady who is a syllabophobe."

"A what?"

"A person who is terrified of words with more than two syllables. Perhaps she'll have learned a few by the time she graduates from high school. But in this case Bombardier is not a deployer of weapons, it is a brand of ale. Rather hard to find over here. I have an arrangement with the Hound and they order it for me. Ah, thank you, my dear."

"The Hound" was *The Hound and Badger*, Jack's favorite pub in Santa Monica, though its name sounded more like what a debt collector does.

"Now then," he asked, "what incomprehensible Gordian knot requires slicing this time?"

Over the next couple minutes I laid out the case, for lack of a better term, as best I could. When I was finished I heard a whistle.

"This is definitely going to be a two-pint problem," Jack said. "What you are describing are two stories circling around each other like boxers in a ring, and ultimately joined in an infinite loop. There is a technical literary term for such a configuration."

"And that is?"

"A sodding mess."

"That's very helpful, Jack."

"I'm not finished. You are absolutely certain that it was your client, the granddaughter of the allegedly-murdered man, who you saw in the lawyer's home?"

"The only way it could not have been her is if she's one of identical twins."

"Oh, good lord no, not twins! You never play that card in writing a mystery. It's not allowed."

"But, Jack, a recent case of mine revolved around twins."

"Yes, but as I recall they were not identical. Besides, that was reality. Anything is allowed in reality."

"Is it possible that Karen Robinson and Jay Leach were having an affair?" I thought out loud. "If that's the case, I think I witnessed the breakup."

After an audible swig of beer, Jack said, "No, no, no, that won't do either. In a city of, what, four-million people, the idea that a woman you literally met by chance through a tragedy should prove to be the lover of an attorney whose gaga client you also met by chance is too monumental a coincidence. The only thing worse than stories with twins are stories with coincidences. It is a little-known fact that the reason Charles Dickens was never knighted was because Queen Victoria hated coincidences, and his books are full of them."

"Really?"

"No, I just made that up. It's what I do. The point I'm making, David, is that the coincidence you have proposed is simply too vile to be allowed to live. So assuming, as we must, that there is no coincidence involved, it means that every player in this conundrum belongs there. That being the case, looking at it novelistically, I have to say that there is one person who is your key player, the nexus of this puzzle, if you will. That person will prove to be at the center of everything, with ties to everybody else."

This was the kind of insight I had been waiting for. "Who is that, Jack?"

"I haven't the faintest idea. But there has to be one."

"Is that really all you can think of?"

"You haven't given me much to work with, dear boy, or rather, you've given me too much. The case is going off in all directions. Now, if there is nothing else I can help you with, I must take my *inbrexit*."

"*Inbrexit?*"

"Short for 'inebriated exit.' You know how it is, everything must be short, short, short. No large words to confuse the reading public. I must get back to reducing the English language to a compendium of catch phrases in order to please my teenaged taskmaster."

"I'm sure she appreciates all your effort."

"Yes, well, editors. Can't live with them, can't run them over with a bus. Oh…oh, my."

"What?"

"There's a title in there somewhere if I can render it tersely enough. Now I really must go and get back to my desk before the thought goes away. Ta ta, David."

Jack hung up.

The bizarre deaths of Tony Marsh, Wilbur Constable, Edie Gogos, and Michael Baroni; Baroni's attempts to contact Marsh without revealing he was Boris Verdugo; and the strange drama acted out by Jay Leach and Karen Robinson…could they really all center around one person? I asked myself.

And if so, who?

Who d'you think, luv? the voice of Audrey Hepburn, as Eliza Doolittle, said inside my head, which I interpreted as: *Who do you think?…LOVE.*

Could it really be that Miranda Love was the nucleus of this, in Jack's words, sodding mess?

Can it really be that obvious?

I knew from experience that Jack disdained the obvious solution as much as he did coincidence.

And twins.

Suddenly realizing I'd skipped dinner, I went to the fridge to see what I could find that wasn't crawling. I'd exhausted my stash of frozen pot pies. There was some lunch meat that I couldn't even remember buying, some cheese that I could probably slice the mold off of, and a half-empty jar of strawberry preserves, which sounded promising, as long as I also had bread and peanut butter.

Like I said, examining one's fridge reveals a lot about their person. In my case, it revealed that if L.A. was not the fast-food capital of the world, I'd likely starve.

As I started to close the fridge door, the realization struck me like a falling rock.

I still had evidence in my pocket; that from Verdugo's fridge.

I pulled it out and ran to my laptop. Still leery of my last experience with a strange drive, my hand hovered over the port.

I had no evidence that it was contagious. If it was a booby trap, it would have more likely been found sitting out in the open for anyone to pick up. Still, despite Karen Robinson's advance in the bank, I could ill afford to replace yet another computer.

Oh, come on, handsome, go ahead and stick it in, Mae West's voice taunted inside my head.

After counting to three, I put the drive in the port and closed my eyes.

Cracking one open again, I saw a plain drive folder on the screen.

Opening it up, I found several files comprising the known history of the Valley Slasher, including scans of newspaper articles. I had already read a couple of them in my own research, but included in the files were voluminous notes Verdugo had made about the case. Unfortunately, a lot of these were written in truncated form, using initials, contractions and abbreviations, few of which I could decipher. Among the ones I could were "LB" and "RB," which I deduced stood for Leonard Baroni and Rosemary Baroni, Michael's parents.

The rest, though, was as incomprehensible as hieroglyphs.

One file labeled *PHOTOS* contained a series of shots of the family house, the one that Tony Marsh had sold them, a few pictures of Leonard and Rosemary, and a few more of Michael himself. If there was any significance to these other than normal, ordinary family snapshots, I could not see it.

Well, what were you expecting? the smirking voice of Vincent Price asked inside my head.

Vinnie had a good point; what *had* I been expecting? The identity of the Valley Slasher, laid out with irrefutable proof? A confession for the allergy murders, followed by a suicide note reading, *Goodbye, cruel world, I'm off to drown as a clown?*

Maybe tomorrow's fresher eyes would find something, but at the moment I was suffering from the dueling distractions of fatigue and hunger.

I put in a call to Checker Pizza and ordered a pepperoni and olive pie for delivery. It would be late show time when it arrived, but I suspected I would still be hungry.

The pizza came within twenty minutes. Either I was more famished than I thought, or it was better than their usual deliveries. I ate the entire thing.

Once my hunger had been assuaged, the fatigue started kicking in.

I got into bed around half-past-midnight, late for me, and fell asleep immediately.

The next thing I knew, something was ringing in my ears.

I was still in bed, and the ringing was my telephone. The clock on my nightstand announced it was 10:13 in the morning. Wow. I must have been more fatigued that I realized.

Getting up and stumbling to the phone, I heard an hysterical voice at the other end. It took me a good minute to figure out it was Hannah Skaal. Knowing there was only one thing that could upset Hannah this much, I swallowed hard, assuming that the day I had been dreading for quite some time had finally come.

Palmer Hanley must be dead.

He was in his nineties, I told myself, *that's longer than most people get.*

Even so, the weight of sorrow was settling in my chest.

"Dave! Dave, are you listening to me?" Hannah was sobbing.

"I'm sorry, Hannah, I zoned there for a moment. This is about Palmer, isn't it?"

"Yes, he's...he's...gone."

"I'm so sorry, Hannah," I said, feeling sorry for both of us. "But he went out on top. I wish all of us could go that way, particularly at his age."

"NOOOOOO!" she wailed, and I had to hold the phone away from my ear. I'd anticipated Hannah taking Palmer's passing hard, but this was a little excessive.

Dames, Bogie sneered, but I mentally shut him up, which I'd never done before. Hannah was not normally prone to hysteria.

Something was wrong.

"Hannah, are you okay?" I asked.

"I...I...I..."

"Do you want me to come over? Do you want me to call the police for you?"

"Dave...he's...he's..."

"I know, Hannah, Palmer is dead."

"No!" she shouted again. "He's been murdered!"

That feeling of sorrow in my stomach suddenly froze into a snowball. "How do you know he was murdered, Hannah?"

"Because...because...the head!"

The head?

I suddenly had a grisly vision of Palmer's skull bashed in.

"Is anyone else in the apartment, Hannah?"

"N...no."

"Okay, just try to hang on, I'm on my way over," I said.

After hanging up I took the world's quickest shower, threw on some clothes, and headed out.

This time of morning was the smack-middle of rush hour, which meant it took an agonizing thirty-five minutes to get to Los Feliz. Finding a place to park was another ordeal, and once I had gotten to Palmer's building, I buzzed his apartment and waited for Hannah to answer.

She was still crying.

"It's Dave, buzz me in," I said.

Once inside I went to the guard desk.

"Remember me?" I asked desperately. "I think there's something wrong with Palmer Hanley, something serious. I have to get up there."

"Do we need to call the police?" the guard asked.

"I think we might. Hannah seems too upset to call herself."

"Okay, I'll let you up and call them from down here."

The elevator ride seemed to take forever.

On the ninth floor, I raced to Palmer's apartment, where I met a still-distraught Hannah at the door. Immediately I noticed the place did not smell good. In fact, it smelled a lot worse than it should, and I couldn't identify the reek.

Going into Palmer's bedroom, I found him in the bed, but not at rest. He had clearly died in distress. His dead hand was still wrapped around his throat and there was a grimace on his face that the relaxation of muscles could not eradicate.

When I saw what he had reacted to I nearly vomited last night's pizza onto the floor.

Staggering back out, I sank into a chair.

Hannah sat on my lap, still sobbing, and held onto me as though her survival depended on it.

As I attempted to comfort her, I struggled to rid my mind of what I had seen in the bedroom.

It was the body of Palmer Hanley, whose own head had been untouched.

But he now shared his bed with the severed head of a horse.

Inside my brain, the soft, raspy voice of Marlon Brando purred, *I made him an offer he couldn't survive.*

11.

I waited for the police to arrive. I seemed to be doing a lot of that sort of thing of late.

I had closed the door to Palmer's bedroom, taking care to handle the knob with a Kleenex. I did this mostly out of respect, but also so the combined smells of a horse's severed head and a dead body would be minimized in the rest of the apartment.

Hannah's story, sobbed out while I held her and tried to comfort her, was that she had received an early-morning phone call from a delivery man, who was double-checking her address. The caller had asked her to come outside and wait for him on the street so he could pull up, make a quick drop-off, and then speed away to his next stop. She had complied, going outside to wait, but when no one had shown up within a twenty-minute window, she went back inside, assuming he would call her back from the street.

He never did.

Upstairs she had found the apartment door wide open, and Palmer and Mister Head were sharing a bed.

Hannah had been set up by one of the oldest pretenses in the business, the delivery man ruse, though usually that gag is employed for obtaining someone's address over the phone. Never before had I heard it used to lure someone out of a place so a crime could be committed.

Whether the cause of Palmer's death would prove to be a result of his allergy, or shock, or if there was a more direct cause was not yet apparent. What I did understand was that whoever forced the horse head on Palmer knew of his allergy, just like Tony Marsh's killer knew of his peanut intolerance and Michael Baroni's killer knew of his deadly reaction to latex rubber. Circumstantially, one probably could add diabetic Wilbur Constable to the list, though the nature of his affliction made murder a harder call, and the jury was still out regarding Edie Gogos.

While shocked and sickened by the horse head, Hannah had no

idea of its significance. How someone managed to get into their mid-twenties without ever seeing *The Godfather* was beyond me, but Hannah Skaal had experienced an unusual life.

After I explained the grisly connection, she asked: "Is this somehow connected to that actor show?"

"I have no proof, but I think it is," I said.

"A crazy fan?"

"Maybe."

"Dave, do you think Mr. Hanley knew I loved him?"

"I'm sure he did, Hannah."

"He was like a grandfather to me. I never knew mine."

"It's okay."

"I feel like I…I…didn't do enough for him…"

The sobbing started in again and she clung onto me like Harold Lloyd grasping those clock hands. There was little I could do but let her sob. It took a while, but Hannah finally cried herself out.

Then in a sudden fit of logic she asked: "Dave, where do you even get a horse's head?"

I hadn't thought to wonder about that. For me, it was simply someone copying an old movie scene. But Hannah had asked the perfect question.

The first sirens were wailing off in the distance. "Hannah, it's going to get a little crazy here," I said. "This apartment is a about to become a crime scene, and I'm not sure they're going to let you stay here."

"I don't think I could, anyway," she said.

"Do you have anyplace else you can go for the next day or so?"

"No. Can I stay with you?"

"Um…we'll see." While that did not sound like the worst idea, I wasn't positive it was the best, either.

The police, accompanied by the manager, arrived a few minutes later. Among the cops I recognized the hawkish face of my old friend Detective Dane Colfax, who was now working out of Robbery-Homicide. He seemed to have added a little more salt to his salt-and-pepper hair since the last time I saw him. When he saw me, he shook his head.

"Beauchamp, what is it with you?" he asked. "Whenever you show up people die. Are you the Angel of Death, or something? And if the answer is yes, can I give you a list?"

"I showed up after the fact this time, Dane," I said. "You remember Palmer Hanley, don't you?"

"How could I forget? That's why I'm here. I happened to hear the report and recognized the name, so I decided to swing by. Being a celebrity case it would have come our way anyway. What say you and I have a little talk out in the hall?"

Turning to Hannah, I told her I'd be right back and encouraged her to answer any question the police asked her.

She nodded.

In the hallway, Colfax said, "Okay, Dave, let's hear it."

"Everything?"

"Everything."

I rattled off the details as I knew them but left out the part about seeing Karen Robinson at Jay Leach's house because I still had yet to make any sense of that. Even without it, the story as it bounced back to me sounded pretty nuts.

Screwy, ain't he? Mel Blanc as Bugs Bunny commented inside my head.

"Don't you ever get involved in simple cases?" Colfax asked. "Infidelity? Skip tracing? Anything that doesn't involve corpses?"

"I did find a missing cat for a woman once," I replied.

"So how does the Valley Slasher fit into this?"

"I really don't know, other than the fact that one of the victims was the son of two of the Slasher's victims."

"The guy in the clown mask."

"Right."

"And you think your friend in there was killed because he was allergic to horses?"

"Well, I don't think his allergy was the motive, just the means."

"Wouldn't shooting him have been easier?"

"Yes, it would have. So would stabbing, or strangling, or poisoning, or putting a pillow over his face, or just about any other method of murder I can think of. There must be some reason to go to such extremes."

"Like what?"

"Dane, I don't know!"

"Do you know who else knew about Hanley's horse problem?"

"Hannah knew, since she overheard him talking about it. I don't know of anyone else."

"And I take it you don't think Hannah could have done it?"

"Not in a million years."

"If you say so, but you understand I'll still have to check her out."

"Yeah, but trust me, there's no way. She loved Palmer."

"Wouldn't be the first time a young woman kills her older lover because he's rich."

"Dane, you're not getting it. She wasn't his lover, she was his surrogate granddaughter. She's taken care of him for a couple years, starting back at the Temple. She's torn end-from-end over his death. It is absolutely impossible that Hannah Skaal could have done this."

"But she did know about the allergy."

I threw my hands up in the air.

"All right, all right," Colfax said, "don't get your boxers in a bunch. Like I said, I still have to check her out, because that's my job, but I'll take your *amicus curiae* into account."

"*Amicus curiae*? Are you studying law now?"

"Night classes at UCLA."

"Don't tell me you're going to become a lawyer."

"Hell, no. I just thought it would be a good idea to know what I'm up against as a cop."

"So am I done here?" I asked.

"I think so. I know where to find you if I need you."

"How about Hannah?"

"I'll talk to her and then she can go."

"She lives here."

The detective's eyebrows raised. "Sleeps here, too, eh?"

"I told you, it wasn't like that! Hannah was Palmer's live-in caregiver and assistant. Palmer was a pretty state-of-the-art ninety-five, but even so, when you're that old you need a lot of assistance."

"This place isn't going to be very comfortable over the next few days," Colfax said.

"I'm planning on finding someplace else for her."

"Okay. Let me know wherever it is."

Detective Colfax was finished with Hannah in less than twenty minutes, after which she sounded desperate to leave. I walked her outside to my car, which I hoped was not being blocked in by an emergency vehicle. It wasn't.

"What's going to happen to the apartment now?" she asked.

"That's tomorrow's problem." I turned over the ignition.

"Are we going to your place?"

"For the time being, at least. We just need to get out of the police's way for a while."

"I don't want him to be dead, Dave."

"I don't either."

She whimpered all the way to my apartment.

Once there, I got her to nibble on some toast while I looked online for a nearby motel. There was one not far away, for a reasonable rate, which I told her about.

"I need to use the bathroom," she said.

I directed her there, regretting that I had not yet cleaned it as I had promised myself I would do since last October. When I heard the door open again, I said, "I think I've found a good place, Hannah."

"I think I have, too," she replied.

I turned to face her and my jaw dropped like the wolf in a Tex Avery Red Hot Riding Hood cartoon.

Hannah Skaal was completely naked. Her red hair, taken out of its pigtails, cascaded over her white shoulders. Her breasts were larger than I'd imagined and her waist was slimmer than her usually dowdy outfits revealed. Hannah Skaal was, in short, a knockout.

"I hope you're not angry with me," she said.

"Uh, well, I'm feeling a lot of things right now, Hannah, but anger isn't one of them," I stammered back.

"I just don't want to be alone. I want to stay here with you. I'll earn my keep. Honest."

"I, uh…Hannah, I…"

"Please, Dave, don't make me go away."

She rushed up and pressed herself against me. I could feel her through my clothes.

Since that rendered my clothes redundant, I got rid of them.

We barely made it to my bed before I thrust inside her, exploding there a few minutes later.

Some time after that, Hannah began softly crying.

Good god, I thought, what have I done?

If you don't know, sport, I can't explain it to you, the voice of

Errol Flynn said in my head.

"Hannah, I didn't hurt you, did I?" I asked.

"I used to do this to get what I wanted, in my old life," she whimpered. "Usually drugs. When I cleaned up, I swore I'd never do this again. Yet here I am."

"I'd like to think I had a little bit of say in the matter."

"Really? You wanted to do it, too?"

"Hannah, I'm not in the habit of having sex with people I don't want to have sex with." I'd said that to assuage whatever feelings she was wrestling with right now, but the truth was I was seriously wondering whether helping Hannah Skaal into bed had been a good idea.

She, on the other hand, took it at face value.

Two more times she took it at face value.

I was nearly asleep, half from exhaustion, and half from exquisite abrasion, when Hannah nudged me.

"Dave," she whispered, "I need to get in the shower. Have you ever done it in the shower?"

"Uh, yeah, I have, actually."

"Care to show me how it works?"

"Hannah, I don't know if I can. I'm not sure I can stand up."

My standing up, though, wasn't as important as Little Dave's ability to stand up, and he—unbelievably to me—was at attention and saluting.

For the next half-hour, all I heard over the rush of water coming through the showerhead, and the gasping, moaning, and chuckling sounds rising from our soaped-up bodies, was the voice of W.C. Fields inside my head, saying: *Ah, to hell with the drought.*

I couldn't have agreed more.

By the time we had finally gotten out of the shower, spent, pink, and wrinkled, I didn't even have to be asked whether Hannah could move in.

The only question was whether or not to call Detective Colfax to let him know that.

After careful consideration, I opted to not pass along that information just yet, on the grounds that I could always tell him later, but I couldn't un-tell him later. Some little part of me (a different little part than the one that had just gotten a workout worthy of a Guinness World's Record) thought it best to keep that bit of information to myself.

I went into the bedroom to get a clean pair of briefs, but I noticed that Hannah remained steadfastly nude.

"Hannah, great as it is, I don't think I can do it again right now," I said.

"What? Oh, no, it's not that. I just don't like putting dirty clothes on after a shower, and dirty clothes are all I have. I either need to go back and get more clothes from the apartment or go shopping."

"Shopping is the better idea, but you still have to wear something to go into the store."

"You don't have anything I could borrow, do you?"

I looked through my closet for something that might come close to fitting her, settling on an old, white t-shirt and a pair of shorts I rarely wore anymore. She happily put them on, and the sight of Hannah in the synched-waist shorts (which she wore without panties) and tight shirt, (which she wore without a bra), made me question whether my Twinkie really was out of crème filling.

But we had things to do.

Since my place was only a mile or so from a name-brand discount clothing store, we tried there first, and it proved to be a good choice. With my input, Hannah tried on outfits that better suited her body. Looking at herself in the triple-mirror while trying on a tight-fitting sweater and slacks, which enhanced every arc of every curve, even she seemed shocked.

"I never knew," she said. "No one ever told me I could look like this."

Armed with about a week's worth of new outfits, Hannah wanted to go back to the apartment, but I wanted to stop off at my office first. I figured she might as well see where I spent my days sitting around waiting for work to come in.

"Oh, this is…nice," Hannah said upon entering.

"It gets the job done," I responded.

"You don't have a cleaning lady, do you?"

"Um, no. Does it show?"

She gave me a look that expressed, *Are you kidding*? "Do you have any cleaning supplies?"

"There are a few in the other room, but I didn't bring you here to be the maid."

"I'm not a maid, but I don't like dirt, either."

She started for the supplies.

"All right, thank you," I called, knowing I couldn't stop her.

While she was working to make my office look less like a set for a horror movie, I powered up my laptop to try and find out where one might procure a horse's head. I knew that Francis Ford Coppola had obtained the one used in *The Godfather* (yes, it was real) from a dog food manufacturer, so that seemed like as good a place as any to start.

I typed in *Dog food manufacturer Los Angeles* and was surprised to find five within the greater Los Angeles area. Only one, Perfect Friends Pet Food, boasted in their advertising of putting horsemeat in their product.

I probably could have called them, but I felt that the best bet would be to inquire in person.

After all, that always worked in *The Rockford Files*, didn't it?

After telling Hannah where I was going, I recommended she call a cab if she needed to go anywhere. She said, "I'll be fine until you get back."

"You sure?"

"Positive. Just don't forget to come back."

She smiled seductively.

The voice I heard this time was coming from inside my little head, not my big one.

12.

Perfect Friends Pet Foods was located in Cudahy, a small town in south Los Angeles County just off the 710, which was one of those freeways even people who have lived here for years tend to overlook. It ends up in Long Beach, but before getting there cuts through a handful of the so-called "Gateway Cities."

To what they serve as the gateway I have no idea.

After exiting the freeway I drove around until I finally found the nondescript building that housed Perfect Friends Pet Foods.

The first person I encountered inside was a bored looking African American receptionist.

"Hi, would it be possible to talk to the plant manager?" I asked.

The woman looked up at me in a way that indicated she was looking down on me at the same time. "You're not one of them, are you?"

"Them?"

"The ones who think animals are more important than people?"

"Would it help me see the plant manager if I was?"

"Definitely not."

"Then no, I'm not one of them."

"Mm-hmm."

I don't think she believed me.

"Look, ma'am," I tried again, "I'm in kind of a bind, and I was hoping I could get someone here to help me. I'm working for a film company, and we're shooting a thriller—"

"And you need horse parts for one shot," she said.

"Um, well, yeah, but how did—"

"Someone was in here a day or so back wanting a head."

I tried not to look excited.

"Oh. Did you give it to him?"

"I didn't. Someone else here might have."

"Can I talk to that person?"

She leveled an unblinking gaze at me. "You don't really work for a film company, do you?"

So much for *The Rockford Files* approach.

When all else fails, there's always the truth.

"Okay, you've got me," I said. "I'm not with a production company. I'm a private detective investigating a case in which a horse's head turned up, quite possibly the one you provided to someone a couple days ago."

"Are we going to get in trouble?"

"Only if it's illegal to sell somebody a horse's head."

"I wouldn't know about that."

"Off hand, I wouldn't either," I admitted.

"What's your name, again?"

I gave it to her and she picked up the phone and punched in a number.

"Hi, Mr. Mazetta?" she said, her voice sweetening. "There's a fellow here named Dave Beauchamp who'd like to see you. It's about that request we had a day or so back. Right. Hmm? No, I don't think so. If he is, he must have joined the force straight out of high school."

Holding the receiver down she said, "You're not really a cop, are you?"

"Like I said, I'm a private detective. And I'm thirty-three."

Her eyebrow arched like she didn't believe me about that, either.

"He says he's a private detective," she said into the phone. "All right." She hung up. "Someone will be out in a minute."

"Thank you. So, what kind of pet food do you make here?"

"Cheap kind, but I didn't say that. You have a pet?"

"No."

"Then I guess you won't be asking for a free can."

Another woman soon appeared through a door at the rear of the lobby. She was wearing a sleek gray suit over a white sweater, and her platinum blonde hair was pulled back tightly in a bun, which screamed: *No, I'm not Kim Novak, but thanks for asking.*

"Are you Judy or Madeline?" I asked when she came close.

"Well, someone finally gets it," she responded. "You like Hitchcock?"

"Of course, and *Vertigo* is one of my all-time favorites."

"I'm neither Judy or Madeline, actually. I'm Marnie." She stuck her hand out formally. "Marnie Thorpe."

Well of course you are, Sean Connery's voice rumbled inside my head, as I shook her hand.

"Dave Beauchamp," I said. "I'm a private investigator."

"So I've heard. I work with Mr. Mazetta. Come on back."

On the way to Mr. Mazetta's office we passed at least a dozen framed posters hanging on various walls showing dogs and cats of all breeds chowing down on Perfect Friends Pet Food. In a strange way, it was actually making me hungry. When we finally arrived at the head man's office, I was surprised how small it was, given the buildup.

Vince Mazetta was seated behind his desk. He wore a perfectly pressed blue shirt with a white collar, and a bright red tie. He was maybe sixtyish, and had a grey bouffant hairstyle the likes of which I thought went out in the 1970s.

Maybe it wasn't real.

When he stood up, I was surprised how small he was, too. The guy must have been all of five-foot-one.

Maybe four-eleven without the hair.

"Siddown," he ordered, and I did. "So, you're really a private dick?"

"I'm afraid so."

"You look like my daughter's boyfriend. He's in eleventh grade."

I shifted on the chair in order to reach into my back pocket, and Vince Mazetta suddenly tensed, which in turn caused me to freeze. "Um, I was just going to get out a wallet-sized copy of my license," I said.

"Whatever you got in your pants, leave it there. I'll take your word for it. So you want me to tell you why I sold somebody the head of a horse."

"If you don't mind."

Mazetta shrugged. "It was a little weird, to be honest. This guy comes in and says he works for a prop shop somewhere in town. He wanted to put that goop they smear all over someone to make one of those life masks, but do it on a horse, so he could get the perfect replica of a head. I told him I didn't get it, because animal effects these days are all digital, right? I have a son in the industry, so I know this shit. But the guy, he says that was the problem, that digital can only get so realistic. So he wanted to make a cast. He knew no horse is going to stand there and let you trowel that shit all over their head, and even if it did, it wouldn't leave its eyes open. But a horse that's already dead, no problem, even the eyes. So I asked the boys downstairs if we had a nice fresh head, and it turns out we did. I had 'em pack it in a styrofoam case with some dry ice and he took it. Now, are you tellin' me that the guy didn't use the head to make a mold?"

"I think you could say that the head was used instead to pull a spectacularly unfunny joke," I offered. "Are you familiar with *The Godfather*?"

"You talkin' about the movie or Joey the Match?"

"Um, the movie."

"Aw, shit, are you tellin' me the guy did the head-in-the-bed gag with my horse?"

"Somebody did the gag. I can't prove the head came from you."

"What'dya want from me, then?"

"Ideally, the name of the person to whom you sold the head, so I can find out."

"What're you going to do him when you find him?"

"Well, there may be some legal action."

"If it's legal action that'll splash back on me, forget it."

"Mr. Mazetta, what if I were to offer you a guarantee that you would not be involved in any legal action?"

"How you gonna do that?"

I leaned forward, smiled, and prayed he wouldn't see that I was about to start lying like a rug. "I feel confident in saying that the man I'm working for would never allow this case to go to the courts?"

His eyes narrowed. "What's that mean?"

"If I could identify the man who approached you about the head, and then deliver him to my employer, you would never have to worry about that man, or anything he says or does, again."

Vince Mazetta glared at me for a minute, and then broke out laughing. "Jesus, where do they recruit you guys from these days, the local Montessori? Who are you working for?"

"Tony," I said, taking a shot in the dark.

"Which Tony?"

"Little Tony."

"I don't know any Little Tony."

"That's the way he likes it."

"Are you bullshitting me, Mr...what the hell was your name again?"

"Beauchamp. Do I look like I'm bullshitting you, Mr. Mazetta?"

"Yeah, frankly."

We stared at each other for a few seconds, and then he laughed.

"Aw, screw it," he said, hitting a button on his desk phone. "Hey, Marnie? Would you bring in any information we have on that guy who wanted the head?"

"Yes sir," I heard her reply.

After jabbing the button again to cut off the call, he looked up at me.

"I'm gonna tell you somethin,' kid," he said. "I think you're so full of shit you'd steam in the morning dew, but you got balls. I don't see much indication they've dropped yet, but they're there somewhere."

He leaned forward.

"Now I'm gonna tell you somethin' else. If any of this crap splashes back on me, I'll find you."

He smiled, and I smiled back, though I was probably the only one of us struggling mightily not to wet himself.

Marnie Thorpe came in with a piece of paper, which she handed to Mazetta, who glanced at it, then handed it to me.

I glanced at it and groaned.

"What's the matter?" Mazetta asked. "You know the guy?"

"Yeah, you could say that." I rose and extended my hand. "Thank you, Mr. Mazetta. I intend to keep my promise to not involve you any further."

"Hey, you got a pet? Marnie, give him a few cans on the way out."

After retrieving a six pack of Perfect Friends Cat Food, I wondered internally how effective my performance had been.

Don't quit the day job, junior, Robert Mitchum said in my head. *Then again, maybe you should, for everybody's sake.*

Okay, I walked into that one.

As I went past the receptionist in the lobby, she glared at the cans, then at me, and muttered, "You told me you didn't have a pet."

"I've been inspired to get one," I said, running for the exit.

In my car, I looked over the piece of paper again. It was a photocopy of a simple bill of sale, handwritten, probably because of the unusual nature, and it told me that the price of a horse's head these days was $320—less than a carpool violation. It also told me that the person who claimed to be buying it was fictional, since the signature read *J. P. McGillicuddy.*

You don't remember J. P. McGillicuddy?

That was the slug-in name Barry Fitzgerald's character Lt. Muldoon used for any unidentified suspect in the classic film *The Naked City.*

It didn't tell me much.

Sure, and how can you be sayin' that, boyo? Barry's voice said inside my head. *It tells you something worth a pot o' gold.*

He was right. It did.

It told me that the person responsible for the deaths of Tony Marsh, Palmer Hanley, Michael Baroni, and probably Wilbur Constable and Edie Gogos, was as an old film buff, just like me.

It also tells you that you've just stepped into a big, knee-deep problem, Bogie chimed in.

He was right too.

If the police followed this same line of inquiry, and figured out the significance of J. P. McGillicuddy, they would also realize the suspect was an old film buff, and who had some kind of connection with all of the victims.

Just like me.

13.

When I got back to my office I almost didn't recognize it.

I don't think I'd ever seen the place looking this clean and neat, even before I moved my stuff into it.

It was Hannah's doing.

The real sign that a hand other than mine had been at work was the fact that the thrift store painting of a moody, rain-drenched, *noirish* street, which had hung at an angle since forever, had been straightened.

I'd have to change it back when she wasn't looking.

"Hi, Dave!" Hannah said brightly, then her face dimmed. "Something's bothering you."

"Why do you say that?"

"I can just tell. I could always tell when something was bothering Mr. Hanley, too."

"I'm just a little concerned is all."

"Not about me, I hope."

"No, no, of course not."

"What, then?"

I seated myself behind my newly-polished desk, and Hannah took my one and only guest chair.

"Well, my hunch regarding the source of the horse's head proved to be correct. But the more facts I uncover, the more the responsibility for the killings appear to point to one person in particular."

"Who?"

"Me."

"*What?*" she screamed. "Dave...you...you didn't...you couldn't!"

"No, no, of course not. But the clues make me look like a suspect."

"Oh, that's crazy!"

"You know that and I know that, but getting the police to see it our way might be a challenge, given the evidence so far."

"What evidence?"

"Well, I knew, or at least met, every one of the victims. And it seems the killer is an old film buff, like me."

"There must be lots of old film buffs. Look at how many people came to the actor show."

"I know, but there's a level of film-buffery that goes deeper than the opportunity to meet actors. Half the people there were probably buying signed photos to sell on eBay. I'm talking about the kind of film buff who can identify a movie simply by hearing a line of dialogue?"

"Well, you mean like, what is it... 'Play it again, Sam?'"

I smiled grimly.

"You've just proven my point, Hannah. That's not a real line of dialogue from *Casablanca*, even though most people think it is. The line is really, 'Play it, Sam,' and it's not spoken by Bogart, either, it's spoken by Ingrid Bergman. Film buffs know that."

"So what does the killer know that you know?" she asked.

"J.P. McGillicuddy."

"Who's he?"

"He's nobody. He's a made-up name from an old movie that a lot of people have heard of, called *The Naked City*, but only a real film buff would understand the significance of someone signing a piece of paper J.P. McGillicuddy."

"*The Naked City*? I didn't realize you liked *those* kinds of films."

I had to laugh.

"It isn't one of *those* kinds of films, Hannah, though I did have to watch a few of those kinds of films for a case once, and I assure you, I didn't like them. They made me feel kind of sad, in fact."

"So do you think some other film buff is trying to frame you? That's the right word, isn't it?"

"Yes, that's the right word, but I don't know. I can't imagine why anyone would."

"What are you going to do?"

"Be careful, I guess. Try to stay a step ahead of the police, if possible. This place looks fantastic, by the way."

"Thanks," she replied, smiling. "I had a hard time getting that painting over there to hang straight. It wanted to go crooked. Hey, do you think we could get something to eat? All of a sudden I'm hungry.

I know I shouldn't be."

"There's no reason you shouldn't be," I told her. "Let's go out and grab a bite."

We went to an old-style diner just down Ventura Boulevard from the office, where Hannah ordered the turkey sandwich and I got a burger.

The food had only just arrived when my cell rang. It was Colfax.

"Dave, I'm having a problem running a history on that girl, Hanley's caregiver."

"Let me guess," I said. "There's a period of several years where she just falls off the grid, right?"

"Yeah, but how did you...ohhh, because she was part of the Temple."

"Yep."

"You wouldn't happen to know where she is now, would you?"

"Yeah, she's right here."

Hannah looked up from her plate.

"Put her on."

I handed the phone to Hannah. "It's Detective Colfax," I said.

"What does he want?"

"He wants to talk to you."

She looked at me apprehensively.

"It's okay. He's on our side."

I hoped.

Taking the phone as though she was forcing herself to, she whispered: "Hello?" After a few seconds, she said: "No, I'm pretty sure there's no next of kin. Right. No, I never heard Mr. Hanley talk about wives or children or siblings, or anything like that. Why are you asking me this? Oh."

Holding the phone down from her ear, she whispered: "He says if Mr. Hanley had no next of kin, then I'm the one who's going to have to deal with his burial, or else the county will do it."

"Tell him that's fine. I'll help you."

"Hi, it's me again," she said to Colfax. "Okay, I'll do my best. What? Where am I staying? With Dave."

Suddenly looking like she'd just been caught doing something naughty, Hannah added: "Yes, at night, too."

"Here, let me talk to him," I said, and she handed the phone back.

"Dane? Hannah will be living with me until further notice, though she'll need to get back into the apartment to get some stuff. When do you think she'll be able to go back in? Maybe tomorrow?"

I nodded hopefully to Hannah.

"With police supervision. Right. Also, there's a car that belonged to Palmer. Can she pick that up? Okay, great. Anything else?"

He told me what else.

"That's not going to be a concern of yours at this time," I responded.

Hannah looked worried.

"All right, then yes, if you want to put it that way. Happy now? I can take care of myself, Colfax. Right. Bye."

I put the cell phone back in my pocket.

"What did he want to know that was none of his concern?" Hannah asked.

"Oh, uh, whether we were…you know…an item," I said.

"We are, aren't we?"

"Yeah, it looks that way."

I didn't tell her what Colfax had really said, which was, *Every time you hook up with a broad, I have to save your butt from getting killed.*

As far as I was concerned, that was simply coincidence.

"He thinks I killed Mr. Hanley, doesn't he?" she said.

"What makes you say that?"

"There was something in his voice. He didn't sound friendly."

"He's a cop doing his job. I've already told him there a far greater chance the Man in the Moon killed Palmer than you."

We ate in silence for a few minutes, then Hannah said: "All this stuff that I'm going to have to do for Mr. Hanley, that you offered to help with?"

"What about it?"

"Do you think they'll let us keep him?"

"Keep Palmer?"

"Keep him with us, instead of burying him?"

"Um, that I don't think they'd allow."

"Not even in one of those jars?"

"Oh, you mean his ashes?"

Her face took on a puzzled expression.

"What did you think I meant?" she asked.

"I guess I blanked for a moment and wasn't really listening," I told her, trying to cover for my own stupidity in wondering whether she wanted to have Palmer stuffed, like Roy Rogers did with Trigger. "Yes, that would be possible."

"I remember him saying one time that he would rather be cremated than…how did he put it?…'boxed up and put into dirt storage.' It was kind of funny at the time, but now it's real."

I could see she was fighting back tears again, so I reached over and took her hand. Honestly, I wasn't sure if I really wanted the cremated ashes of a former friend hanging around my apartment, as much a looming presence of the past as the painting of Rebecca De Winter in *Rebecca*, but neither did I want to argue with her.

Instead I asked: "Do you happen to know if Palmer left a will?"

"He met with a lawyer not long after we…got out…and I'm pretty sure it was to make out a will. I wasn't involved. The lawyer was someone his new agent recommended, and the meeting was in the agent's office. But there's a small safe in the apartment with all his important papers in it, so if he has a will, it's in there."

"You have the combination?"

"Two-turns left to twenty-two, one turn right to—"

"No, Hannah, you don't have to say it aloud, as long as you know what it is. It's going to be a day or so before you can go get things from the apartment, according to Colfax. But he did say you can pick up the car any time you want."

"The car keys are in the apartment, too, on a hook in the kitchen."

I sensed that dealing with Palmer Hanley's arrangements and the disposition of his stuff was going to become a part-time job. But there was no way to back out now, even if I wanted to.

"After lunch we'll go to the apartment and see if the police will let you take the car," I said. "I doubt we can get to the safe."

When we had finished eating and I paid the bill, I drove back to Palmer's building, feeling Hannah tensing in the passenger seat as we got close. A couple police cruisers were still present, but, almost unbelievably, there was a spot on the street out front. I pulled in and told Hannah, "We'll be as quick as possible."

Getting into the building was not a problem, of course, since Hannah had the key, but the apartment was still blocked off.

Flagging down a policeman, I said: "Hi, we were here earlier. She actually lives here, and she needs to get her car keys. They're hanging on a hook in the kitchen."

"Hold on," the cop said, disappearing into the place. He came back a moment later holding keys. "These them?"

"Yes," Hannah said. "Do I need to sign for them or anything?"

"No, it's okay. We know how to get in touch with you, though, right?"

I pulled out my wallet to hand him a business card, but I was still out. "Hannah," I said, "when we get back, remind me to put more cards in my wallet."

I knew she would.

After telling the officer that Detective Colfax knew how to reach us, we retreated. Taking the elevator to the building's garage, Hannah walked straight to Palmer's turquoise Mini Cooper—which looked like it should have *Tonka* stamped into its underside—and got in.

"You can follow me back to the apartment," I told her, then ran out to my car on the street.

Hannah proved to be a slow driver, like someone who had not been driving for long, but it was easy to keep her in sight through my rearview. We made it home without incident.

After six attempts to parallel park the Mini on the street a block from my place, she finally made it, within a foot or so of the curb.

Back inside the apartment, she stretched out on the couch. For a second I thought maybe she wanted me to stretch out on top of her, but it turned out she was simply fatigued.

"The next few days are going to be hard, aren't they?" she asked.

"Yes, I'm afraid they are," I told her. "Palmer's passing is going to get picked up by the media, if it hasn't already, so any time you turn on the TV you will probably see a story about it. It's not like in the movies where people die and are either just left there, or are put in an ambulance and whisked out of sight. In real life there are a ton of procedures to follow and details to take care of."

"Dave, where do you think we go when we're dead?"

"Well, I don't know, really. I don't believe people come back as ghosts, if that's what you're asking."

"What do you think heaven is like?"

"Hannah, I'm not a theologian," I said, noticing that she flinched when it sounded like I was about to say *Theotologics.* "I think maybe each person's heaven is personalized to them. I guess mine would be an old movie. I'd be seated at a roulette table in a casino while Humphrey Bogart extended my credit to the house."

She looked over at me. "I didn't know you gambled."

"I don't. But who knows what I'll be doing after I pass?"

"One of the people…back you-know-where…had a gambling addiction," she said, softly. "He thought…the place…would be able to help him. It didn't."

"Well, you don't have to worry about me," I promised, lightly stroking her face.

She closed her eyes and smiled.

"What do you think Mr. Hanley's heaven is?" she asked.

"You knew him better than I did, Hannah. What do you think it is?"

Keeping her eyes closed, she said: "Maybe he's at an actor show like the one we went to. He had so much fun doing that, meeting people and signing pictures. Only in heaven, only nice people would be there, not people like Miranda Love."

"I don't think anyone in heaven has to worry about running into Miranda Love."

She seemed on the verge of falling asleep when I gently nudged her and said, "Hannah, you still awake?"

"Mm-hmm."

"I need to go back to the office, just for a little while. You'll be okay here, while I'm gone, right?"

"Mm-hmm. Oh, and put some cards in your wallet."

Smiling, I dug out my stash of business cards and restocked my billfold. Then before leaving, I wrote down my office and cell phone numbers and sketched out a map to my office building, just in case. She was lightly snoring as I went to the door. Looking at her, peacefully stretched out on the sofa, asleep, I felt a slight pang in my chest.

It was either the onion on that hamburger I had for lunch or love.

You're such a romantic, Katharine Hepburn dead-panned inside my head.

On the way to my office I pondered calling Karen Robinson under the guise of asking advice about funeral planning, but really to find out what she was doing at the home of Jay Leach.

Upon getting there, I discovered she had saved me the effort.

This is Karen Robinson, her voice said on my answering machine. *Do you know how to kill someone and get away with it?*

Jeez, now what?

After a pause, her voice went on: *Shit. Why am I doing this? I'm not really going to kill anyone, I'm just frustrated and angry. I was wrong to call you. Please disregard this. But go ahead and call if you have any updates on my grandfather's case.*

After rattling off her number, she hung up.

I called back immediately, getting her machine. But only a second after I instituted the "you're it" phase of phone tag, she picked up.

"Dave, I'm sorry about that call. I was just…well, I don't have a husband to yell at anymore. Your number was right by the phone, so…"

"It's all right, Karen," I said, "as long as you really don't kill anyone."

She laughed. "Be kind of dumb now, wouldn't it? So do you have some information for me?"

"I've managed to find Michael Baroni."

"Really? What did he have to say about those letters?"

"Nothing. He's dead."

There was a pause, then: "Dave, you don't think—"

"Palmer Hanley is dead, too. So are a couple other people from the Celebrity Expo."

"What's going on?"

"I don't know yet, but when you first claimed your grandfather's death was murder, I frankly didn't put a lot of stock in it. But Palmer's was definitely foul play. Whatever's going on, I'm pretty sure it's connected to the expo."

"Since that's where Granddad was killed, I've always assumed that."

"Then you're going to love this. Michael Baroni changed his name to Boris Verdugo."

There was a commercial-length pause, then: "Are…you…shitting…me?"

"I don't have DNA evidence, but I'm convinced they were one and the same."

"My god. So Verdugo, or Baroni, killed my grandfather and the others, and then killed himself?"

"No, I think he was murdered by the same killer as the others."

"Jesus. There's a serial killer out there so I call you up asking how to get away with murder. Now you probably think it's me."

"Of course, I don't, though it wouldn't hurt to tell me who has made you so mad you want to kill them."

"Oh, it's this asshole lawyer named Jay Leach."

After taking a deep breath I said: "You mean the man whose house you were at last night."

"Yes, and—"

She suddenly stopped for a pause so pregnant it could have been carrying triplets; then: "How...would you...know that?"

"I was there," I said. "I brought Leach home. I saw you."

"Shit! We need to get together and talk."

"All right. Do you want me to come out to your apartment again?"

"No. I have a recording session this evening in North Hollywood. I have to be at the studio by four. Can you meet me there?"

Since North Hollywood was a skip down the road for me, I agreed.

To kill the hour-and-a-half before I had to be there, I put into my laptop a disc of *Borderline*, a nifty little romantic crime drama starring Fred MacMurray and Claire Trevor that was nobody's must-see film of 1950, but I liked it.

Once it was finished, having ended the same way as it had the last time I'd watched it, I headed out.

Chanticleer Sound was located on Lankershim Boulevard in the NoHo Arts District. I got there a few minutes early and waited in the lobby for Karen, who came rushing in like she was being escorted by a windstorm. Going to the receptionist, she said: "I need the conference room for a few minutes."

"It's open," the woman behind the desk said.

Karen whisked me away to a small, glass-enclosed room with barely enough space to hold the conference table and executive chairs, and closed the door.

"God, what a day," she said, taking a chair. "I've been dealing with Garden Glades Memorial Park, and they're trying to rip me off at every opportunity. But that's where my grandmother is, so Granddad wanted to be there, too. Okay, what happened to Hanley?"

"Another allergy-related death."

"How can this be happening?"

"Believe me, I wish I knew. When I find out, you'll be first on my list to inform. But for now, tell me about your problem with Jay Leach."

She rolled her eyes. "He thinks he's a player, but he's nothing but a drunken asshat. But if you know him, you already know that."

"I only barely know him. The guy was threatening to sue me."

"Over what?"

I gave her the condensed version of the story, including his admission that the threat was so much hot air.

"Well, mine isn't," she said. "I'm going to sue his ass, and that's not a bluff. See, when I was going through my grandfather's papers I found a contract between Granddad and Leach for a different collector show, one that Leach was trying to organize on his own. The deal with Leach would have been exclusive. He promised money up front if Granddad did his show instead of the one that Boris Verdugo… Michael Baroni…organized."

"That's interesting," I said. "And Tony signed the contract?"

She nodded.

"But I met Tony at the Celebrity Expo. How could he be there if he had an exclusive agreement with Leach?"

"Because Leach never came through. The contract was dated 2012 and it was valid for three years, and during that time Granddad didn't do the Verdugo show. He was very conscientious when it came to contracts. But my reading of the one he signed with Leach was that it was pay-or-play, which means Granddad should have gotten his exclusivity stipend no matter what. It was only a thousand dollars a year, but that plus a supposed signing bonus of two-thousand, added up to five grand. I couldn't find any record that the money had ever been paid, and believe me, Granddad saved everything. I contacted Leach about it. He gave me the runaround, so I tried going to see him at his home."

Ah, now the plot is thickening, William Powell said inside my head.

"And you threatened to take him to court over it?" I asked.

"Yeah, but I'm not sure he really heard me. See, I went to his house and rang the doorbell, but no one answered. I tried the door and found it unlocked, so I went in, but no one was home. Who goes off and leaves their house unlocked in L.A? I was in the process of writing Leach a note when he came stumbling in, drunk as a bastard. But I guess you already know that if you drove him home. I confronted him and he started blubbering about how he had no money, how Miranda Love was the devil incarnate, and how his connection to her was destroying him, and how all women were out to get him. He wasn't making a lot of sense. I finally gave up trying to talk about the contract and left, figuring it would have to be straightened out in court. Honestly, though, I'd probably spend more than five grand on an attorney."

While that satisfactorily answered the question of what Karen was doing in Leach's house, it also opened up another potential lead.

"You say your grandfather saved everything?" I asked.

"It's almost unbelievable what he saved."

"Do you think there's any other paperwork relating to this deal with Leach."

"Like what?"

"Like a form asking for information about health issues, such as allergies."

She frowned. "I'll be on the lookout for anything like that and let you know." Glancing at her watch, she added: "I'm going to have to go into the studio in a few minutes."

"One of your songs?" I asked.

"Yeah. I try to produce my own stuff whenever I can. So where do we go from here?"

That was a great question. The best I could come up with by way of an answer was that she keep searching through her grandfather's papers to try and find any documents relating to Jay Leach or Boris Verdugo, while I paid another visit to the charming Mr. Leach.

Agreeing, she went into the studio and I left the building.

I was nearly to my car when my cell rang.

It was Hannah.

"Dave, did you know somebody named Gayne Prescott?" she asked.

"He was one of the guests at the Celebrity Expo, but I can't say I know him."

Then the other shoe dropped.

On my head.

"Wait, you just asked *did* I know Gayne Prescott, not *do* I. You used past tense."

"It was just on the television. He was found dead."

"Jeez," I moaned. "Okay, thanks for letting me know."

Even though I had no proof, logic argued that Prescott's death was not simply coincidental or random, but the latest one in the string of murders. News of his death also made me feel a little better about my status on the suspect list, since I had never even met the man, only his neighbor who liked to dress up as a cop.

"Will you be home soon?" asked.

"I still have some things to do," I said. "I'll be home for dinner."

"Which means I'll have to go the store. What do you want?"

"Hannah, you don't have to do that."

"I live here now, don't I?"

"Okay, surprise me. But no calamari."

"I don't even know what that is."

"That's why I love you. I'll see you later."

"Dave...you just said you loved me."

"Uh, yeah, I guess I did."

"I love you, too."

"I guess we'll have a lovely dinner, then."

That made her laugh. She was still laughing when I disconnected the call.

Feeling that strange pang in my chest again, I headed back to the office. Once there I powered up the laptop to see if I could find a phone number and address for the Law Offices of Jay Leach.

It turned out Leach had a website complete with his picture (which made him look more respectable than the last time I had seen him) and a phone number, which surprisingly did not translate to 1-800-SHYSTER. But I could not find an address. Maybe he worked out of his house.

Or maybe he had to move a lot.

Trying the number, I got a machine.

What else was there these days?

I didn't bother leaving a message, and instead decided to run out to Leach's house in person. Burning up gas to get there might not yield any results, but it would make me feel like I was doing something.

I managed to squeeze through that narrow traffic window separating morning rush hour (six a.m. to three p.m.) from afternoon rush hour (four p.m. to midnight) and made it to Leach's house in good time, though my Corolla was getting thirsty. Parking on the street, I went up to his door and rang the bell.

As had been Karen Robinson's experience, there was no response.

As had also been Karen Robinson's experience, the door was unlocked.

As had not been Karen Robinson's experience, Leach was already there.

He was dead, but he was there.

14.

When Detective Colfax's voice came on the line I said: "Hi, Dane, it's Dave Beauchamp. I, uh, well, I found another one."

"Christ in a Chrysler, Beauchamp!" he shouted. "What is it with you?"

"I don't know. But this one is a lawyer named Jay Leach."

"Leach? That's really his name?"

"If he changed it, I'd hate to hear from what."

"Where is he?"

"Hollywood."

"My old stomping grounds. Are you at the scene?"

"I'm here."

"You didn't touch the body, or anything, did you?"

"I'm not totally stupid, Dane, and shut up Mitchum."

"Who's Mitchum?"

Oh, jeez, had that been out loud?

"Never mind. I didn't touch anything."

"You think he had help dying?"

"I can't tell. There's no puddle of blood or visible bullet holes, or a knife hilt sticking out anywhere I can see."

"All right. Call it in."

"What was the name of Mendoza's partner at the Hollywood station?"

"Willford, but don't call the D's directly. Try to pretend you're a normal person and call 911. They'll probably send Willford out anyway, but if you call him straight up he might think you're somehow involved. You're not, are you?"

"No. In fact, Leach's death makes my life more difficult, since there were things I needed to ask him and now I can't."

"Hey, how'd you get inside his house, anyway?"

"He had a bad habit of leaving his front door open."

"Interesting. Okay, call 911, but first give me the guy's address."

I reeled it off for Colfax, who then disconnected. Then I called

911.

While waiting for the first emergency vehicle to arrive, I wondered whether I should update my resume to include *Babysitting corpses until the police show up.*

A paramedic truck was first on the scene, then some prowl cars started showing up, followed by an unmarked car, and a familiar looking plainclothesman.

Detective Bruce Willford almost walked past me, but then stopped and turned back. "I know you," he said. "Why do I know you?"

"The Temple of Theotologics case. Dave Beauchamp."

"Oh, right. Beauchamp. So what are you doing with a new body?"

"Stumbling over dead people is my mutant talent."

Willford didn't laugh.

"Okay, detective," I went on, "I came here to see the victim and found him this way. I called it in."

"What did you want to see him about?"

Not wanting to give an elevator pitch for the case again, I replied: "We had a legal misunderstanding that I was hoping to clear up."

"You know the guy well?"

"I've had some dealings with him."

"Well enough to know who next of kin is?"

"He mentioned a wife who is out of town this week."

"So you did talk to him before he died."

"Yes, but not today. Last night."

"Okay. Do you have a name for his wife?"

I hesitated a moment, trying to remember. Then Gene Kelly's voice said: *Leslie.* Like Leslie Caron, his co-star in *An American in Paris.* Jeez, I wish I could train my surface mind to work this well, without the help of the Hollywood Victory Caravan.

"Leslie," I said.

He wrote it down. "You don't know where she went, do you?"

"No idea."

"I'm sure we can find her, wherever she is. In the meantime, you have any theories about what happened to Mr. Leach?"

"Me?"

"Am I talking to anyone else?"

"Well, I'm not really in a position to theorize, but I think it's safe to say that the man had a drinking problem. He was extremely drunk last night. Alcohol might be a contributing factor."

"Okay. We'll see what the ME says."

"Can I go now?" I asked.

"Yeah. If I need you some more, I'll let you know."

I have to say that Willford had toughened up considerably since the last time I saw him. I assumed that came with the job.

Back in my car, I took stock of the dead end I'd hit where the lawyer was concerned. Maybe Karen Robinson could come up with something in her grandfather's papers.

With no better ideas coming to mind, I headed back to the office.

Walking in, I was startled all over again at how clean it was; so clean, in fact, that I could now see how badly the walls needed to be repainted. I made a note to call building management, though I wasn't about to hold my breath for a response.

While ruminating about my walls, the desk phone rang.

It was probably Hannah.

I thought about answering "Hey, sexy," but then thought better of it, just in case it wasn't her. "Beauchamp Investigations," I said instead.

Boy, did I make the right decision!

"Hi, Mr. Beauchamp," a man's voice said, pronouncing it *bow-champ*, with equal emphasis on the syllables, making me sound like an Olympic archer. "This is Terry Brucker. We met at the Hollywood Celebrity Expo. You gave me your card. I was with Mr. Prescott."

"Oh, right."

It was the guy dressed as a policeman.

"I don't know if you heard," he went on, "but Mr. Prescott died."

"I have heard. I'm sorry."

"He was always really nice to me. We lived next door to each other."

"Mm-hmm. Is that why you called, Mr. Brucker?"

"No, no, there's something else. They took Mr. Prescott out this morning on one of those rolly things. Covered up, you know, 'cause he was dead."

"That's the standard procedure."

"Right. But last night there was a woman over at his house, kind of snooping around."

Now he had my full attention.

"A woman?" I said. "Did you recognize her?"

"No, but when I saw her I went over and asked if there was anything I could do for her. I kind of look out for Mr. Prescott. And when I came over, she said she was Mr. Prescott's sister, and came to see him. Then she got in her car and drove away. I thought it was kind of weird at the time, but today, I really wonder about her."

"Mr. Brucker, what made you think it was weird at the time?"

"Because Mr. Prescott told me on more than one occasion that he didn't have any brothers or sisters, but she said he was his sister. And today he's dead. So I had to wonder who this woman was, why she lied to me, and what she was doing at his house."

"Mr. Brucker, have you told this to the police yet?" I asked.

"Yeah, when they were here, but they asked me for a description of her, and I just said old. Old and kind of stretched."

"I'm sorry. Stretched?"

"Her face was tight, like she'd had a facelift."

"Do you recall the color of her hair?"

"Red, I think. Wait, brown, maybe. Or reddish brown. Light reddish-brown, maybe blonde."

"Okay, not black hair. What about her size?"

"Oh, you know, not real big, not real little. Woman-sized."

"Woman-sized," I repeated.

"Yeah, you know. Smaller than a man, bigger than a kid."

"What about her clothes?" I asked.

"Oh. Well, nothing special, as I recall."

"Professional dress?"

"I don't think she wore a dress at all."

"Pants suit?" I tried.

"I don't know, a sweater, maybe. Slacks."

"All right. Now, you said she got in her car and drove away. Did you notice the make of the car?"

"Silver."

"Silver isn't a make, Mr. Brucker, it's a color. Was it a Ford? A Chevy? Toyota?"

"No, just a car. A silver car. The reason I'm calling you is because I don't think the police believed the woman had anything to do with it. But you're a private detective, and they're smarter than police, right?"

You can say that again, Bogie replied inside my head.

"Sometimes," I said. "All right, Mr. Brucker. Thank you for calling, and if you ever see this woman again, please write down the make and model of the car, and the license number, if possible. Okay?"

"Okay," he agreed. "Or should I say ten-four?"

"Okay is fine."

"By the way," Brucker went on, "Because of you I've decided to change characters."

"Really?"

"Yeah. I don't see myself as a policeman anymore. I see myself as a detective."

I could envision him standing in front of the Chinese Theatre in Hollywood, his girth stuffed into an army surplus store trench coat and a cheap fedora plopped on his head, offering to pose for tourist selfies for a dollar a pop.

"Mr. Brucker, do you mind if I ask what you do for a living?"

"Well, I was a building inspector for the City of L.A., but I took an early retirement after a building I inspected fell over a hill. It wasn't my fault, though, it was the rain."

"I see," I said. "Well, it could happen to anyone."

After I hung up the phone I rested my head in my hands.

How do they find me? Zero Mostel asked plaintively inside my head.

I wanted to go home, particularly since I now had someone there waiting for me.

As I drove back home, I tried to figure out why a woman would pretend to be the sister of a man who had no family. Why lie? Until I knew who the woman was, I couldn't begin to understand.

Business as usual, in other words, the ever-helpful Robert Mitchum said inside my head.

Instead I turned my thoughts to Hannah. She wasn't the most sophisticated of young women; she wasn't the most knowledgeable of young women; she wasn't the most self-reliant of young women; but she was...

...Hannah.

I hoped she was equally smitten with a babyfaced, possibly

schizophrenic, failed lawyer and only marginally successful private detective.

I was home in no time.

Hannah's Mini Cooper was still parked in the same spot in front of my building, and I found myself smiling as I drove past it and into the drive, and on to my parking spot.

Going up to my apartment, I started to put the key in the lock, but then wondered if I should give Hannah some kind of warning that I was home, so she wouldn't be startled. I gave a light rap and called out, "Hi, Hannah, it's me" before opening the door.

What I saw upon opening the door stopped me in my tracks.

For a moment I thought I had entered the wrong apartment.

Hannah had moved the furniture around in such a way that the apartment now looked twice as big as it had before. The sofa was pushed up against a wall, which created a much larger open area. The back of my old battered lounge chair now abutted a different wall, giving ample space for small tables on each side of it. The television stand meanwhile had been shifted to a point where it was visible from every spot in the living room.

Hannah walked out of the kitchen, beaming.

"Hi, Dave," she said. "You like it?"

"Hannah, how did you do this all on your own?" I asked in amazement.

"It was pretty easy, actually. The secret of moving anything heavy is leverage. Believe me, I've had to move enough sick people on and off beds to make sofas a piece of cake."

"But how do you *know* to do this?"

"What do you mean?"

"Everything is in its perfect place. How did you figure that out?"

"I don't know. I just moved things where it looked like they should be. You do like it, don't you?"

"Yes, yes, I do. I'm just startled. I wonder if your real talent is in interior decorating."

She beamed more brightly at that.

I sat down on the sofa and leaned back. "I wish you could rearrange all the facts of this case I'm on so they fit together this well," I sighed.

She sat down beside me. "Lean your head forward."

I did and she began lightly massaging the back of my neck. I liked that.

"What parts of the case are bothering you?" Hannah asked.

"Everything. It keeps getting more and more complex. There are more and more angles, more and more people involved, more and more strange circumstances, and nothing is adding up to anything."

"You're home now. Try to put it out of your mind."

Hannah proceeded to give me a professional-quality massage, which made me moan and gasp like an actor looping sound effects into a porno. At the end of ten minutes the outside of my head felt great, but the inside was still a cranial swirly.

"Lie down if you want," she said, getting up and moving to the lounger. Looking at her sitting there, I could not help but envision her as a client. Who would she be played by in a movie? Not Mary Astor, not Lauren Bacall, not Faye Dunaway…

Don't be such a chump, Bogie said in my head. *It's Ann Sheridan or it's no one.*

Danged if he wasn't right.

I doubted Hannah knew who Ann Sheridan was; these days, most people probably didn't. But now that it had been pointed out to me, Hannah completely captured her combination of subtle ginger beauty, innocence, and unlabored sexuality, with the added level of being totally unaware of any of the above. Hannah's hair was a little kinkier than Ann's…at least the Ann I saw on screen and in photos… and she was a bit more sturdily built, but now that the resemblance had been pointed out to me, it was unmistakable.

"You're looking at me kind of funny," she said. "Do you want to…you know…do it again?" she asked.

"Well, some time, sure. Right now I'm just looking."

She smiled self-consciously. "It's kind of funny that you didn't already have a girlfriend. I mean, you're so nice."

"Well, some of the women I've met haven't appreciated niceness very much."

"I like niceness. I haven't had a lot of it in my life. Mr. Hanley and you have been about it."

"It's a wonder he didn't propose to you," I joked.

"Oh, he did. A couple times."

I sat up. "Really?"

"Yeah. I don't think he was serious, but he did."

"And you said no?"

"I just laughed. Besides, when I was back in…you know where…
I used to hear about members, young women, who would be pushed
to marry really rich old men to get control of their fortunes, which of
course would end up going…you know where. I hated that, and if I
actually had married Mr. Hanley, people might think that about me."

"You know, Hannah, marriage or not, it's possible that Palmer
named you his beneficiary in his will. If he has a will, that is."

"So that means I'd get whatever he left anyway?"

"Yep."

"I never even considered that."

She thought in silence for a few moments, then said: "Dave, you
don't think *they'd* try to take it for themselves, do you?"

"Who knows what the Temple might try to do," I said, "at least
what's left of them. But if they did try, I think they'd have a very
hard time succeeding. But this is all moot until we find out what is in
the will, so as soon as you can get back into the apartment, you need
to get the paperwork out of the safe. Colfax said you might be able
to get in tomorrow."

"Okay." She got up and started toward the kitchen. "I went out
and got some ground beef for dinner. I'm pretty good at making
things with ground beef."

"Sounds great."

"Does your oven work?"

That was a good question. Throwing something frozen in the mi-
crowave is the extent of my culinary expertise.

"Turn it on and see," I called back.

While she puttered in the kitchen, I sank back into swirling, gray
thought.

I couldn't tell Hannah this; despite her herculean efforts to ease
my mind, she had actually roiled it further. What if Palmer Hanley did leave a sizeable estate to Hannah? What if the Temple of
Theotologics did make a play for it by contesting the will on the
grounds that Palmer was a mentally unsound man under the control
of a young, calculating gold-digger who influenced the writing of his
will for personal gain?

Even worse than that, what if someone from the Temple had

managed to infiltrate the apartment, find the safe, open it, and either destroy the will or plant a false one, or both?

Since I'd gone that far, I might as well throw paranoia to the wind and hurl the other shoe off the cliff.

What if the Temple of Theotologics was behind the murders?

15.

I worried all the way up until Hannah called me for dinner. When I sampled the dish she had somehow whipped up out of ground beef, pasta, tomato sauce, cheese, and whatever spices I had laying around, it put all else out of my mind.

It was unbelievable.

"Seriously, Hannah, how do you do this?" I asked after filling my plate for the second time. "How do you take whatever you find and make it better?"

"I just do what seems right," she said.

For the first time I felt a measure of sorrow for her. Had she not had as rough a start in life, she might have already conquered the world.

I had nearly re-cleaned my plate when the phone rang.

"You want me to get it?" Hannah asked.

Since my mouth was full, I nodded.

After picking it up, she called: "Dave, it's someone named Leslie Leach. Wasn't that awful lawyer named Leach?"

"Yes, it's his wife," I said, wiping my mouth and getting up from the table.

I kissed Hannah on the nose before taking the phone and saying, "This is Dave Beauchamp."

"Hello, Mr. Beauchamp, this is Leslie Leach, Jay Leach's wife… I mean, widow. I found your name and office number on my husband's telephone pad. I tried your office, but you weren't there, so I found this number online on White Pages."

I was still listed in the L.A. directory, chie
never afford to become unlisted.

"I hope I'm not disturbing you," she said.

"No, it's fine. I'm sorry for your loss."

"Thank you. I was out of town and was called by the police and told that Jay was dead."

"It must have been quite a shock."

"Ye-es," she answered hesitantly. "I mean, I didn't expect it, exactly. But the police tell me you discovered his body, and that you're a private investigator."

"That's right."

"Were you working for my husband?"

"No. He was threatening to sue me, actually. But I don't think he meant it."

She made a sound that might have been a bitter laugh.

"Mr. Beauchamp, did you see my husband before he died?"

"Yes. He mentioned you."

"Did he? Did he tell you why I was gone?"

"Um, no."

"So he did not hire you to follow me?"

"No, not at all. May I ask why you were gone?"

There was a sigh, and then she said, "I went away to try and clear my head, to decide whether I was going to remain married to him or come back and institute divorce proceedings. I'd gotten to the point where I didn't know how much more I could take. His drinking, the people he worked for, his crazy get-rich-quick schemes. It was like being married to a sitcom character, only without many laughs."

"I'm sorry to hear that. What did you decide?"

"It doesn't matter now, does it?"

"I suppose not. But, Mrs. Leach, how is it I can help you?"

I heard another sigh, this one longer and more rueful.

"Mr. Beauchamp, when you saw Jay, did he seem like he was going to kill himself?"

"Kill himself? No, I don't think so. He was drinking heavily, and I sensed he wasn't exactly in a good place in his life, but I wouldn't characterize him as despondent. Do you think he killed himself?"

"I don't want to think that. I don't want to think that my running off to try and figure out what to do with my life drove him to do something irrational."

Since this was not the best circumstance in which to reveal Leach's comments about wanting to "murder the bitch," I deflected. "Mrs. Leach, I did get the impression he was angry at someone else."

"That hideous Miranda Love creature, no doubt," she said. "Jay couldn't stand her, but for some reason, he wouldn't drop her."

So, the missus doesn't know the story, Bogie pointed out inside my head.

"He used to tie one on and then start moaning, 'There are eight-million stories in the naked city, and I had to become a supporting player in hers!' But it was his own damn fault."

"I'm acquainted with Miranda, and she does seem to have that effect…" I began, then stopped dead. "Mrs. Leach, could you repeat what you just said?"

"About it being my husband's fault?"

"No, his comment to you."

She did, and its significance came at my brain like a freight-train.

"It's a quote from Jay's favorite film," Leslie Leach went on.

"*The Naked City* was his favorite film?"

"You know it, too? Is this some kind of guy thing?"

"Mrs. Leach, did he quote the movie often?"

"Oh, god yes. He had a DVD of it, which he'd watch time and time again and then start pontificating about the common man simply trying to do his job, against all odds. I think on some level he identi-fied with it. This may sound insensitive, Mr. Beauchamp, but I'm really rather happy I'll never have to see that movie again or hear dialogue from it."

My mind was in overdrive. "Yes, well, like I said, if you're wor-ried that your husband did something drastic because you left, I am quite convinced that is not the case."

"Okay, well, I'm sorry I bothered you."

"Not a problem. Goodnight."

I didn't even wait for her to say goodbye before I hung up.

"Dave, what is it now?" Hannah asked. I hadn't even realized she'd been hovering over me while I was on the phone.

"He said it in the bar, too. Jeez, why didn't I catch it then?"

"Who said what?"

"Jay Leach said, 'With me, one's too many and eight-million aren't enough.' I thought he was misquoting Howard da Silva in *The Lost Weekend*. The eight-million part didn't even register."

"Would you still love me if I told you I don't have any idea what you're talking about?" Hannah asked.

I took her in my arms, felt her warmth as she reciprocated.

"It means one little piece of the puzzle has just fallen into place," I said. "I know who procured that horse's head from the pet food company."

"That horrible Jay Leach?" Hannah asked.

"That horrible Jay Leach," I confirmed.

While I had no proof that Leach had signed the name *J.P. McGillicuddy*, the hypothetical person of interest mentioned in *The Naked City*, on the bill of sale for the horse's head, Jack Daniels had convinced me not to believe in coincidences.

"So did he kill the others, too?"

"That I don't know."

But he is looking to be your one single connection, dear boy, Jack now chimed up inside my head.

He was right; every road seemed eventually to lead back to Jay Leach. An even grimmer conclusion was the thought that if nobody else died now that Leach himself was dead, it would strongly indicate that he was indeed the murderer.

But the drunken lost soul of a man that I had met seemed hardly the criminal mastermind type.

All this was not doing much to lift the fog inside my brain regarding this case, but it did force my brain to start working again.

After a while Hannah came up and started stroking my head again. "Dishes are all clean," she said. "Want to go to bed?"

"Hmm? Oh, sorry, Hannah. I'm still working on this danged case. I don't know how much good I'm going to be for the rest of the night."

"Okay." She kissed my head and went to bed alone.

It was a little after one when I finally joined her, my head hurting from the strain of thinking, not from the weight of the results.

* * * *

The next morning I awoke to a warm hand slipping underneath my sleep shorts.

Before long it was too hard to get out of bed.

A half-hour later, as Hannah rolled off of me, I asked: "Are we going to start every day like this?"

"It beats getting up for morning drill," she replied.

An hour later I was clean, shaved, dressed and ready to go to the office. But first I put in a call to Detective Colfax to see if we could return to Palmer Hanley's apartment that day.

"There are still some men there, but it should be okay," he said. "Just make sure someone sees you, don't go in on your own."

"You know I'd never do that," I told him.

"I have to tell you, Dave," Colfax went on, "even in R-H we don't have a lot of experience in murder by decapitated horse. There's no spatter and only two sets of prints, which are found all over the place. I imagine they belong to the vic and Big Red Riding Hood."

"I'll thank you to speak more respectfully about her," I snapped.

"So, it's getting serious, huh?"

I could hear the grin in his voice.

"Yep," I said.

"Okay."

"Have you dusted the front doorknob?"

"Gee, Mr. PI-in-love, we dumb cops never would have thought of that on our own," he sang sarcastically. "Of course we dusted the front doorknob. Prints there were smudged, like somebody used a cloth or wore a glove to open the door. The only interesting thing we found in the whole place were tracks in the carpet."

"Tracks?"

"Parallel indents going from the front room to the bedroom."

"What do they signify?" I asked.

"Near as I can figure, a suitcase on rollers, like maybe one big enough to hold a horse's head. We've been asking the neighbors if they happened to see someone carrying or rolling a suitcase through the halls, but no one did."

"How did Leach get past the guard in the lobby and into the elevator?" I thought aloud.

"What did you say?"

"Knowing what it's like to get into the building if you don't live there, I was wondering how Jay Leach got in and got the guard to let him up to Palmer's floor in the elevator. Probably lied his way in. Maybe he told the guy he had luggage for a tenant that had been lost by an airline and was returning it, or something like that. That might be what I'd do."

"Are you finished speculating, Beauchamp?" Colfax asked.

"I guess."

"I'm real glad about that, because that means you now have time to tell me why you held back your suspicion that Jay Leach was the man who delivered the head. He's your most recent corpse, right?"

"Oh, uh, it's not that I held anything back, Dane. I just figured it out, in fact, based on something he said before he died. It would be hard to explain to someone who is not an old movie buff."

"Okay, fine, whatever. But you're convinced it was Leach?"

"Yeah."

"Where'd he get the head?"

"A pet food company in Cudahy."

"For chrissake, Beauchamp, when were you planning on telling me *that*?"

"I'm telling you right now," I protested. "I called you, remember?"

"Okay. At least give me the name of the damn pet food company."

"It's called Perfect Friends, but I'd really appreciate it if you didn't hassle the owner."

"You'd really appreciate it, huh? Why is that?"

"Because being locked in a car trunk is not my favorite mode of travel."

"Someone in the outfit?"

"If he isn't, he sure gets off on playing the part."

"So we got a pet food Don and a horse's head that ends up in somebody's bed. If I go see the guy, is he also going to shove an orange peel in his mouth and mumble?"

"I can only report the facts as I know them, Dane. I can't be expected to explain them logically."

"Okay, all right. I don't suppose you happen to have a picture of this Leach character that I can show to the guard in the lobby, do you?"

"There's one on his website. I think it's Leachlaw.com"

"Of course it is. All right, I'll check it out. Hey, I'll tell you what. Since you need to get something from the apartment, I'll meet you and Red at the apartment in two hours."

"Didn't I mention something about showing respect a few minutes ago?"

"I vaguely remember something like that," Colfax said. I think on some level he was enjoying making my back-hair stand up. "One other thing, Dave. If I find out you're holding back any other information from me, you're going to be off my Christmas card list. *Capisce?*"

He hung up.

After explaining the situation to Hannah, we both went to the office. There were no messages waiting for me on the machine, and it was too early for the mail. Hannah spent most of the time trying to get the painting of the rainy street scene absolutely straight.

It was a lost cause.

We arrived at Palmer's apartment a few minutes early. A couple uniforms were still in the apartment, and they resisted letting us in until Colfax arrived.

When he finally showed, he told the cops, "They're okay," as he escorted us inside. Then turning to Hannah, he said, "Go get whatever you need."

"I'm going too," I told him.

"Let's all go," Colfax declared.

We went into Palmer's bedroom, where a small safe was situated in the closet. She deftly turned the dial until I it opened.

"Nothing's been touched," she said after inspecting the contents. "At least that's good. What do you think we should do with this?" She held up a bundle of currency in hundred dollar denominations.

"How much you got there, Red?" Colfax asked.

"Don't call her Red, okay?" I said.

"I've been called worse, Dave," Hannah replied. "I can't pretend I don't have red hair."

She took a moment to count the money.

"About twelve-thousand dollars," she said. "This was for emergencies."

"Twelve Gs covers a lot of emergencies," Colfax commented.

"Can I see what else is there?" I asked, and Hannah handed me an envelope embossed with the address of The Law Offices of Richard H. Neale, which I figured contained a will.

Turning to Colfax, I asked if there was any problem with our taking the safe's contents.

"No, it's fine," he replied, "though I'd recommend you put that cash in a bank instead of leaving it lying around. And if that paper turns out to be a last will and testament, let me know what's in it, would you?"

"Will it have a bearing on the case?" I asked.

"Well, stop and think about it, Beauchamp. Right now we don't have a motive for what appears to be a deliberately-caused death. Maybe it's in those papers."

Hannah shuddered.

"I'll contact the lawyer today," I said. "At some point Hannah's going to need to come back for her personal belongings. The manager is going to want the place cleaned out soon so he can rent it out again."

"We should be out of here in another day," Colfax said. "Like I said, we're not turning up all that much. But before you go, how many people had the combination to the safe those papers were in?"

"Just Mr. Hanley and me," Hannah replied.

"All right. Try to stay out of trouble, Beauchamp. See you later, Red."

"Bye bye, Copper," she said, which surprised both Colfax and me, but only Dane grinned.

We took off.

On the way down to the car, Hannah said: "You don't think I made him mad, do you?"

"What do you mean?"

"I called him 'Copper.' I thought it was funny, because copper's a color, like red, and he's a policeman. A copper. But I don't want to make him mad."

"Hannah, you got a smile out of him. That's harder than getting a dollar out of Jack Benny."

Now cut that out! Benny said in my head, right on cue.

"Let's go back to the office," I recommended. "I have a lock box in my desk where we can put the money until we find a bank. That is, if you trust me with it."

She laughed and punched me in the arm.

It hurt gloriously.

At the office I had a

somebody called, but it was only a scammer claiming to be the IRS, stating that they were coming to get me.

Powering up my laptop, I found the phone number for the Law Offices of Richard H. Neale, and punched in the number.

I reached an efficient-sounding receptionist.

"Hi, my name is Dave Beauchamp, and I'd like to talk to Mr. Neale," I said.

"What is this regarding, sir?" she inquired.

"The last will and testament of Palmer Hanley, which Mr. Neale prepared."

"Is Palmer Hanley deceased?"

"Yes."

"Was Palmer Hanley a man or a woman?"

"Um, a man."

I was about to chalk it up to the kind of peculiar question only a legal secretary could ask, but then realized that *Palmer*, used as a first name, could indeed be considered androgynous.

After several more efficiently officious questions, the receptionist slipped us in to Mr. Neale's busy schedule at three-forty-five.

* * * *

The Law Offices of Richard H. Neale were within the Miracle Mile, a stretch of Wilshire Boulevard that was once home to the city's grandest department stores, and is now known for its museums, including one that contains the bones of unfortunate animals dug out of the La Brea Tar Pits.

Contrary to popular belief, no dinosaur remains have been found there.

That's because they're at the Hollywood Celebrity Expo instead, Red Skelton ad-libbed in my head, laughing at his own joke.

The law offices were in a building that was nondescript on the outside, but large and plush on the inside, complete with new carpet and glass walls. A young Latina wearing bright green cat-eye glasses sat behind a kidney-shaped receptionist desk. The glasses should not have looked good, but they did.

"You must be Mr. Beauchamp," she said.

"Yes, and this is Hannah Skaal."

"Take a seat, please. Mr. Neale will be with you momentarily."

She was as good as her word; within two minutes a tall, tanned, man of about forty emerged from the back. He wore no jacket but his trousers looked expensive.

"Hi, Mr. Beauchamp?" he said, softening the "ch" into "sh" to create *BEE-sham*, which was, at least, original. "I'm Dick Neale, come on back, please."

After leading us to a spacious office, he asked us to sit down.

"First, let me say I am sorry for your loss."

"Thank you," Hannah said.

"I understand neither of you were blood relations of the testator."

"No, no we weren't," I said, "but we have the will."

I handed it to the attorney who opened it, quickly examined it, and pronounced it legitimate. Then turned to Hannah and asked to see identification. Hannah shot a worried look toward me, but I assured her it was all right. She produced her driver's license, which Neale examined.

"I haven't had that for very long," she said.

"It doesn't matter, Ms. Skaal, thank you," he said, handing the license back. "You have been named as the executor of his will. Do you accept this responsibility?"

"What will I have to do?"

"See that Mr. Hanley's last wishes are carried out."

She looked at me again and I nodded.

"Okay, I accept," she said.

"Good, good, now let's go over what we have here. 'I, Palmer Manfred Hanley, a resident of the County of Los Angeles in the State of California, being of sound and disposing mind, memory and understanding'…yada yada yada…would you like me to read it verbatim or simply summarize it?"

"Summarization would be fine," I said.

"Good, good." He read in silence for a few seconds, then said: "Well, in a nutshell, Mr. Hanley's estate at the time of this writing was worth five-point-six million dollars."

Hannah gasped.

Neale looked at her. "You didn't realize it was that much?"

"I tried not to get involved in money matters other than those needed to run the house," she said.

"I keep notes of each person whose will I prepare, and I looked them up before you came. Mr. Hanley's income was rather considerable during the last several months of his life, though I must warn you, part of that income was from a publisher who had contracted with him to write his memoirs. Had he done so?"

"He was working on some kind of book," Hannah said, "talking into a machine, but I don't know how far he got."

"We will have to research that, because it might mean paying back a $500,000 advance. Even if that is the case, however, it still leaves a considerable sum."

"I can't believe he earned so much in such a short time," I said. "I don't know how much of Palmer's history you're familiar with, Mr. Neale, but he was essentially held prisoner by an entity of his own making for decades."

"I know the story," Neale replied, "which is why I know not all of his money came from the resumption of his performing career. The Temple of whatever-it's-called maintained an off-shore bank account in Hanley's name, which they padded with cash every time there were rumblings that its tax-exempt status might be revoked. Unfortunately, no one ever thought to obtain a power-of-attorney over Mr. Hanley. I doubt they felt it necessary. That was an enormous oversight on their part because, when he split with the Temple, the off-shore account in his name legally became his and his alone."

Just hearing that the Temple had managed to bilk themselves out of millions of dollars made my day.

"I suppose you'd now like to hear who the beneficiaries are," Neale said.

"Absolutely."

Richard Neale scanned the paper again, just for good measure, then looked up. "He left me twenty-thousand dollars for making out his will, which I must say is quite generous. Quite generous. But there are three others. Not surprisingly, Ms. Skaal, you are the primary beneficiary. You are named as well, Mr. Beauchamp, as is someone with whom I am not familiar."

"Is it Mr. Hanley's agent?" Hannah said.

"No, no," Neale said. "I know Kenny. He's the one who connected me with Palmer Hanley in the first place. Kenny did quite well from the deals he made for Mr. Hanley, who happily paid him thirty percent of his earnings instead of the usual twenty. No, this is someone different."

He read the name.

Were I an animated character, my jaw would have hit the floor with a resounding clunk, like Tom Cat in those old cartoons.

"Would you say that again, please?" I choked.

"Of course. The fourth beneficiary is someone named Miranda Shawlee," Neale repeated.

16.

"Miranda...Shawlee," I said, in the tone of voice usually reserved for things like *Liver...ala mode.*

"Is there a problem?" Richard Neale asked.

"Palmer left money to Miranda?"

"Some, though the bequeathal is a bit whimsical. Let me read it to you. 'To Miranda Shawlee, I leave the sum of six-hundred dollars, which should cover the amount I cost her during our days in live television.'"

I laughed out loud.

"I assume Ms. Shawlee will know what this means," Neale said. "As for you, Ms. Skaal, Mr. Hanley left you the sum of two-million dollars."

For a moment I thought Hannah was going to pass out. When she finally got her breath she asked, "Did you say two-million...?"

"That's right. In your case, Mr. Beauchamp, he was not quite as generous."

"Well, Hannah was really the one who took care of him for so long. I just came in toward the end."

"Yes, but he did consider your actions the primary reason he was able to free himself from the Temple, therefore he bequeathed you one million."

Even though I was seated, I thrust out my hands to steady myself on Neale's desk.

"One million dollars?" I said.

"That's right," Neale confirmed. "As I said, not quite as generous, but still ample."

"Yeah...I'd say so."

"That leaves some two-million and change, depending on how the book advance situation plays out, for the establishment of a foundation to help people who were harmed in a material, emotional, or physical way by the Temple of Theo...oh, how do you pronounce it?"

"Beauchamp," I said, dazedly. Then: "Oh, sorry, The-a-tuh-log-ics."

"Yes, the-a-t...the Temple, at any rate. As executor of the will, Ms. Skaal, you are responsible for establishing this foundation. I would be happy to help you do this, but you are under no obligation to retain my services."

"You're a lawyer, Dave," she said, "what do you think?"

"Oh, I didn't realize you were one of us, Mr. Beauchamp?" Neale said.

That scene from Tod Browning's *Freaks*, in which all the side-show carnies eerily proclaim their acceptance of a beautiful young woman by chanting, *Gooble-gobble, gooble-gobble, one of us, one of us*, flashed through my head.

"I'm not practicing at present," I told him. "But I can see no reason why you should not be involved in setting up the foundation, Mr. Neale."

"Then I'm fine with it," Hannah said.

"My involvement will entail some separate charges," the attorney continued, "which can be deducted from the estate, once it has passed through probate. Speaking of which, there will also be a charge for opening probate, and that will need to be paid up front."

He named the price, and since I was still more accustomed to being broke than to having a little in the bank, I flinched. Hannah, however, simply nodded.

"Do I pay it to you?" she asked.

"Yes. You may send a check."

"Not cash?"

"Cash would be acceptable, yes, though I would caution you against sending it through the mail."

"We'll provide one or the other," I told him.

"Fine," Neale said, rising. "I trust this answers all or most of your questions. I have another appointment now, so please allow me to show you out." As he ushered us to the lobby, he added: "For what it's worth, even though I did not have that much personal contact with Mr. Hanley, I found him to be a delightful man. Please feel free to call us if you have any further questions, and the sooner you send the money for opening probate, the sooner we can get everything in order."

Before leaving the office I gave a business card to the reception-ist.

Back in the car, Hannah let out a scream, which scared the hell out of me, and then clamped both hands over her mouth, removing them to say: "Dave, I'm going to be a millionaire!"

"I know. So I am. We'll have to find a good money manager and figure out the best way to invest it. We also need to get that cash that was in the safe into a bank account. Do you have one?"

"It's Mr. Hanley's account, really," she said, "but we both used it. Both our names are printed on the checks."

"What's the balance?"

"Around ninety-thousand dollars."

Jeez, suddenly everywhere we turned, we tripped over money!

"You're going to need to open an account of your own, Hannah," I said. "I'll help you open it up."

"I'm glad you're here, Dave," she said. "I just don't think I could do all this stuff by myself."

At once I saw myself as Nick Charles, whose occupation during the course of action in *The Thin Man* was looking after his rich wife Nora's fortune, while solving murders on the side.

We had no sooner gotten home than a reporter from the *Los Angeles Times*, who remembered that I had been instrumental in Palmer's rescue, called for a statement about his death. I had one prepared. Palmer Hanley had not lived an easy life, I told the guy, but in the end he was rewarded with the kind of success and happiness he had come not to expect, but was grateful for every second of every day.

Before he hung up, though, he said someone wanted to talk to me.

After a moment of silence, a woman's voice said: "Hey, Dave."

It was Luisa Sandoval.

"Hi, Louie."

Luisa "Louie" Sandoval was the one who had gotten me involved in the Temple of Theotologics case in the first place. She had been an investigative reporter for the now-defunct *L.A. Independent Journal* and had moved up to the *Times*. I knew her to be relentless when chasing down a story, and also, a least for a brief, intense, and un-likely period, had known her in the Biblical sense. It was the sort of affair one writes about in one's memoirs, but doesn't really bring up to one's current significant other. In fact, I hoped simply talking to Louie was not going to land me in hot water with Hannah.

"How are you?" I asked.

"Doing good. Back at the Indie-J we used to dis the *Times* at every opportunity, but it's actually not bad here. You?"

"Fine. Working on another problem case, but in general good."

"Problem case, huh? Does it involve a bunch of dead actors, by any chance?"

Dead actors? I didn't recall ever telling Louie about my little cranial dysfunction.

Then I figured out what she was really saying.

"Palmer Hanley is dead, but I assume you know that," I said cautiously, hoping to find out what she had pieced together.

"Yes, I know, but so are about a half-dozen other actors who were at one of those autograph shows with him last week. Don't try to tell me you haven't made the connection, either, because I saw you on TV when the first one died, the Shadow guy."

"Tony Marsh," I said. "Yes, I was there that day."

"So why are they dying? Was there something at the hotel that got them? Are we talking about an outbreak of Legionnaire's disease, or something like that? Is there a cover-up going on?"

"Louie, you're getting a little carried away, aren't you?"

"Dave, *something* is happening to these people. You said yourself, you were there."

"I can tell you that neither Tony's nor Palmer's deaths had anything to do with Legionnaire's disease."

"And all the others are just coincidence?"

"I can't speak for any of the others. Look, Louie, if you want to investigate the hotel for Legionnaire's, I can't stop you. Since it's next to the airport, maybe somebody flew in from somewhere with a virus. I don't know. A fan or someone. All I know is that this has been a very trying week. Palmer's death, and dealing with his estate—"

"You're the executor?"

"No, Hannah Skaal is the executrix. You remember Hannah, right?"

"The nurse? Pippi Longstocking grown up?"

"Be nice."

"Why? Oh, good lord, Dave, was that her that answered the phone? Are you playing hide the chorizo with Pippi Longstocking now?"

"Let's say I'm helping her out."

"And helping yourself in."

"Louie…"

"You don't have to explain. I'm happy for you. So happy I'm actually going to take your word that you don't know anything about the other deaths."

"If I find out anything, you'll be the first person I call."

"I'd better be. *Adios*, *querido*."

"Bye, Louie."

I hung up and turned around to see Hannah glaring at me.

"She's the one who punched you in the nose, isn't she?" she asked.

Louie Sandoval had indeed punched me in the nose, and hard. But it was part of a pretense we were performing for the sake of others. Our survival at that moment depended on it. It had to be convincing, and it was.

Boy, was it.

Apparently Hannah still held that against Louie.

"Yes, it was Louie," I said. "Somebody at the *Times* called to ask for a quote about Palmer, and then that guy handed the phone over to her, because she works there now. She's figured out there's a pattern of deaths related to the Celebrity Expo, and wanted to see if I knew anything about it."

"But you didn't tell her anything."

"I told her as little as I could, but that's not going to assuage her for very long. You know how tenacious she is."

"I know how gorgeous she is." Hannah said. "Are you going to see her again?"

"I might talk to her again, but it's not like, you know, *seeing* her."

She walked up to me, and glared at me for a second, then took my hand.

"It better not be," she said, leading me toward the bedroom.

* * * *

Since the next day was devoted to dealing with Palmer's effects,

I pushed Louie and the case out of my thoughts as much as I could. Hannah and I had to get to the bank to set up her private account, into which was deposited the twelve-thousand in cash, and out of which was written the probate check.

From there it was off to the Price Brothers Mortuary in Burbank, which despite their best efforts at making customers welcome, was simply not a fun, inviting place to be.

What's more, it lived up to its name. *Everything* came at a price.

Hannah and I had already agreed that there should be no public memorial service of any kind for Palmer, since it would likely turn into a media event, but it took an hour to convince Raymond, our Price Brothers representative—a short, chubby man whose sympathetic expression had been stamped onto his face like the numbers on a license plate—that we meant what we said.

Of further annoyance to the "post-life representative," as he called himself, was our insistence that Palmer be put into a plain cardboard box for the cremation rather than the stylish wooden casket Raymond was offering. When Hannah explained that it was Palmer who left instructions in his will that his money be spent to help those still living, I thought the man was going to faint.

Eventually, we got what we wanted.

By Saturday, Hannah was allowed back into her apartment.

A professional crime-scene clean-up outfit had done sterling work on Palmer's bedroom, though a flowery scent now permeated the room.

Ironically, Hannah appeared to be allergic to it.

While she packed up her clothing and personal items, I took stock of the apartment's contents. Since neither she nor Palmer had been living there long enough to accrue a ton of stuff, it looked to be a fairly easy move. The problem was that even a tenth-of-a-ton of stuff was more than my apartment could handle. Most of the excess would go to charity shops, though it quickly became evident that renting a small storage unit would be necessary.

Even though the apartment was paid to the end of the month, we agreed to move everything out as quickly as possible. Before we left, Hannah covered her nose with a cloth and went back into Palmer's bedroom. Looking through the drawers of his nightstand, she located a small audiocassette recorder.

"This is what I was telling you about," she said, handing it to me. "Mr. Hanley was talking into this for his memoirs."

I rewound the tape a little and hit play, and heard his familiar voice chime out, mid-sentence.

Hannah fought back a sob, followed by a sneeze.

"I don't know if I can listen to that," she said in a hushed voice. "Hearing him again, it's…"

I shut the machine off.

"I'll listen to it later," I told her. "You don't have to hear it. Let's go, okay?"

Once we were at my apartment I put the tape machine in a drawer, so she wouldn't have to see it, either.

"Well, I think we've solved enough problems for one week, don't you?" I said.

Then the phone rang.

Hannah got it.

"Who?" she asked. "Oh, hold on." Holding the receiver down, she said, "Dave, it's someone named Terry Brucker."

"Oh, *jeez*," I moaned.

"Do you want me to take a message?"

"No, I'll talk to him." Taking the phone from her I said, "Mr. Brucker, you're calling me at home, you know."

"Yeah, I know. Good thing you're not hard to find, isn't it?"

Yeah. That was just swell.

"What is it you want, Mr. Brucker?"

"It's about that woman I saw at Mr. Prescott's house."

"Oh? Has she come back?"

"No, she hasn't come back, but if you remember, when I saw her I said she looked kind of stretched, like she'd had some work done?"

"Yes, so what?"

"Well, I was thinking of having a little work done myself, maybe have a bump put in my nose so I look more like a detective."

"A bump in your nose."

"Yeah, you know, like that old actor Broderick Crawfish?"

"You mean Broderick Crawford?"

"Did he have a bump, too?"

Seriously, *how* do they find me?

"Mr. Brucker, this is why you're calling me? To get a bump in your nose?"

"I wondered if you knew of any good plastic surgeons you could recommend."

"How would…? Why would…? Do you drink?"

"Well, some beer, sure. Why, you want to go grab a brew?"

I started massaging my temple. "No, but I'll tell you what. Why don't you go the bar and get into a fight. That will result in a broken nose and you won't incur the expense of a plastic surgeon."

"Wouldn't that hurt, though?"

That's why we're suggesting it! Broderick Crawford's voice barked inside my head.

"I suppose it would," I conceded. "But I'm afraid I can't help you locate a plastic surgeon. I don't know any."

"Oh. I thought you real detectives could find anyone, but okay. I guess I can look online for them, too."

"Good luck, Mr. Brucker. Goodbye." I hung up before he could say anything else.

"Who was that?" Hannah asked.

"A guy I met at the Celebrity Expo and unfortunately gave my card to him. At first I thought he was just a little dumb, but now I'm starting to wonder if he's not a little bonkers. If the phone rings again tonight, don't answer it, okay?"

We spent the rest of the afternoon finding places in the bedroom for Hannah to put her clothes.

By early evening, I was starting to wonder how long it would be before we outgrew this apartment.

A little before six Hannah said, "I'm kind of getting hungry. I may need to go to the store."

"Look, we've both been working hard today. How about I go get some takeout?"

"Can we have fried chicken? Mr. Hanley always liked fried chicken."

"Fried chicken it is."

She sat down on the couch. "I can't stop thinking about him, Dave. I keep remembering things he said to me. When you were talking to that guy on the phone a while back, I remembered something Mr. Hanley told me."

"What's that?"

"Well, I heard you say that if you got your nose broken you don't have to go to a plastic surgeon, but Mr. Hanley did."

"Palmer had plastic surgery?"

"He told me that one time he was doing a fight scene in a movie and another actor was supposed to swing at him and miss, but the guy really hit him in the face and broke his nose."

"Ouch."

"They re-set it at the time, but years later it resulted in a deviated septum and Mr. Hanley had to get surgery for it. This time a plastic surgeon was involved, to make sure his nose came out looking the same."

Leave it to Palmer Hanley to be the only actor in Hollywood who actually wanted to keep his old nose.

"When did all this happen?" I asked her.

"The deviated septum operation happened before I was at the... you know. When it started affecting his breathing...*they* finally got him a doctor. Mr. Hanley said they actually got the doctor to come out and do the operation in their private medical center. He said by then he was happy to see anyone from the outside, even if they were going to cause him pain."

"Yeah, I remember him joking that he was allergic to horses and pain."

"But he claimed the procedure went smoothly and without much pain. He said the...*they* had gotten the top plastic surgeon in Los Angeles."

"That's something I suppose."

Then it hit me.

"Oh my god!" I blurted.

"What? What's wrong?"

"Nothing wrong. Something might even be right."

"What?"

"A plastic surgeon."

Hannah's face reflected her confusion as I fished out Karen Robinson's number and jabbed it into the phone.

Fortunately, she was home.

"Karen, Dave Beauchamp. No, I'm sorry, I don't have anything concrete yet, but I have a question. Did your grandfather every have any kind of work done on his face? Yes, a face lift, a tuck, anything?

Really. I see. Do you think you could find any record of the doctor who did it? Could you try? Yes, it might be important. Yes, all right, thank you. I'll talk to you later."

I hung up and turned to Hannah.

"It all fits," I said. "Karen says that Tony Marsh had his eyes lifted when he went into the real estate business because he thought they were too squinty and it made him look shifty, and who wants to buy a house from someone who looks like a crook? I didn't see Gayne Prescott, but Wilbur Constable looked decades younger than his real age. It didn't strike me at the time, but he might have had a facelift, maybe more than one. And Edie Gogos barely looked like herself back at the expo. As for Boris Verdugo, his nose job could be seen from the International Space Station. Probably half, if not more, of all the others had had some sort of work done."

"Dave, why is that so important?" Hannah asked.

"Because if you take a group of actors of a certain age, and you try to find some kind of link between them, you might look to see if they all appeared in the same film, or worked with the same director or producer, or maybe another actor. But working actors work with a lot of people. It's like that Kevin Bacon game where you link any two actors together through two or three steps. That's not really conclusive. But there could be another connection that has nothing to do with the actual making of movies."

"What's that?" Hannah asked.

"Plastic surgery. This is Hollywood. Everything's about looks. Even child actors have been known to have a little work done on their faces. But since cosmetic work is the ultimate elective surgery, the doctors have to be as careful as possible to make certain their patients won't have any side effects. A dentist will ask you if you're allergic to anything before they give you Novocain and start sticking rubber-gloved fingers into your mouth, right? I'm sure nurses ask things like that, too."

Hannah nodded.

"So it's not much of a stretch to think that a cosmetic surgeon would take even greater precautions in asking."

"How do you know that the dead people went to the same cosmetic surgeon?"

"I don't," I confessed. "But it adds up. Assuming that a random group of actors all went to the same dentist is just too coincidental. There are too many dentists in town. But cosmetic surgery is a different story, and when one's continued livelihood is dependent on how good they look, they're going to try and find the best surgeon they can. You just said Palmer told you the Temple had gotten the top guy in L.A. to do his work. Someone with that sort of reputation in L.A. is going to have a pretty extensive patient list. Jeez, it actually makes sense."

Sure, kid, it makes sense, Bogie said inside my head, *but aren't you forgetting something?*

What?

Who's going to admit they went under the knife?

That was a good question. Karen Robinson freely admitted her grandfather had a lid-lift, but most celebrities vehemently deny they've ever had work done.

That is where the internet comes in.

I dashed off to get my laptop and went to Internet Images, the largest collection of unrelated pictures on the web, cribbed from everywhere, including personal websites.

It should be called "Big Brother Photo Supply."

I looked up pictures of Gayne Prescott from his *Arrest Squad* days and downloaded a few. Then I looked him up as recently as I could find, coming across a Hollywood Celebrity Expo photo from 2013. I downloaded that, too. Then I popped up both photos and compared them side-by-side.

"Oh, yeah," I said.

The Prescott of 2013 looked like a drumhead with teeth and little bitty eyes.

I did the same for Wilbur Constable, and while his lift had been much more subtle and effective, the difference between Constable in the 1990s and last week was noticeable.

"This has to be the answer," I uttered. "Hannah, did Palmer ever tell you the name of the doctor who worked on him?"

"No. Sorry. Maybe it's on that tape he was making."

"Maybe."

I looked up Edie Gogos, and saw that not only had her face been completely restructured since her heyday, but her teeth were entirely different, too.

Hannah came up behind me and put her hands on my shoulders.

"Is this what being around a private detective is going to be like?" she asked.

"Not now, Hannah," I said.

"That's what I'm talking about. How often am I going to hear, 'Not now, Hannah,' when you suddenly get an idea?"

"Hannah—"

She started tickling my ear.

"I'm still hungry, Dave."

I got up from the computer and turned to her. Putting my arms around her waist, I said, "I can't promise you that being around a private detective is going to be easy. Fortunately, I'm not that good a private detective."

"Oh, stop," she said, squeezing me back. "If you weren't a good private detective I wouldn't even be here. I'd still be back...*there*."

"I love you, Hannah."

"I love you, Dave."

"I guess there's only one matter left to decide, then."

"What?"

"Regular or extra crispy?"

She hit me on the shoulder, but she laughed while doing it.

After making sure I was carrying enough cash to pay for the take-out chicken, I said, "I'll be back in a flash," and left the apartment.

Before I was able to get to my car, however, I ran into a very large, very imposing man dressed in a black suit. He was not inclined to get out of my way.

"Your name Beauchamp?" he asked.

"Yes." The fact that he had pronounced my name correctly indicated this gorilla and I had some sort of prior connection, though I could not imagine what it was.

"Get in the car."

The car in question was a black limo.

"I'm sorry?" I said.

"You'll be sorrier of you don't get in the car," the gorilla said.

"Hey, what is this?"

The back window of the car rolled down and I saw the face of Vince Mazetta.

He did not look happy.

I would not like to be in your shoes, my friend, the voice of Shel-
don Leonard said inside my head.

17.

"Beauchamp, just get in the car, would'ja?" Mazetta commanded. "I promise you'll return."

I got in the car.

"Mr. Mazetta, what's going on?"

"Where were you headed?" he asked.

"I was about to go get some take-out fried chicken for dinner."

"Where?"

"There's a Mr. Clucky's a few blocks from here."

"A *what*?"

"Mr. Clucky's. It's a fried chicken chain."

The gorilla now got in the driver's seat of the limo.

"Okay. Philly, go to...Jesus, really? It's really called Mr. Clucky's?"

"It really is," I said. "It's on Moorpark."

"Gotcha," Philly said, pulling away.

"Who comes up with these names?" Mazetta asked rhetorically. "Why not just call it Stupid Fried Chicken?"

"I agree, it's a pretty awful name," I said, "but the chicken's good. Since you're here already, you could try some."

"Naw, I'm meeting an associate for dinner at Baretta's and you were on the way."

Baretta's Ristorante was indeed less than a mile from my place, and it was one of those old, storied Italian eateries favored by the likes of the Rat Pack in the 1960s. It did not surprise me that it would attract Vince Mazetta, and not simply because the bolognese sauce was reputed to be the best in L.A.

"Okay. What can I do for you, Mr. Mazetta?"

"I was visited by a police detective today," he said. "My recollection of our last conversation was that it included your assurance I would not be implicated in anything involving the police."

"Was the police detective named Dane Colfax?" I asked.

"Yeah. You sent him to me?"

"I sort of directed him that way."

Mazetta turned to me. "You're admitting it?"

"But I specifically told him not to hassle you. I merely suggested to Detective Colfax that he obtain a photo of a man named Jay Leach, and then inquire if he was the one who had bought a horse's head."

"He did that."

"And was it?"

"Yeah, it was him."

"I thought as much."

"Look, Beauchamp, I don't like being visited by the police."

"I'm sorry, Mr. Mazetta, but you weren't charged with anything, were you?"

"No. But you said you'd leave me out of this. Then again, you said you were working for someone named 'Little Tony,' which I checked out, just in case. Turns out that's a bigger pile of horseshit than any you can find at Del Mar."

"Yeah, well, sorry about that."

"Sorry, he says," Mazetta muttered. "I call around town like a mook looking for a Little Tony, and guys are laughing their asses off at me, because there is no Little Tony, and you're sorry."

"Does saying I'm really sorry help?"

Mazetta glared at me for a second, then started chuckling and shaking his head.

"You are really one for the books Beauchamp," he said.

Yeah. Maybe someone will write one about me someday.

Mr. Clucky's was now just on the right, and Philly pulled the car into the lot.

"What were you going to order, Beauchamp?" Vince Mazetta asked.

"Oh, well, uh, a bucket, with biscuits and sides of slaw and mac-and-cheese."

I realized Hannah never told me whether she wanted regular or extra crispy.

"And could you ask them to do half-and-half on the bucket, half regular and half-crispy?"

"You get that, Philly?" Mazetta asked.

"Yeah."

Vince Mazetta pulled a fifty dollar bill out of his wallet and handed it to the gorilla. "Go on, get the cluck bucket," he said.

Philly dutifully got out and headed into the fast food restaurant.

"You really don't have to pay for my dinner, Mr. Mazetta," I told him.

"It's all right. Think of it as a favor. Who knows? Someday I may ask for a return favor from you."

Uh-oh.

"But what I really want to talk about is your cop friend," he went on. "I reiterate, my recollection is that you said I'd be left out of any investigation."

"What I recall, Mr. Mazetta, is telling you that I would do my best to leave you out of any legal action."

"Cops aren't legal?"

"Did Dane…I mean, Detective Colfax, behave threateningly to you in any way?"

Mazetta shrugged. "Well, he's got kind of a sly manner about him, but threatening? Naw."

"Did he imply that you had done anything illegal?"

"No, but I'm cured of selling horse heads in the future."

"Then I don't think you have a problem."

"Look, Beauchamp, at the very least you can tell me what the hell this cockamamie mess you're in is all about."

"I guess I owe you that much."

I launched into a recap of the entire case up to this point, including the procurement of the horse head that killed Palmer Hanley.

When I was finished, Mazetta said: "That's one fucked-up case."

"Yes sir, I know that."

"Has anyone died since this Prescott guy? Anyone from this convention of yours?"

"I don't know. Not that I've heard. Why?"

"Because you've got a string of bodies, one after another, culminating with Prescott. If they stop right then and there, doesn't that suggest something to you?"

I sat in the back seat of the limo, frozen. "Oh, jeez," I uttered, "it suggests they got the person they wanted, and they don't have to do any more."

Mazetta frowned.

"Huh," he grunted. "I was thinking it suggests that Prescott was the killer of the others, and then someone found out about it and whacked him. But your way works too. Well, whichever way, it's your problem, not mine. All I want is a guarantee that you're not going to give my name out to anyone else, cop or otherwise."

"Do you have a quarter?"

"What?"

"A quarter. If you have one, give it to me. A dime would work just as well. Anything."

"Jesus, I'm already buyin' your dinner for you!"

"Humor me, please."

Looking confused, Vince Mazetta reached into his pocket and pulled out a quarter, which he handed to me.

In return I pulled out my wallet and withdrew a business card, which I handed to him.

"Thank you for the twenty-five cent retainer," I said. "This means you are now my client, so I can't say anything to anyone about you without violating attorney-client privilege."

A smile slowly formed on his face.

"I'm startin' to like you, Beauchamp," he said.

Philly returned then with a bag full of food and a fistful of change, which he handed to Mazetta.

"Hey, that does smell good," Mazetta said.

"Feel free to have some," I said, taking the bag.

"Thanks, but I gotta go eat a plate of sausage and peppers. That's what's expected. Some other time, maybe. Philly, please drive back to Mr. Beauchamp's apartment."

No other words were spoken until we reached my building, but by then the aroma of the fried chicken in the car was overpowering.

"Ah, fuck it, give me a wing," Vince Mazetta said.

I dug out the biggest one I could find and handed it over.

"Thanks. You can let yourself out now, Beauchamp. Enjoy your dinner. And give my best to the redhead."

Reaching for the car door handle, I said, "I'll do that, thanks, and...um, Mr. Mazetta, how do you know my girlfriend's a redhead?"

He looked to Philly and laughed.

"How do I know she's a redhead, he says! You're funny, Beauchamp. It's my hobby to know things." After taking a bite of chicken, he said: "Hey, this shit's pretty good. Mr. Clucky. Who'd a thought it? Okay, Beauchamp, get outta here, and the next time I see you, I hope it's because you want some cat food."

"Yes sir, thank you," I said, getting out of the limo, which pulled away a few seconds later.

I had no way of knowing whether Vince Mazetta really was connected to what was left of the Mob or simply liked to pretend he was. The way he had said *That's what's expected* when talking about eating like a Mafiosi implied he might be pulling an elaborate pretense, like the one-time Hollywood producer who enjoyed pretending he was a made man because it gave him an edge in business. If that was the case, Vince Mazetta deserved an acting award.

I only hoped I wouldn't read any headlines tomorrow about a customer dying at Baretta's Ristorante.

As soon as I got back into the apartment, Hannah said: "Ooh, that smells great."

"Yeah, it does. Hannah, do you know Vince Mazetta?"

She shook her head. "Doesn't sound familiar. Who is he?"

"Oh, just an acquaintance. He may have helped me with a case."

That part was true, because in addition to the free chicken bucket (minus a wing), Vince Mazetta had led me to an insight that I probably would not have reached on my own, but which made sense.

After we had eaten Hannah took care of the plates, which I presumed was simply rote by now having taken care of Palmer for so long. I knew I'd have to at least attempt to ease her out of the role of housemaid at some point, but for the time being, I felt it best not to interfere.

Plus you get your house cleaned up, Bogie commented, cynically.

While Hannah was in the kitchen I said, "Hey, mind if I go back online?"

She sighed and answered, "Go ahead."

I researched every celebrity that I could remember seeing at the expo. I hadn't given much attention to Mitchy Salens, the one-time kid actor, but a photo dated 2016 showed him to be as wrinkled as an old chamois cloth, which argued against a lift. Then again, I had heard no report of his death.

The last name I entered was Geneva Merrill, and the results from that photo search did not even require close comparison.

Photos of Merrill from the Golden Age showed a lithe, dark-haired woman with large eyes, a full, straight nose and dimples in her cheeks; not quite a classic beauty, but certainly attractive, and someone who knew how to flirt with the camera. Much more recent photos showed a woman with blonde hair, a full face, a much thinner nose, much thicker lips, and horizontal creases extending from the corners of her mouth; not unattractive, but not the same face. In several of the images, old and new photos of her had been pasted side by side and labeled *Before and After*.

The differences were clear.

Just then, Hannah came into the living room. "I rearranged the dishes in your cupboards a little," she said. "I hope that's okay."

"Hmm? Oh, as long as I can still find things on my own." There weren't so many dishes for it to really matter anyway.

"Are you discovering anything good?"

"Just that Ms. Merrill had a facelift, or several, but I suppose that's not really surprising."

"She's not the actress who keeps winning Oscars, is she?"

"Geneva Merrill? No. I don't think she's won any."

"Oh. There's another Meryl?"

It took me a second.

"Are you talking about Meryl Streep?"

"I guess so. She played that famous French chef in a film?"

"*Julie & Julia*, yeah. But I wasn't talking about her. I meant Geneva Merrill, who was a dancer and actress from the 1950s who became an anti-drug activist. But I can see how you'd make that assumption since Merrill and Meryl sound alike."

Then a voice sounded in my head.

It wasn't one of the usual members of the Hollywood Victory Caravan. It wasn't even an actor.

It was Jay Leach, a very drunken Jay Leach, from only a couple days ago.

"Oh, jeez," I uttered. "Hannah, you did it again."

"I did what again?"

"You just jogged my brain into realizing something. It was something Jay Leach said the other night, and it didn't make much sense at the time, but I assumed that it was because he was so drunk. He was complaining about Miranda Love, and he said something like 'That old mare will be the death of me.' Mare, as in female horse, because the bartender mentioned a horse. But now I don't think he meant Miranda, because he slurred the words, *mare'll*."

"Like Streep?" she asked.

"No, like Geneva Merrill, since she had a connection to the expo. Oh…oh, that must be it!"

"So does this mean you've solved the case?" she asked.

"No, it means…"

Okay, bright boy, what does *it mean*? Robert Mitchum asked in my head.

"I'm not sure exactly what it means, outside of the fact that I can now link Jay Leach to another guest of the Celebrity Expo."

"Is Jay Leach the killer? He sounds like the type."

I put my hand on my forehead.

"I don't know," I admitted. "If he killed the others, then maybe he died of natural causes. Or drank himself to death. Man, every time I think I'm onto something, it turns out all I've done is make the case more confusing. This never happened to Philip Marlowe."

Oh? Bogie said inside my head. *So* you *know who killed Owen Taylor, the Sternwoods' chauffeur*?

"I think I need to think," I uttered.

I tried approaching this mess of a case from every angle:

Operating under the assumption that Geneva Merrill was still alive, because I had not heard any differently, and she was someone whose death would certainly be reported, then maybe the murders had stopped with Jay Leach. If, in fact, he had been murdered. If not, then they had stopped with Gayne Prescott. So if the theory I put forth to Vince Mazetta was correct, either Jay Leach or Gayne Prescott was the primary victim, and the others just to throw investigators off the trail.

But as of yet, I had no evidence that either Leach or Prescott had been murdered, only that they had died.

So I tried instead assuming that Mazetta's theory was the right one, and that Jay Leach had killed all the actors for whatever reason, and then had died himself, either by his own hand (on a bottle), or else someone had discovered his crimes and murdered him. That threw a beam of suspicion on Leach's wife, who, maybe, wasn't really out of town, or who, maybe, secretly came back to kill him.

But that was an awful lot of maybes.

It also didn't explain why, if Leach was the killer, he would not have murdered the one person for whom he had a clear motive to kill, Miranda Love.

Could the two theories be combined? Could it be that *Miranda* was the intended victim all along, but Leach did not live long enough to kill her?

Or could it be that Miranda was the one who found out about Leach's murders and took care of him herself?

"This is giving me a headache," I said, rubbing my temples.

"You should lie down, Dave," Hannah suggested.

"No, I'm too keyed up right now. I have to find the connection between Geneva Merrill and Jay Leach, and there's only one person who can tell me that...if she's still alive."

"Can you call her?"

"I could if I had her number. Wait! Amber Holmes must have it."

"Who?"

"Verdugo's assistant, Amber. She did all the paperwork for the Celebrity Expo, so she must have it."

"Then call her."

I had already started for the phone when the cold water bucket overturned on my throbbing head.

"I could if I had her number," I sighed.

"Maybe she's in the book," Hannah said.

"Some days I think I'm the only one left in the book," I said. "I have another idea."

I dug out the number for Verdugo & Associates and punched it in.

After two rings, a recorded message in Amber's voice stated: *We are very sorry but Verdugo and Associates is no longer in active business for new clients. If you are an existing client, please call...*

A valley number was left as reference.

That's what I was hoping for.

I called it and got another recording, also by Amber, simply asking for a message after the beep. I had gotten as far as "Hi, Amber, it's Dave Beauchamp, the private investigator who found Boris's body with you, and..."

The line picked up and Amber said, "What do you want?"

She did not sound happy.

"I'm sorry to bother you," I said, "I just have one quick request. I need to get hold of Geneva Merrill. I know you have the records, but I need her address or phone number. It's really important."

"Everything's really important, isn't it? You know what? Fine. You can have her number. Hold on."

After a minute or so on hold, she came back and rattled off Merrill's phone number and address, which was in the affluent Holmby Hills district of L.A. Since I don't believe she had worked in the last thirty or so years, she must have saved everything from the money days. Or else her position within the anti-drug foundation she operated paid a handsome stipend.

I thanked Amber and wished her well, which she took semi-graciously, and then hung up.

I tried calling Geneva Merrill first. After four rings the call was answered by a man who sounded like Kenneth Williams.

You know Kenneth Williams, right? From the British *Carry On* movies? Possessor of the most flaring nostrils in the entirety of show business? If you heard him, you'd know him; his was a voice that originated in the spleen and came straight through the nose.

"Hello," the voice prompted again.

"Oh, I'm sorry," I said, "I might have the wrong number."

"Since this number is unlisted and I do not recognize your voice, I daresay you do."

"I was trying to reach Geneva Merrill. Maybe I wrote the number down incorrectly."

There was a long pause, after which the man said: "Miss Merrill is not in."

"Oh, well, can I—"

"To whom am I speaking?"

"My name is Dave Beauchamp, and I'm an investigator here in town, and—"

"What, pray tell, do you investigate?"

"Um, right now I'm investigating a certain lawyer named Jay Leach."

In the background I heard another voice, a man's say: "What is it, Jeffries?"

"A man who purports to be investigating a leech, sir. Or perhaps I am mistaken and it is the other way around."

Definitely Kenneth Williams.

A second later the new voice said: "Who is this and what do you want?"

"I was hoping to speak with Geneva Merrill."

"About what?"

"May I ask who you are?"

"The man who lives here! What do you want with my wife?"

"Well, I guess first I was trying to find out if she was still alive."

"*What?*"

"Look, sir, I was at the Hollywood Celebrity Expo a few weeks ago, and I happened to see her there, so—"

"God, I hate it when she does those things! It always leads to some fan like you trying to get in touch with her. How did you get this number? Never mind, I don't care. Do not call here again."

The receiver at the other end of the line slammed down like Thor's hammer, causing my eardrum to ring. The ringing quickly turned into a high-pitched, cackling laugh.

Robert Mitchum, ladies and gentlemen. For such a big, tough guy, he laughed like Hugh Herbert.

I hung up the phone.

There was little I could do tonight. I'd have to try again tomorrow.

Hannah was standing behind me now, gently rubbing my shoulders and neck.

"I know how to get rid of headaches, you know," she said.

I turned around and saw that she had slipped out of her clothes.

She pressed her breasts into my eyes.

"What's a headache?" I asked, fumbling out of my clothes before picking her up and carrying her to the sofa.

18.

A major chunk of Sunday was spent securing a storage facility for the overflow furniture and items from Palmer and Hannah's apartment, but we had yet to get into the apartment to start moving. It wasn't that the police were still keeping Hannah out. It was simply more fun to go back to bed once we'd gotten home.

I got up later than usual Monday morning (blame Hannah for that), and shuffled to the bathroom. Catching sight of my naked countenance in the mirror, I'd swear Little Dave was staring at me wide-eyed and saying: *Please, sir, I'd like some more.*

That was probably just my imagination, though.

Hannah was up by the time I got out of the shower, and was making overtures about pushing me back into it and joining me.

"Hannah, I have to get some work done," I said, reluctantly, as we wrapped our arms around each other. "But god, you feel good."

So okay, it was even later by the time I actually managed to get my clothes on, but I doubted it made any difference in terms of trying to contact Geneva Merrill. If I were to show up at her house in person I doubted I would get a more convivial welcome than I received last night on the phone, and showing up ninety minutes earlier than it was now would not have changed things.

Maybe her husband would feel compelled to talk by someone more official.

Fishing out the card for Dane Colfax, I put in a call.

"Hello, Beauchamp," he answered. "Funny, I was about to contact you. You were right about that horse head. The guy who runs the meat-grinding plant recognized Leach."

"Yeah, I know. I heard from him."

"Oh? Interesting character, isn't he?"

"Seems to come from a good...*family.*"

Colfax chuckled.

"Well, he had an uncle who ran with Mickey Cohen back in the fifties, but this is L.A., who didn't? But that's all we can find on him.

Either he's a genius at not leaving fingerprints, or he's painting the lily about his own involvement with the outfit. What have you got for me?"

"A hunch."

"Did you say lunch?"

"No, I said *hunch*."

"I heard *lunch*. I have to go into a meeting in a minute. You know where Pierre's is?"

"Of course."

Pierre's was a Los Angeles legend. Located only a few blocks from City Hall, it claimed to be the birthplace of the Monte Cristo sandwich. Whether it actually was or not seemed not to matter. The cross between a veggie-less club and French toast was the specialty of the house and ordering anything else was akin to asking for chow mein at In-N-Out Burger.

"Meet me there at 12:30," Colfax said.

Knowing that finding a parking spot in downtown L.A. was only slightly more possible than cold fusion, I left several minutes early. After spending a gallon's worth of gas driving around the maze of one-way streets, most of them under construction, I finally accepted the inevitable and pulled into a fifteen-dollar parking lot.

It was 12:40 by the time I got to Pierre's. Colfax was nowhere to be seen. I got in line anyway.

After another minute, a familiar voice behind me said, "Sorry I'm late."

"Not a problem, Dane," I replied, turning around. "I was running a bit behind, too."

It took another five minutes to reach the order counter. We both got the Number One, which was a Monte Cristo, sweet potato fries, slaw and a drink, and after paying, I managed to score a table in the corner.

Colfax splattered his fried sandwich with hot sauce—something that made my stomach complain on behalf of my eyes—and took a bite. Somehow, he survived it.

"All right," he said, "here we are, so play your hunch."

"I've been operating under the theory that Jay Leach was some-how at the center of all this, but I think I'm wrong, in part because he's dead, too. But another name, Geneva Merrill, has popped up."

"Who's Geneva Merrill?"

In between bites I gave Colfax a brief rundown of her career, and then finished with her more recent history as an anti-drug crusader.

"So what's her connection to the rest?"

"I don't know, exactly."

You don't even know vaguely, Robert Mitchum said in my head.

"There's something else, too, Dane," I went on. "Not just Palmer Hanley, but all the victims so far have died from a severe allergic reaction to commonplace items, information that not everyone would have. Except for a doctor."

"So they all went to the same doctor?"

"In a sense. I think they may have all gone to the same cosmetic surgeon."

Detective Colfax stopped chewing and looked at me. "Cosmetic surgeon," he said through a mouthful of food.

"Each of the DBs had some sort of work done. It is common procedure to ask a patient during consultation whether they have any kind of known allergies before the surgery is done. The patient files of a plastic surgeon would contain all that information."

"DBs? When did you start speaking Lapdese?"

"Lapdese?"

"L-A-P-D-ese."

"Around the same time you started saying things like *amicus curiae*."

"Fair enough. So you're saying that information regarding the deadly allergies could have been gleaned from the confidential medical files held by a cosmetic surgeon, and not a regular doctor or dentist."

"Yes, because nine-times-out-of-ten you get nose jobs or facelifts purely for your own ego, not because you're really sick. I'm speculating that a cosmetic guy would take more than the usual precautions with a patient because these are most often elective surgeries. Also, I can't imagine anyone risking a malpractice suit because of a chemical or substance reaction during the procedure. Seems like it's enough of a risk if your patient comes out looking like the Elephant Man instead of Mr. or Miss Universe. I've already ascertained that everyone who's died, with the possible exception of Jay Leach, underwent some form of plastic or cosmetic surgery."

"You realize that this theory only holds water if each one went to the same plastic surgeon, right?"

"Yes, I do. I also realize that the LAPD probably has more resources than I do to find out whether or not that is the truth."

Colfax nodded his head slowly, either a sign that he was processing what I had told him, or that he'd gotten a bit of ham gristle that was hard to chew. I had only taken a few bites out of my sandwich, before finding it too rich for my blood. Washing it down with ice tea helped a little, but I knew I would never finish this grilled heart-attack on a plate.

"Okay, I'll try to check out plastic surgeons for you," Colfax said. "But I can tell you one thing about Leach. If he had an allergy, it was to poison."

"Something showed up on the tox scan?"

"Come on, Dave. You could order a custom-made car from Germany, have it delivered by rowboat over the wrong ocean, and have it held up in customs for three months, and it would still arrive faster than a tox scan. But our eagle-eyed ME found a small bruise with a tiny puncture hole in its center on the deltoid region of his left arm, the kind made by a needle."

"Is it possible he killed himself?" I asked, sincerely hoping not, since I had convinced Leslie Leach otherwise.

"If that were the case he would have jabbed himself in the leg or hip or the front part of the arm, or some other place that's possible to reach, but not the delt. We would have found the syringe he used, too. No, he had help."

"So he just stood or sat there and let someone stick a syringe in him?"

"Jabbing someone with a needle is pretty easy to do if your victim isn't expecting it. It's even easier if you already have experience with syringes."

"Like a doctor."

"Like a doctor. If your poison is fast-acting, it's even better, and if your victim is already blotto, it's a slam-dunk. Or maybe a slam-drunk."

"Monte Cristo sandwiches have a bad effect on you, you know that, Dane?"

"Speaking of which, are you going to eat yours or let it go to waste?"

I slid my plate over to him. "Knock yourself out. Do you know for a fact that Leach was drunk when he was killed?"

"Blood alcohol level of point-three and change," he said, then took a bite out of my sandwich. "He was, as the saying goes, feeling no pain."

"So if everyone else died as the result of an allergic reaction, but Leach was poisoned, maybe his death isn't related to the others. Unless he was the killer of the others."

Colfax popped the last of his sweet potato fries into his mouth; those were another culinary trend for which I had little palate. "We can't ask him, obviously," he said.

He looked at his watch and shook his head.

"Cripes. Another damn meeting I have to get back to. They keep trying to shove me into this administrative B.S. But that's not your problem." He got up and stuck out his hand. "I'll keep you posted."

When I got back to the office, I noticed a call on my machine. It was from Hannah, asking how I felt about potato soup for dinner. It sounded great, but before I called her to tell her so, I punched in the number for Jack Daniels.

Since it was early afternoon, Jack sounded fully, lucidly sober.

"Is this a professional call?" he asked. "Am I going to have to charge you by the pint?"

"This is probably an easy one, Jack," I replied. "I know you've made a study of poisons, so are there any that, say, could be shot into someone's arm and kill them immediately?"

"Only dozens."

"Well, let's say you have a limited time to kill the person, so it has to work the first time, and quickly, and you are, say, in the medical profession and have access to different drugs. What would you select?"

"I hope this does not pertain to a real case."

"I'm afraid it does."

"Oh, dear. Well, if I were on a mission to kill and it was do-or-die, so to speak, I would use botulinum toxin, which is perhaps the most lethal poison out there."

"Is it available to a doctor?"

"Oh, good lord, yes. For the right kind of doctor it is eminently available. In its refined state, it is known by the name Botox."

"Botox?" I repeated.

"Yes, that is why it is called Botox, it is a contraction of *botulinum* and *toxin*. You'd think they'd have given it a different commercial name since in its purest state it is the sort of poison used in chemical weapons."

"So any plastic or cosmetic surgeon would have access to it?" I asked.

"Of course, it is one of the tools of their trade. Dare I ask why you are inquiring?"

"Thanks, Jack. I'll talk to you later."

I hung up and immediately punched in Colfax's number.

"Robbery-Homicide," a voice answered.

"Detective Colfax, please," I said.

"He's out. I'm Detective Rod Lopez. Is there anything I can help you with?"

"My name is Dave Beauchamp, and I—"

"You're the peeper who exposed the Temple, aren't you?"

"That's me."

I hadn't realized the term *peeper* was still in use.

"You on to something now?" Lopez asked.

"Possibly. Please tell Colfax he should ask the ME to specifically check for traces of botulinum toxin in the screens on a DB named Jay Leach."

"Wait, what's that called again?"

I repeated it.

"Botulinum toxin," he repeated. "Okay, I can do that much. Call the ME, I mean."

"Good, thank you."

"Say, Beauchamp, how come you're not working for us?"

"I'm too dumb to pass the tests," I said.

There was a beat, then the guy laughed.

"You're obviously too honest, too. I'll tell Colfax you called."

"Thank you."

For the next half-hour I sat and tried to figure out what, if anything, in this case made sense. Since sometimes writing my struggling thoughts down on paper makes them clearer, I took out a sheet and jotted down the names *Miranda Love, Karen Robinson* and *Ge-*

neva Merrill.

Why those three? Easy: no one else involved in this mess was still alive.

Wha' abou' the redhead? Desi Arnaz asked inside my brain.

Sorry, Desi, but there was no way she was involved in any of this.

Are you...sure of that? Raymond Burr chimed in.

"Yes, dammit," I said aloud, "I'm sure of that." The truth is, I was never so sure of anything in my life.

Underneath the names I wrote: *Knew Boris Verdugo.* Since all three women had been connected with the Celebrity Expo, they had to have known him at some level. I put the initials of each next to the question.

Next I wrote: *Facelift,* followed by: *ML claims not; KR unknown but grandfather yes; and GM oh, yes.*

The next category was *Known allergy.* I jotted: *TM, peanuts* under Karen's name; *GM unknown;* and *ML unknown.*

Though anyone who had ever met Miranda could argue she was allergic to common human decency.

Knew Jay Leach was next, with yeses for Karen and Miranda, but only supposition for Geneva.

So far it was Karen Robinson, four for four, but only by proxy.

Now it was time for the $64,000 question: *Who knew Verdugo was Michael Baroni?*

Only Karen had any connection with the Baroni family, since her grandfather had sold them their house, but she had seemed genuinely surprised by the deduction that Verdugo and Baroni were one and the same.

Then again, I had told her that over the phone, which meant I was not able to gauge her reaction visually. She might have been faking.

Was Karen the one behind the killings?

Trying to look at it the way Jack Daniels, or any other novelist would, Karen's involvement made no sense. It was she, after all, who had gotten me involved in this in the first place. If she were somehow implicated in the deaths, why would she be the one who first cried murder? No matter how one viewed Karen's culpability, it plainly defied logic.

There is no logic to this, the voice of Orson Welles said inside my head, *but I can't help it...it's my character.*

"Holy crap," I uttered. "*Mr. Arkadin!*"

Mr. Arkadin was arguably Welles' most obscure film, a semi-reworking of *Citizen Kane* in which a man is hired to investigate the lost history of a mysterious millionaire, by the millionaire himself, who claims to have had an amnesiac period in his life. It turns out that the millionaire (played by Welles in community theatre-caliber makeup) has only hired the investigator as a way of finding out if unsavory parts of his past can still be discovered, and if they can be, the investigator will be killed.

That was a potential answer as to why she would hire an investigator and be culpable at the same time.

Looking down at my paper, I wondered if I should steer Colfax to Karen Robinson as well when he called back.

If he called back.

Don't do anything rash, kid, Bogart admonished. *It's not like you've cleared the other two.*

He had a point. I hadn't really looked into the backgrounds of Miranda Love and Geneva Merrill, outside of looking up their photos online. While researching them might not yield any useful results, it was not like I had anything better to do at the moment.

Going onto my laptop, I got into Wikipedia. I'm not the world's biggest fan of Wikipedia, since its information can be manipulated and controlled by the subjects of the articles themselves, or their heirs, or their fan clubs, or, for that matter, their enemies. But sometimes you can glean some useful information, or at least sources.

The article on Miranda Love seemed to prove my point regarding manipulation, since it contained a banner warning of unsourced, and therefore possibly unreliable, information.

There was no mention of her former name, Shawlee, and her stated birth date, May 27, 1941, was not only unsourced and unreliable, it was ridiculous. It meant she would have been about twelve when she didn't make her TV appearance with Palmer Hanley, and all of eighteen or nineteen when she appeared opposite Jimmy Stewart in *The Man From Tucson*. While the latter was technically possible—Ida Lupino was headlining films in adult roles at fourteen, after all—the former was out of the question, particularly if she was also carrying on with a producer.

The rest of the article was impossible to take any more seriously.

According to Wikipedia, Miranda Love was considered the finest actress in Hollywood by most major directors, and had been the original choice for every notable starring role of the 1960s and '70s, from the title role in *Cleopatra* to Nurse Ratched in *One Flew Over the Cuckoo's Nest*.

It was tempting to log-in and add that she had also been the original choice for the shark in *Jaws*, but I did not want to overdraw my Karma account.

There was virtually no personal information on Miranda, except that she was a "fan favorite" at conventions and autograph shows.

Next I typed in Geneva Merrill's name.

The article that popped up was not only longer than Miranda's but seemed to be much more accurate.

Geneva had been born Genevieve Esmeralda Castillo in Del Rio, Texas on November 28, 1931, which sounded perfectly reasonable, and she had gotten her start as a child performer in vaudeville as Ginny Castle, probably an attempt to persuade audiences that the young dancer was related to Vernon and Irene. Her family moved to Los Angeles in 1947 and she was enrolled in Hollywood High School. Only two years later she was signed by MGM, first as a dance double for Patricia Medina, for a really terrible film called *The Pirate's Daughter*, and later as a featured dancer and contract player. She continued in the business, dancing less and acting more, into the 1980s, at which time she lost her son to a drug overdose, and retired from the business.

Her work as an anti-drug crusader was a major portion of her Wikipedia article. Her son, Wesley, had been twenty-two when he died in 1984, and her husband at the time, Edmund Sperry, the boy's father, did not last much longer. Young Wesley's death hit Edmund, who was an attorney, particularly hard. He was killed six months later when his car went off the road on Angeles Crest Highway and tumbled down a ravine. He was found to have had an overabundance of sleep medication in his system. While it could not be proven, the speculation existed that it was suicide.

If anything, the loss of her husband and son seemed to make Geneva a stronger person. She embarked on her new career as an activist and in 1993 remarried, this time to a…

"Aw, *jeez!*" I said aloud.

I read the sentence on the computer screen over again to make certain I'd not been mistaken.

I hadn't.

Geneva Merrill had married a man named Dr. Jerome Torgesson.

Who was renowned as one of Los Angeles's most accomplished cosmetic surgeons.

19.

Once the numbness abated, I typed Torgesson's name into the computer. A dozen articles popped up naming him as the go-to man in the Southland for a new, younger look. One, from trade magazine devoted to the special effects industry, described how he consulted with computer animators who would be tasked with making an actor look younger through digital means on screen.

None of this proved he had any direct connection with the recent killings, of course, only that his files might contain the necessary information that the murderer required.

So might any other Hollywood skin sculptor's.

But Torgesson was the only one married to a former actress.

But you don't know that for a fact, do you? Bogie asked me.

He had me there; I didn't. There might be another cosmetic surgeon out there who was the husband of a 1950s or '60s starlet.

What the hey, this was Hollywood: maybe there was another cosmetic surgeon out there who was the partner of a 1950s or '60s leading man.

But there was only one who had a direct link to an attendee of the Hollywood Celebrity Expo.

So far as you know, kid.

Oh, do something to *help* me, would you, Bogie?

This case was beginning to resemble "the *Vertigo* effect," which Hitchcock created by having the camera zoom in while tracking backwards, resulting in the illusion of coming and going, getting closer and further away at the same time, but remaining essentially in the same place.

It looked like I would have to take that list from the expo and look up each and every person online to try and determine if they were personally connected to a plastic surgeon.

Fortunately, right then my phone rang. It was Richard Neale.

"Hi, Mr. Beauchamp, I've come up with a little problem regarding Miranda Shawlee, in connection with her bequeathal in the will of Palmer Hanley, and I'm wondering if you can help me."

"What do you need?" I asked.

"Her address. I haven't been able to locate her."

"I'm sorry, Mr. Neale, I should have told you at the time that she now goes by the name Miranda Love."

"Miranda Love? Didn't I see someone of that name on the news recently?"

"That's probably the only place you've seen her. I'm certain I could find an address for you."

"I'd appreciate it. If it takes a substantial amount of your time to do so, feel free to bill me."

"I don't expect it will, but thank you. Since you're here, though, Mr. Neale, may I ask how long it's going to take for the money from the estate to be disbursed?"

"Best case scenario, two-to-three months," Neale said. "Worst case scenario, it's delayed indefinitely in court. Since Mr. Hanley had no family, that should expedite things, but given the circumstance of that religious organization he founded, and what I understand to be their litigious history, I cannot promise anything."

Which was precisely what concerned me. "Okay, I'll get back to you with Miranda's address."

After he hung up I thought about my options for finding her, since her contact information had been redacted on the list Amber Holmes had given me for the expo. There was always the database, providing that Miranda Love was her real legal name. I could also try the PI databases, but the same *caveat* existed there.

You could try looking under 'Lucrezia Borgia,' the measured, tenor voice of Dwight Frye sneered inside my head.

You remember Dwight Frye? Renfield? Fritz, the hunchbacked assistant from *Frankenstein*?

I decided that the quickest way to find out was to call Leslie Leach. Surely her husband had records of Miranda somewhere in his files.

I put the call in, but got a machine. I didn't leave a message.

Phone machines…cell phones…smartphones…there are definitely days when I wish I had been around in the 1940s and '50s, when the phones were still dumb enough to be controlled by the caller, not the other way around.

In my day I had a car and a pair of shoes, Bogie told me, *and on good days enough ration coupons to put gas in the car.*

Right. I decided to put my shoes and my car to good use.

I'd go see Leslie in person.

I was already halfway to the Leach residence in Hollywood before I bothered to wonder whether or not she would be there. That was one advantage to movie and television detectives: the witness they sought was *always* there.

And if it was a woman you were visiting, they often answered the door in nothing but a towel, the unmistakable voice of Fred MacMurray said inside my head.

When I arrived at Chez Leach, I saw that the front door was hanging wide open.

Either Mrs. Leach was home or the place was being burgled.

I knocked on the jamb and within seconds a tall, dark-haired, statuesque woman appeared in the front room, clad in a form-fitting blouse and jeans instead of a towel. But that door having been mentally opened, I couldn't help but wonder what she looked like in a towel.

Hey, knock it off, a woman's voice said inside my head.

It was Hannah's.

Sorry, honey.

I put the woman to be a step or two from forty in either direction. Her blue eyes were wide-set, but that only enhanced her looks.

"Who are you?" she asked.

"Mrs. Leach?"

"That can't be, since I'm Mrs. Leach. You have one more chance."

"No, I'm Dave Beauchamp. We spoke once by phone."

"Oh, right, Mr. Beauchamp."

"Your door was open, so…"

"You'll find everything in the house open. Do you know how long it takes to get the smell of a dead body out of a house?"

I imagined the manager of the Los Feliz Parkview Apartments, where Palmer Hanley had expelled his last breath, could probably tell me, but all I said was: "Um, no I don't."

"Pray you never have to find out. What is it you want, Mr. Beauchamp?"

"I was hoping to get some information about one of Jay's clients."

"Really. Well, come on in."

I went in. I couldn't smell a dead body, but the place did seem a bit musty.

"Again, I'm very sorry for your loss," I said.

She sighed and seemed to be trying very hard not to shrug. "I wanted to be out of his life, but I can't honestly say I wanted him to be out of mine. Does that make any sense at all?"

"Yes," I lied.

"There were good times," she went on, more to herself than to me. "It wasn't always bad. Then he started taking the kind of mistresses that came from distilleries. I knew he was unhappy, but there was nothing I could do about it. I came home to find a huge styrofoam cooler out back, big enough to hold about three cases of beer. Must have had a helluva party while I was gone."

If only she knew what had really been in there.

After staring off into space for a moment, she seemed to re-notice that I was still there.

"I'm sorry, Mr. Beauchamp," she said. "You don't want to hear this. Which client is it you're asking after?"

"Miranda Love."

She winced upon hearing the name and turned away.

"I'm trying to get contact information for Miranda," I went on. "I have to see that something gets mailed to her."

"Anthrax, I hope," she said over her shoulder.

"Just a simple letter, ma'am, though I can't help but notice that you seem a little more hostile towards Miranda than the last time we spoke. Have the two of you been in touch?"

She turned back to me, her arms folded.

"She called. She was looking for Jay, and didn't know he was dead. Finding out seems to have upset her greatly."

"At least she had some consideration for him."

She widened her baby blues and I felt like I was under a spotlight.

"None whatsoever," she said. "She wasn't concerned that he had died and she didn't offer any condolences. She was upset because she wanted him to do something for her and his death meant she couldn't get what she wanted."

"I'm sorry. All I need is an address or a phone number, some way I can contact her, and then I'll be on my way and out of your hair."

"Oh, you're not really in my hair. If you'll wait a minute, I'll check Jay's address book."

As she walked into the next room, I could not help notice that her sashaying gait seemed practiced.

Like a B-movie actress's.

When she returned, I had it. I knew who she reminded me of.

"Here you are," she said, handing me a piece of paper with Miranda's information written on it.

"Thanks for this. And, uh, I don't want to seem forward or obnoxious, or anything like that, but has anyone ever told you that you look like Marie Windsor?"

"Who's Marie Windsor?"

"A film actress of the 1950s." *And one of the sexiest movie stars of all time.*

Dave! Hannah's voice scolded in my head.

Leslie Leach sashayed toward me still wearing that ghost of a smile.

"Is it important to you that I look like Marie Windsor, Mr. Beauchamp?"

"Oh, no, not really, it's that…I mean, I just…"

I just had this crazy thought that you might be one of those people who wants their face to be recreated as another person, which means you would have gone to a plastic surgeon to do so, which means it might have been Dr. Torgesson, which means I might be able to put you on the suspect list in place of Karen Robinson because you're acting like such a femme fatale, *but upon reflection I realize what a stupid idea it was and one I handled like a rank amateur, and now here I am trying to explain, and, oh, jeez, don't blush! Don't blush! Don't blush! Don't—*

"You're blushing, Mr. Beauchamp, which I take to mean that you must like this actress. Some kind of fantasy, perhaps?"

"Uh, well, no, it's just a…well, it's not really anything, but I…"

Her smile widened. She had perfect teeth. Strong and white.

"I'm flattered. But honestly, I try not to see old movies. I don't see many new ones, either. Once you've seen Leonardo DiCaprio raped by an animated bear, there's not much left to see."

Nyea hey hey hey hee hee! Yogi Bear said inside my head, and it was going to take a long time to rid my mind of that image.

"But this Marie Windsor," she went on, "was she in *The Naked City* by any chance?"

"No."

"Well, that's something. I'd hate to find out that's why he married me."

"Thank you again for the information," I said.

"Not at all. Don't close the door on the way out, okay?"

I was perspiring when I left the house.

At least that was better than blushing.

Back at the office I called Neale and gave him Miranda's address. Then, since the potato soup Hannah had promised was starting to sound good, I headed home.

It was well before dinner time when I got to the apartment, but I could detect the aroma of savory soup, even through the door. Going in, I was greeted by Hannah, but a different Hannah than the one to which I was accustomed. Her complexion was the color of yogurt and her hair was wild and flying in all directions.

"Hannah, what's wrong?" I asked.

"Dave, I've done something terrible."

"What?"

"I didn't mean to, but she...she..."

"Hannah, please tell me what happened."

She stepped aside and let me into the apartment, then pointed at the floor of the living room.

The body of a woman was sprawled across the floor.

"Jeez, Hannah, who is that?"

"She showed up and started screaming and acting crazy. I didn't know what to do."

I went to the body on the floor and examined it. Then I let out a moan.

"Dave, am I going to jail?" Hannah asked.

I didn't answer. Instead I put my fingers on the wrist of the prone figure of Miranda Love to check for a pulse.

20.

Miranda was unconscious, but alive.

"Hannah, tell me what happened here," I said.

"Like I said, she knocked on the door and when I opened it she burst in and started yelling and making threats and in no time she became obnoxious and I was afraid she was going to try and hurt me so...I crimped her."

"You did what to her?"

"Back at the...you know where...if you were part of the medical staff, you were taught how to subdue people, just in case they tried to escape or something. There's a place in the neck you can pinch in a certain way and it causes people to pass out. They called it crimping. I didn't want to do it to her, Dave, but I was scared. Do I have to leave now?"

"What? Why would you have to leave?"

She suddenly looked like a frightened six-year-old girl.

"Because now you know what I'm really like."

"Hannah, have you ever actually hurt anyone doing this?"

"No, but I've seen it happen. Back *there* one time I saw a person's carotid artery crimped long enough to induce a stroke."

Nice place, this Temple, the voice of Eve Arden snarked inside my head.

Before I could worry about Miranda Love suffering a pressure-induced stroke in my living room, her eyes began to flutter.

Then she threw up on the carpet.

The apartment no longer smelled of potato soup.

"Jesus Christ," Miranda moaned, "what happened to me."

"I'm sorry," Hannah said, "you were just so threatening."

I gave Hannah a *shush* gesture, then helped Miranda up—pulled her up, really—and walked her to the kitchen sink, drew a glass of water, and handed it to her. "Rinse your mouth with this," I said.

"It's probably poison," she muttered, taking a gulp of water and swishing it in her mouth before spitting it out. "I imagine you expect me to thank you," she went on, "but I want to know what happened to me."

"You passed out," I told her, before Hannah could say anything.

"I'm not usually given to passing out," Miranda said.

"There's a first time for everything."

"Like you trying to be nice to someone," Hannah said.

Miranda set the glass down and looked up at her and I could see she was about to let Hannah have it, but then something happened to her face. It softened, looking almost regretful.

"You are so young, child," Miranda said softly, walking to the closest chair, which was at my tiny dining table, and sitting down. "So young, and so beautiful. You are beautiful, you know."

"No," Hannah said.

"Don't argue with me. You are beautiful. I was young and beautiful once, too. I doubt you can understand what it's like to be a lamb at a convention of wolves. That's what the business was like in the 1950s. Women complied with whatever was asked of them, on or off camera, or they were turned away. I played the game at first, as I was expected to, but it backfired, thanks to that miserable friend of yours!"

"I'm not sure it was entirely Palmer's fault," I began, but Miranda cut me off.

"Be quiet! You weren't there. After that debacle, I came to realize that if being a whore no longer paid off professionally, it was time to try the only remaining option. Become a bitch. Instead of sleeping my way up like the others, I started scratching and clawing, removing the eyes of anyone who got in my way. It became my style, what I was known for, and producers and directors would hire me just to see if they were the only one in Hollywood with a big enough ball sac to tame the great lioness. And you know what? No one ever did. It may have come at a cost, but I am still here."

She raised her head as though looking for her key light.

If this was a performance, it was the best one she ever gave. But it seemed to be genuine, like maybe for a tiny second she was allowing us to see the real Miranda Love, a vulnerable woman who had to forge her own suit of armor out of attitude.

While Hannah took paper towels and an old sponge from the kitchen and went to work on the mess on the floor, Miranda edged back to normalcy by asking: "You got any booze around this dump?"

"I don't drink as a rule."

"Not old enough, huh?"

"Miranda, why don't you tell me why you came here in the first place. How did you even know where I live?"

"You're in directory assistance," she replied. "As to why I am here, I need your help."

"In what way?"

"I am going to be murdered!"

"What are you talking about?"

"Don't you watch the news? Don't you know what's going on? All those others from the autograph expo have been murdered, probably by some crazed fan."

Having done the best she could with the towels and sponge, Hannah carried them into the kitchen and threw them away, then poked around under my sink until she found a spray bottle of cleaner, and went back to work. Not once did she complain or even allow her face to register the unpleasantness of the job.

"Okay, look, Miranda, if you know for a fact that Tony Marsh and Wilbur Constable and Gayne Prescott and Edie Gogos and Palmer Hanley were murdered, you really should talk to the police about it. A friend of mine is working on the case. I'll call him."

I pulled out my cell.

"Wait!" she cried. "Obviously, I don't know for a *fact* that they were murdered. Only the murderer knows that for certain. But it's the only thing that makes sense, isn't it? A group of people all together in one place suddenly begin dropping like flies? What else *could* it be? I *know* how these things work, young man. A number of years ago I played Emily Brent in *And Then There Were None* at the La Jolla Playhouse. I was *brilliant*, too."

"So you figure that you're next to get offed?"

"Must you be so vulgar in your terminology?"

Very well, the cultured voice of Clifton Webb said inside my head. *Let's say instead that you believe yours will be the next ticket punched at the Celebrity Toes-up Tango Soiree?*

I'm afraid I laughed out loud at that one.

"I don't see what's so *funny*, you cretinous infant!"

"Sorry, Miranda, but you had to be there. Let me ask this, though.

Do you have any allergies?"

"Allergies?"

"Yes, something that you can't eat or drink or be around without becoming seriously ill."

"Why are you asking?"

"The other people from the expo appear to have died because of allergic reactions, and somebody knew about those allergies. So if you're not allergic to anything, you probably don't have to worry."

"They could use a gun, couldn't they?" she asked. "I mean, who *isn't* allergic to a bullet?"

She's got a point, kid, Bogie chimed in.

"All right, let's say you are next on the list to be murdered. How am I supposed to prevent it?"

"Act as my bodyguard. I will pay you."

"That's a little out of my skill set, Miranda, but I think I can direct you to a security agency that will be able to help you."

Back when I was at the law firm, bodyguards had to be employed a time or two to protect court witnesses for a big case. The agency we used was Timmons Security, and it had a good reputation and competitive rates. I told all this to Miranda, but I got the impression she wasn't listening.

"If you like," I went on, "I can call them on your behalf."

"And take a fifteen percent agent's fee? No thank you. I can call them on my own. It appears I've wasted my time here." She rose to her full height, somehow managing to sneer down at me, even though I was about five inches taller.

The Miranda Love I knew and couldn't stand was back.

"I have other places to be. Good night."

She spun around and stormed out of my apartment.

"She's so mean," Hannah said. "But kind of sad, too. Maybe I shouldn't have crimped her."

"What did she say to get you so angry?"

"She came in like she owned the building, and demanded to see you, and when you weren't here she started calling me names, names I didn't much like. Usually I don't get that mad. I probably shouldn't have this time."

"Hannah, don't beat yourself up over it. No matter what misfortune she may have endured in her youth, the Miranda Love of today could incite the Pope to violence."

"Dinner will be ready soon," she said.

I used the time to check an online entertainment website to see if any other elderly actors had died. Fortunately, none were reported.

The soup turned out to be excellent. Restaurant-quality excellent. I was beginning to wonder if there was anything Hannah couldn't do.

"This is really, really good," I said, and she beamed.

"I was hoping you'd like it. I learned the recipe from one of the chefs back…back *there*."

After dinner I mentioned that I wanted to listen to more of Palmer Hanley's tapes, understanding that they would still be too difficult for Hannah to hear. After searching the apartment for about ten minutes, I finally found an old headset that came with a CD player I'd bought some years ago.

As Hannah puttered in the kitchen, I sat down on the sofa, rewound the tape back to the beginning, and hit PLAY.

The first thing I heard was Palmer Hanley clearing his throat, and then saying: *Is this thing on now?*

Hannah's voice sounded next: *Yes sir, as long as that red light is lit up, it's recording.*

All right. Well, then, this is Palmer Hanley speaking, and I suppose I should start at the beginning. I was born the nineteenth of October, nineteen-hundred-and-twenty-one, which makes me ninety-five years old. Being ninety-five years old is a helluva situation to find oneself in, though I suppose it's better than the alternative. I'll bet Ty Power and Julie Garfield would have been delighted to make it to ninety-five.

Or even forty-five, I thought. Tyrone Power had died at forty-four, and John "Julie" Garfield at a mere thirty-nine.

Anyway, I was born in Walla Walla, Washington. Yep, there really is a Walla Walla, Washington. It's not just a silly lyric from some World War II song.

Palmer went on to talk about his childhood in Walla Walla, but would often stop in the middle of a story, such as one involving a pet dog who had gotten skunked, and say, *Oh, heck, nobody wants to hear about this.*

It was clear that the idea of dictating his life for publication was one with which he was not entirely comfortable.

He talked about his interests in architecture as a kid, and how he thought that was what he might want to do when he grew up. That was least until the age of twelve, at which point he saw a vaudeville show, and had his eyes opened to the world of entertainment. After that, he wanted only to be an actor.

Upon graduating from high school he managed to get hired—and fired—by a string of stock and repertory companies throughout the Northwest. He had plans to go to New York, plans that were delayed by his being drafted into the army during World War II. Palmer never saw oversees combat, however; he spent his military years with the Armed Forces Entertainment Division, mostly working in the technical aspects of the show. Based on that experience, he finally made it to the Big Apple, jumping into a large pool of recently mustered-out talent.

He managed to get hired as an assistant stage manager for a show called *Hear That Trumpet*, which closed in a week. Demonstrating that even young, starving actors had to maintain a sense of humor, Palmer related how he would tell people who asked if he was working that he was currently understudying the title role in *Harvey*.

The only person who seemed impressed by his struggle, he recalled, was a young dancer that he came close to marrying, until he learned that his bride-to-be was only fifteen.

After about forty recorded minutes, Palmer stated on the tape that he was growing tired and his throat was becoming sore, and signed off. After a two-second gap, his voice returned, sounding energized. Apparently his memory had been, too, since he related more details regarding the stories he'd already recorded, to be retrofitted into whatever text would result. These included several more wartime stories, including his working in the AFE with a funny young soldier named Jesse Knotts, who mustered out and dropped his first name in favor of his middle one, Don, and gained immortality by creating the character of Barney Fife.

Another story was surprisingly poignant: *Some of you out there might have heard of a little picture called* Citizen Kane, Palmer's voice said on the tape. *I'm not in it, so don't bother to look for me, but there's a scene in that movie where a fellow named Birnbaum, or Bernstein, or some such, is talking about a girl he once saw when he was young. Now he's old and he's telling the story to a reporter, but he says something like, a day never goes by when he doesn't think of that girl. That's the way I feel about Jenny Cass—*

He stopped talking here, as though he suddenly choked up. After coughing, he went on:

Like I said before, Jenny and I were going to get married. At least that's what we told each other. When her parents found out what we were up to, they liked to have a fit. They took her away someplace and I never saw her again. It near tore me up at the time, but looking back on it now, I wonder if they didn't do me a favor. Given Jenny's age, I might have ended up in court like Errol Flynn. A couple years earlier he had gotten himself into some major trouble by playing dock the sloop with a high school girl. But it's been seventy years since I last saw that girl, my Jenny, and there's hardly been a day I haven't thought about her, and wondered whatever happened to her. During the bad times, when I was kept locked up by a monster of my own creation, and not allowed to live a normal life, sometimes it was the memory of her that got me through each day.

He took another pause after that and cleared his throat again before dictating more.

The rest of the tape side was taken up with the menial jobs he had while looking for acting work in New York. The worst of these which, according to Palmer, was as a dishwasher at Horn & Hardart Automat, including time spent in the company of a cook who constantly mourned the passing of the "good old days" when he was a fixture at German-American Bund gatherings.

Side two of the tape started off with Palmer talking about understudying the role of Happy in the original production of *Death of a Salesman*, including a funny story about Lee J. Cobb's toupee falling off one night during his big scene. The stories of his experiences in live television were equally vivid. In one show he worked with Boris Karloff, and while he found Karloff to be a kind and generous gentleman, he also remembered the star gently suggesting to Palmer that maybe he didn't have the requisite "fire in the belly" to sustain a career in acting.

He also related a version of the story involving Miranda Love and the live TV show that got preempted, which resulted in Miranda's six-decade vendetta against him. What was interesting was that he never referred to her by name, saying only that she was an up-

and-coming actress of the time "whose name is one that no one today would really remember."

I wondered if a reader who did not know the full story would question how he could remember an old girlfriend by name, and wonder about her after all that time, and not a one-time up-and-coming co-star. What I assumed was that this might have been Palmer's subtle vengeance against Miranda: if she wanted to come forth and identify herself as the desperate, angry, not very admirable young starlet of the story, she could do so at her own risk, or else simply seethe in silence.

But even I couldn't place his almost-fiancée, the teenaged dancer Jenny Cass. *Peggy* Cass, sure, but to my knowledge she was not a dancer, and she would have been more than fifteen in the late forties. I made a mental note to myself to see if I could dig up any information on this Jenny Cass.

That was when the thunderbolt hit, sparking my brain to life like Frankenstein's monster on the slab.

'Bout time, Robert Mitchum said.

"Oh, no…oh, *jeez*," I uttered, probably loudly since my ears were covered and I couldn't hear anything but Palmer's voice.

"Did you say something?" Hannah asked, coming into the room.

"Oh, jeez." I clumsily shut the tape machine off and pulled down the headphones. "Hannah, have you ever heard of Jenny Cass?"

"I don't think so. Why?"

"Did Palmer ever mention her?"

"Not that I recall. Did he talk about her on the tape?"

"Yeah, he did. They were almost married."

"Oh, her. I remember him talking about almost getting married when he was young, but he found out the girl was like fourteen. But her name wasn't Cass. I thought he said it was *Castle*, you know, like Windsor Castle?"

I nodded. I no longer thought her name was *Jenny*, either.

It was *Ginny*.

And if I went back and listened again to Palmer saying the name on the tape, I'd probably detect the second syllable of the name, uttered right before he choked up.

Castle.

Ginny Castle.

The vaudeville moniker of Geneva Merrill.

21.

If, in fact, Palmer Hanley's one-time betrothed had grown up to be Geneva Merrill, it was safe to assume he did not know that. One does not spend decades mooning over a woman only to ignore her when they're in the same convention hall.

The question now was whether Geneva Merrill remembered and recognized Palmer Hanley at the Celebrity Expo. My gut was telling me that she must have, since "Palmer Hanley" was not so common a name that there could be two of them in show business. Even if there were, the Screen Actors Guild would force one of them to change it.

But did that equate to Geneva Merrill having anything to do with the murders? Sure, she had physical proximity with all the victims, while her husband may have had information regarding their allergies, but what possible motive would she have for killing the people?

There had to be a connection I wasn't making.

Then I made it.

"It's him," I whispered aloud.

Torgesson had to be the killer, and his wife, Geneva Merrill, must be the primary intended victim, the one whose murder was covered by all the others! Had Geneva died under mysterious circumstances, Torgesson would have been suspected immediately, because that's the way the police work. The spouse is always Suspect No. 1 until proven innocent. So he set up this insane string of murders to cover for the fact that it was really his wife who he wanted to kill. Jay Leach must have been the person who found out about it, and that's why Leach was killed.

It was now imperative that I find out if Geneva was still alive.

But how?

Telephoning Geneva's home earlier had been a flop, so I couldn't see any alternative but to show up at her doorstep in person, though chances were I'd be physically ejected from the place instead of simply hung-up on. Torgesson or his snide servant might even call the police.

Then again, because of the lead I'd given Colfax, the police might have already paid a visit to the house.

Why don't you ask your detective friend if you can accompany him there? Bogie suggested. *Bernie Ohls took me places.*

Sure, but this wasn't *The Big Sleep.* In a movie or TV show, that might make sense, particularly if it advanced the plot, but this was reality, and the police didn't take civilians with them on calls.

If I wanted to try and get through to Geneva Merrill, I was going to have to use a pretense, and a dang good one.

What you really need, sport, is feminine companionship, Errol Flynn said inside my head.

I looked over toward Hannah, who was still moving dishes around in the kitchen. I had a distinct feeling I wouldn't be able to find my coffee cup tomorrow morning on the first try.

No, not her, Flynn went on. *The other one.*

"The other…" I muttered, and then got it.

Louie Sandoval.

That actually made sense; I knew Louie was far better at pulling off pretenses than I could ever hope to be, and she wanted me to keep her posted in regards to the case. There was nothing preventing me from calling and asking if she would like to become involved in the investigation itself.

"How's the listening going?" Hannah asked, having come into the front room when I wasn't looking.

Okay, maybe there was *one* thing.

"Oh, something really interesting came up," I said. "An idea for which I might need, uh, help."

"I'll do whatever I can. You know that."

"Right. Well, I was really more thinking about asking…uh, well, you know how, er, Louie Sandoval helped us get out of the Temple complex, and—"

"*Her?*" Hannah demanded, her expression morphing between anger, hurt, humiliation, rejection, fear, and back to anger with more speed and definition than the best computer special effects could have accomplished. "She called you and now you want to get back together with her, is that it?"

I rushed to her and took her in my arms.

"Hannah, it's not like that. This would be purely professional.

Finding Palmer's killer is what's at stake."

I felt her soften.

"Okay, but what can she offer you that I can't?" Hannah asked.

"Deceit."

"What does that mean?"

"It means that Louie will do anything to get a story. I know you remember when she belted me in the face to convince the guards we were at each other's throats, a gesture that helped gets us out of there. Would you have gone that far?"

After a long pause, she said: "No."

"Louie would do it again in a heartbeat. That's why I need her. I have to get inside the house of a man who I think is responsible for these murders, and I don't think I can do it successfully on my own. I need an expert professional liar like Louie."

"I didn't think reporters were supposed to lie. I thought they were supposed to only tell the truth."

"That's once they've gotten the story and are writing it. Until then, it's the Wild West. No rules."

She sighed. "All right."

"Thanks, Hannah."

She looked into my face.

"But Dave," she said, "if I find out that you're getting more from her than lies and deceit, I might just have to crimp you into the hospital. Her, too."

Then she kissed me lightly on the nose, turned, and went back to the kitchen.

Do I know how to pick women or what?

I picked up the phone and dialed in Louie's number.

"You have her number memorized, I see," Hannah called.

"I have it written down," I lied.

After three rings, Louie's answering machine picked up.

This is future Pulitzer Prize winner Luisa Sandoval. I'm not here. Leave a message. Make it good. Thanks.

BEEP!

"Louie, it's Dave Beauchamp. You had asked me to contact you if—"

I heard the receiver pick up. "I'm here, Dave," she said.

"Yeah, hi. Do you still want to know more about the Celebrity

Expo murders?"

"Damn right I do."

"Can we make arrangements to meet sometime?"

"Now okay?"

"It's not the best."

Hannah aside, I doubted there was any way we could bluff our way into Torgesson's mansion tonight.

"Tomorrow morning?"

"Yeah, good."

"You still in Studio City?"

"Yes."

"Breakfast at Lapeer's, then. Say, nine?"

"Fine."

"Can't you give me a little hint of what you're going to tell me?"

"Well, do you have any insight into a cosmetic surgeon named Dr. Jerome Torgesson?"

"'The Michelangelo of Mastopexy?' That Dr. Jerome Torgesson?"

"I believe so. Don't tell me you've gone to him."

"You think I need a titty tuck?"

"Uh, no, not at all. It's just that you seemed to know him right off the top of your head, so…well, that's all."

"I love hearing you blush over the phone," she said with a laugh. "I interviewed Torgesson when I was back at the Indie-J. He used to take ads out all the time. I think we did a piece on him once in return for all the ad revenue."

"You stooped to advertorial? All this time I thought you were crusading journalists fighting for truth, justice and the American way down there."

"Sometimes you have to find ways to pay for the crusade. Crowd-funding didn't exist then. So you think Torgesson is your celebrity killer?"

"I have no proof, but I believe he's somehow involved. I also think his wife, an ex-dancer named Geneva Merrill, might be in danger."

"Shouldn't you call your detective friend, then?"

"If I call the police and I'm wrong, then I've lost all credibility. I want to check him out myself, but I need a plan. You're better at pretense than I am."

"All right. Breakfast at Lapeer's. Is Pippi Longstocking going to be there, too?"

I glanced over at Hannah, who was staring back at me, arms folded, and smiled to her.

"Wouldn't be at all surprised."

"She's standing right there, isn't she?"

"Um, yeah."

"Mm-hmm. Okay. Tomorrow, then. Enjoy the rest of your night in Bloodnut Valley."

"Louie—" I started, but she'd already hung up.

Hannah was still staring at me.

"When are you going to see her?" she asked.

"Tomorrow," I said. "We're having breakfast, all of us."

"All three of us?"

"Absolutely. You have to admit the three of us worked pretty well together when we rescued Palmer from the Temple."

"Except when she socked you in the face."

"Don't worry about that. Just think of it as the threesome getting back together again."

"You're trying to set up a *threesome* with me and her?" Hannah cried.

"No, no," I protested. "I mean, that was an unfortunate choice of words! Honest!"

Then she started giggling.

"You should see the look on your face," she said. "C'mon." Taking my hand, she led me into the bedroom, where she did her best to make me forget I'd ever met anyone named Luisa Sandoval.

I was grinning like an idiot the next morning when Hannah and I entered Lapeer's. Louie was already there, waiving to us from a table.

Because my traditional finances had not allowed me the luxury of eating at a sit-down restaurant very often, I'd not been in Lapeer's for quite some time. Since then, the place had installed two large televisions, one in each dining area, both turned to cable news networks. The sound was down on each, but I could tell that one was tuned to MSNBC and the other to Fox News.

Now that smoking in public has been banned in California, I suppose restaurants compensate by creating Thinking and Non-Thinking sections.

At the table, Louie got up and gave me a quick hug, and then did likewise to Hannah. "You both look well," she said, grinning.

"You look great, too," I said.

Hannah coughed dramatically, and I got the message. We all sat down.

"Thanks for coming," I said.

Louie grinned, turning her face into a dimple factory. "It doesn't take that much to make me come. But of all people, you should know that, Dave."

Fasten your seatbelts, it's going to be a bumpy breakfast, Bette Davis cautioned inside my head.

I took Hannah's hand in mine to keep her from picking up any silverware.

"So, Louie, how's the book coming?" I asked, desperate to change the subject.

She responded with a detailed account of how idiotic book publishers were. The release of her book on the demise—or, at least the diminution—of the Temple of Theotologics had been postponed as a result of the publishing house having merged with another publisher. An excerpt of it had run in *Vanity Fair*, prompting a series of threatened lawsuits from what was left of the Temple. Louie also suspected that the studio head who had optioned the book for a film was secretly a Theotologician himself. He may have purchased the rights in order to sit on them, making certain that the film would never be produced.

After we'd ordered our breakfasts—an omelet for me, a muffin and fruit for Hannah, and for Louie the most expensive thing on the menu, New York strip steak and eggs—Louie said: "Okay, now tell me what's going on here."

Unlike my recitations of the fact of the case for the police, I left nothing out for Louie, who responded with flashes of interest and excitement in her eyes. When I was finished she said: "So you're telling me that all these people died because one guy wants to kill his wife?"

"It appears that way," I said.

"And you don't know if he's gotten to her or not yet?"

Glancing at the television, I prayed I would not see a breaking news flash announcing the death of Geneva Merrill.

"I don't know," I answered, "but until we hear otherwise, I'm assuming she is alive. That's why it's so important I talk to her, and that's why I need your help, Louie. I need to get through to Geneva, but I've already kind of blown it by calling up and leaving my real name."

"Well, I could ask for an interview with her," Louie said. "Working for the *Times* opens a lot more doors than working for the Indie-J."

"What would your questions be?" I wondered.

"Oh, you know, tell me about your life, your career, your cause, do you know you're husband's a serial killer? That sort of thing."

"We might need a little more finesse than that," I said. "Besides, I'd hate for you to get in trouble with your editors."

"What are you talking about? They love me."

"Would they still if you interviewed Geneva under the auspices of the *Times* for an article that never comes out, because it's all a pretense, and then she or Torgesson calls the paper and demands to know what's going on, and they're in the dark?"

"Okay, so I make up a newspaper or magazine. That way they can't check up on it."

"That might work," I said. "Would you be prepared to do the interview right then and there?"

"I would be, but of course I can't guarantee *your* person would be."

"And you might get no further on the phone than I got."

"Okay, how about I show up at the door pretending to be taking a survey, or something?"

"I think it would have to be something bigger, like maybe pretend you're working for the gas company, and you have to come in to check out a leak."

"Do you have a gas company uniform in my size by any chance?" Louie asked.

"Well, no—"

"Even if you did, why would I have to talk to the woman personally to check out a gas leak? I mean, if the butler says, 'Oh, she's not here,' what do I do then? Say, 'Never mind, there was never any gas leak, anyway?' What you need, Dave, is a pretense so big they wouldn't dare turn us away."

"How about you pretend to be the police?" Hannah asked.

Louie and I exchanged glances, and I could sense that Louie was about to comment, but I shook my head. I said: "I'm afraid you can go to jail for that, Hannah."

"That's one of the first rules a reporter learns if we're going undercover," Louie added. "You'd have to be an idiot to impersonate a police officer."

"The security guys did it back at…you know where," Hannah said, defensively.

"Well, then maybe we should hire one of them and let them take their chances," Louie said.

Then a better idea struck me.

"Or maybe some other idiot," I said.

"Like who?" Louie asked.

I smiled at her.

"I think I know the perfect person."

Our food came then. Louie's plate was twice the size of either Hannah's or mine.

Since I was paying, I asked her for a bite of her steak, which I chewed still smiling.

* * * *

It was shockingly easy to convince Terry Brucker to go along with the scheme Louie and I had concocted at Lapeer's, over Hannah's skeptical objections.

Brucker arrived at my place shortly after one in the afternoon, dressed like a Central Casting cop and ready to go. He looked convincing enough for what we needed.

About an hour later the two of us arrived at the Holmby Hills estate of Dr. Jerome Torgesson and Geneva Merrill. Entry to the estate on North Carolwood Drive was prevented by a high fence with an ornate gate that looked like two Irish harps shoved together. Behind the gate was a circular drive that went up to a structure that was somewhere between a mansion and a palace.

Clearly, the nip-and-tuck business was booming.

While I had not figured on the gate, it made sense for this neighborhood. It also added an unexpected level of complexity to actually getting inside the house.

I pulled over and let Brucker out, and then parked my Corolla (which was seriously outclassed by the surroundings) up against the hedge, hoping it wasn't trash day for the street.

"Now remember, Terry," I said as we walked to the gate, "don't actually call yourself an officer. Just let the costume talk."

"Got it," he replied.

I hoped he did.

A freestanding communications box was positioned on the right side of the drive. It had a keypad and a small sign that instructed visitors to hit *37. I did, and a second later a voice came through: "Yes?"

Even through that one word I recognized the voice of the pseudo-Kenneth Williams.

"Hi, I'd like to talk to the lady of the house," I said.

"Who is this?"

"I'm a detective," I replied. "Carlson."

I'd like to state in my own defense that I was not, strictly speaking, lying. I am a detective, and since my father's name is Carl, I am *Carl's son*.

"The lady of the house," the voice sniffed. "Are you certain you are the police and not Avon?"

"I need to speak to the woman who lives here, pal," I said. "We're investigating a burglary in the neighborhood."

"We?"

"I've got a uniform with me."

Again, strictly speaking, that was not a lie. I was in the company of a uniform. Just not a uniformed officer.

Slicin' the truth a little bit thin there, ain'tcha, buckaroo? Pat Buttram asked inside my head.

I ignored him.

"We've not been burglarized, nor have we burglarized the neighbors."

"And hopefully it'll stay that way. Now, are you going to let me talk to someone or not?"

"You may talk to me," he said.

Brucker leaned toward the box. "All right," he said, "we came here to see the lady of the house, but if the shoe fits—"

I shot him a look and gestured for him to shut up, which hopefully did not look like a *Gilligan's Island* comedy take if we happened to be on a security camera.

A second later I saw a man come out onto the porch of the house, look at us, then go back in. Then an electric whine sounded and the gate began to open.

"Come on," I told Brucker, as we strode to the house. "And don't say anything else!"

The guy who met us, named Jeffries if I remember correctly, was somewhere between forty-five and seventy, medium height, and tanned, which gave his gray hair and trimmed moustache a silvery cast. He wore an expensive sports jacket and slacks whose creases could have cut cheese, and a silk shirt with no tie.

The voice of Kenneth Williams in the body of Douglas Fairbanks, Jr.

"You should really be talking to Dr. Torgesson," he told us. "But he is presently at the clinic. Now, what is this about a burglary?"

"A couple houses here on the drive have been hit over the last week and purses were taken, so we're talking to everyone else to see if they've happened to notice anyone suspicious prowling around," I lied.

"I've seen no one."

"Do you speak for the lady of the house?"

"Yeah," Brucker ad libbed, "it's not your purse we're concerned with."

Oh, how I wish I could kick him in the shin.

Instead Jeffries regarded him with withering disdain.

The situation was saved by the sound of a woman's voice behind the servant, asking: "What is it, Jeffries?"

"Police, madam," he called back.

Through the front door came Geneva Merrill, whom I recognized immediately from her online photos (the recent ones, anyway), though she was shorter than I had imagined.

The larger point was that she was still alive.

"Sorry to bother you, ma'am," I said. "You're Geneva Merrill, aren't you?"

She smiled. "Yes, yes I am. Would you fellows like to come in?"

"Yes, thank you."

As we entered the house, which looked like it was perpetually ready for a photo shoot for *Architectural Digest*, I noticed that a strange expression was darkening Brucker's face. We were invited into the stark-white living room and asked to sit down, but I thought it best to stand, as that would imply we were not going to be there for very long.

I went through the same spiel with Geneva Merrill, who appeared genuinely disturbed at the thought of a burglar being in the exclusive neighborhood. "I don't know what we pay that security patrol for if this is the result," she said.

"Well, sometimes these things happen no matter what," I replied, "but that's why we're talking to people and cautioning them to keep an eye out for anyone who doesn't belong in the neighborhood."

"I'm glad for that. I imagine when they catch this man, he'll be another horrible drug addict. They should all be imprisoned."

"Yes, ma'am."

"Or shot."

"Well, that might be a little drastic."

"If you know who I am…what is your name, anyway?"

"Detective Carlson, ma'am."

"As I was saying, Detective Carlson, if you know who I am then you must know the cause to which I have dedicated myself. I would like to see any and all drug use completely eradicated so no mother ever has to endure what I did." She gestured to a large framed oil painting that hung over the room's fireplace and added: "That is all I have left of my son. I painted it myself. I am an artist as well as a performer."

The painting, which had clearly been done by an amateur, showed a young man with longish, dark hair, a clear complexion, and a broad smile posing in a jacket and tie. But the position of the head was slightly stilted and unnatural, like you see in high school graduation portraits.

"Very accomplished, ma'am," I fibbed. "Well, if you do happen to see or hear anything unusual, please don't hesitate to call us. And, as a precaution, lock up your purse and any other valuables."

"I will, thank you," Geneva said. "Let me show you out."

When we got to the door, I had an inspiration.

Pulling a handkerchief out of my pocket, I sneezed into it a couple times, and then begged Geneva Merrill's pardon. "Allergies," I said. "Something's blooming out there and getting me. It's really annoying."

"Oh, I am sorry, detective," she said. "That's something I've never had to worry about, fortunately, but I know a lot of people who do suffer from them. Well, goodbye, and thank you again, both of you."

Then she put a hand on Brucker's arm.

"Have we met somewhere?" she asked him. "You look familiar."

A sliver of panic shot through my gut. This wasn't part of the script.

"I don't think so," Brucker said, his voice barely above a whisper.

"Well, goodbye, then."

As I walked back to the gate, I mentally ran over what I had learned from this rather speedy pretense. First and foremost, Geneva had not been murdered. And apparently, she had no allergies. But then how did she fit into the pattern?

Could I have been wrong about Torgesson being the killer?

Could it actually be that his being a cosmetic surgeon really was just a coincidence?

The gate reopened as though by magic as we approached it. Once we were out, and out of sight, Brucker took my arm and practically ran me to the car.

"Hey, Terry, what are you doing?" I asked. "If you're worried about your performance, you did fine. I mean, I could have done without your ad lib about Jeffries being the lady of the house, but—"

"She recognized me," he interrupted.

"She thought she recognized you."

"No, Mr. Beauchamp, you don't get it. She recognized me."

"You mean from the Celebrity Expo?"

"No, from my home."

"Terry, I'm not following you."

"That woman we just talked to was the one I saw snooping around Mr. Prescott's house," he said. "The one who claimed to be his sister."

22.

As far as headaches went, the one that had hit me as I drove away from Geneva Merrill's house was murder.

"Terry, are you *certain* the woman you saw at Prescott's house, the one who told you she was his sister, was Geneva Merrill?"

"She recognized me, too," he replied.

"Okay, but forget for a moment that she seemed to recognize you. Just concentrate on her. Are you *absolutely sure* it was Geneva."

"It sure looked like her."

"Would you feel confident going into a court of law and under oath swear that it was her?"

He looked alarmed. "I have to go to court?"

"No, I'm speaking hypothetically. Is there any doubt in your mind that it was Geneva Merrill you saw?"

"Well, like I said, she looked stretched, just like the woman we just left."

"Right, but this is L.A., and a lot of people look stretched," I said. "Cosmetic surgery is very common, and sometimes people who have had facelifts come out looking like other people who have had facelifts."

"Really? I didn't know that."

"Does knowing it make a difference in your assessment?"

"You mean, do I now think it wasn't Geneva Merrill? Well, no. I'm sure it was her. I mean, I'm pretty sure it was her. I mean, if it wasn't her, then who was it?"

"I don't know," I moaned, rubbing my forehead as I drove.

"I do know that Mr. Prescott didn't have a sister."

"Right."

"So why would Geneva Merrill say she was his sister?" Terry asked. "That doesn't make any sense. If you can explain that one, you're a genius."

"I'm not a genius, but I have known people who were such close friends that they referred to each other as siblings."

"Huh?"

"Let's say it was Geneva Merrill you saw at Prescott's house, Terry. Maybe they're old friends. Maybe they worked together. Maybe Prescott did some sort of work with her foundation. Maybe they'd become close enough pals that they called each other 'brother' and 'sister.' I just don't know."

"Well, I know I saw *somebody* at the house, and it was a woman with a tight face who told me she was Mr. Prescott's sister," Brucker averred.

I tried to make a mental note to look for any connection between Geneva and Prescott when I got back to my laptop, but my head was already too full of pain at the moment to allow a note to be thumbtacked onto it.

Back at my apartment I pulled up to let Terry out. He wanted to hang, but I told him I had things I really needed to do.

Like try to keep my head from exploding.

"Since I'm suited up," he said, getting out of my car, "maybe I should stop off at a cop bar on the way home."

"I really wouldn't do that, Terry," I said. "I'll be in touch."

Maybe I would, too.

Sometime.

Once inside the apartment I called Louie and asked her to try and dig up everything she could on Geneva in addition to researching Torgesson. There must be a ton of background material on that anti-drug foundation. Then I asked Hannah if she could pinch my nerve until I was unconscious so as to escape the pain in my head.

She didn't take me seriously. Instead she did her best to rub it away, but it wasn't working.

I could always give you a new brain, the voice of George Zucco offered inside my aching head, adding: *I'd rather enjoy it, in fact.*

Some other time, maybe.

"Dave, you should go lie down," Hannah said. "I'll bring you a cold rag."

I retired to the bedroom—alone—though Hannah did bring in a cold washcloth for my forehead. The combination of the darkness, the quiet, and the cool compress was having some effect. The pain had reduced in intensity enough to allow me to be drowsy.

I had nearly dropped off when I heard Hannah quietly enter the room.

"Dave," she whispered.

"Hmmm."

"Karen Robinson is on the phone. Do you want to talk to her?"

"Yes," I said, getting out of the bed and going into the living room.

Taking the receiver, I said: "Hi, Karen? What's up?"

"I tried your office but you weren't there," she said. "I'm going through Granddad's stuff like you asked me to and I think I might have found something. There's a file that contains some strange hate mail that includes a reference to the Baroni family."

"When can I take a look at it?"

"Do you want to come over now? I'll probably be here for a while."

"You're at home?"

"No, at Granddad's house in Tarzana."

She gave me the address, and I said I'd see her within the half-hour. But before I hung up, I asked if she knew the name of the doctor Tony Marsh had gone to for his eye lift.

"I really don't," she said.

"Could you check your grandfather's medical files to see if the name Torgesson pops up?"

"Torgesson?"

"Yes, he's a cosmetic surgeon, and I think he might be at the center of this case."

"The murderer is a crazed cosmetic surgeon? That sounds like a bad horror movie."

Send the script over and if it's ridiculous enough, I'll do it, the voice of Vincent Price said inside my head.

After hanging up I went into the bathroom and took a couple of ibuprofen caplets, hoping to kill the last lingering trace of my headache, and explained to Hannah where I was going.

"Don't you have any male clients?" she asked.

"I'll come back home, I promise," I said, kissing the tip of her nose.

Tarzana, just as it sounds, was named after the venerable Lord of the Jungle. It grew up around property that had been owned by Tarzan's creator, Edgar Rice Burroughs. A hundred years ago this area was nothing but sprawling land and hills, but today it was one more tangle of tract house neighborhoods, strip malls and commercial buildings. About the only trace of the original Tarzana estate is an enormous walnut tree facing Ventura Boulevard, under which the ashes of Burroughs are buried.

Following the directions I'd hastily written down, I navigated a twisty street in the middle of a residential ant farm to Tony Marsh's house. I didn't even have to check for the address: the door of the house's adjoining two-car garage was open, and I could see Karen Robinson standing in front of what looked like a castle wall of cardboard boxes.

I was pretty sure it was Karen, anyway, since her formerly bright-orange hair was now a rich blue color. She was wearing a black workout tank-top that revealed colorful tattoos on her shoulders and upper arms.

As I parked and got out of the car, she waved to me.

"You're in your blue period, I see," I said, when I got there.

She shook her tresses. "You like it?"

"It's different."

"I don't know if I'm going to keep it, though. I may go back to my natural color."

"Which is?"

She took a step closer to me.

"I don't remember," she said. "Maybe we should go inside and see if you can find it."

Wait for it…

You're trying to seduce me, Mrs. Robinson, Dustin Hoffman's voice said inside my head. *Aren't you?*

"I uh, um, I…well…"

She offered a sympathetic smile. "I'm guessing the woman who answered the phone at your house isn't your mom."

"Were you hoping it was?"

She shrugged, then turned and reached back to a stack of boxes, taking from the top one two sheets of paper stapled together.

"I think this might be what you're looking for," she said, handing them to me.

It was the carbon copy of a standard surgical consent form from the medical offices of Dr. Jerome H. Torgesson, M.D., FACS, dated

September 24, 1993.

"Yes, this is exactly what I was hoping to find," I said.

I was holding the first actual bit of evidence directly linking Torgesson to one of the victims.

"What's it mean?" Karen asked.

Flipping the top page over, I found Tony Marsh's faint but readable signature, and above it, a word written into a blank space. Holding the paper out to her, I pointed to the filled in space.

"Peanuts," Karen read.

"Written into a space that asks for any known allergies."

"Dear god. So Dr. Torgesson knew about Granddad's allergy. He's the one who killed him."

"That has yet to be proven," I said. "But it's getting harder to come up with an alternate theory."

"But why? Why kill a man who had been his patient?"

"This is probably going to sound pretty awful, but I don't think Tony was the primary victim. I think he was killed as misdirection from another murder, the victim Torgesson really wanted to kill. There are several other misdirections, too."

"Jesus fuck," she uttered, running a nervous hand through her blue hair. "Can you prove this?"

"No, I can't. Not yet, anyway. Right now it's just a theory, and I have a feeling that few, if any of the other victims would have this kind of clue lying around. Not everybody was as good at saving papers as your grandfather."

"But Torgesson would still have patient files, wouldn't he? Couldn't those be checked?"

"Well, it would take a court order to obtain them, and even if one were granted, any lawyer worth his salt would prevent the files from being opened, citing doctor-patient confidentiality. I've been to Torgesson's house. He can afford a lot of salt."

"The files remain private even if the patients are dead?"

"Maybe not permanently, but it would take a lot of arguing in court. Still, this document might be enough to open the argument. May I keep this?"

"Go ahead," she said. "I found something else, too."

Turning, she reached for a file folder that was sitting on the same box and handed it to me. Its tab label had a series of question marks written on it. "Is this what you called the hate mail?" I asked.

"Read it for yourself and then decide."

The folder contained a handful of letters that could best be described as crank mail. A few might have qualified as genuine hate mail, but even those were vague enough to be non-threatening. One was from a man who charged that he had actually created *The Purple Shadow* and that Tony Marsh was ripping him off, but the fact that it was written in purple colored-pencil by someone who spelled it *shadoe* spoke volumes.

"Am I looking for anything in particular?" I asked.

She took the folder back and pulled out a particular sheet, then handed it to me. It was actually two pages stapled together, and the one on top was written in small, neat block print, such as an artist or architect might use.

MR. MARSH:

MY LIFE HAS BEEN MISERABLE SINCE YOU SOLD OUR HOUSE TO THAT FAMILY.

MY MOTHER AND FATHER FIGHT ALL THE TIME NOW AND MY MOTHER BLAMES ME FOR HAVING THE HOUSE TAKEN AWAY, BUT I DIDN'T DO ANYTHING. IT'S NOT LIKE I HELD UP A BANK OR MURDERED SOMEBODY. IT WASN'T EVEN COKE! ALL IT WAS WAS SOME POT PLANTS IN THE BACK YARD, AND I WASN'T EVEN MAKING THAT MUCH MONEY FROM IT. THE LAWS IN THIS COUNTRY ARE FUCKING STUPID, AND IF YOU DON'T KNOW THAT THEN YOU ARE FUCKING STUPID TOO!

BECAUSE YOU BOUGHT OUR HOUSE OUT BEFORE MY DAD COULD TRY AND GET IT BACK, AND THEN SOLD IT TO SOMEONE ELSE, MY LIFE HAS BEEN SHIT.

YOU HAD NO RIGHT TO DO THAT! YOU HAD NO RIGHT TO DESTROY MY HOME. IF YOU WERE A DECENT PERSON YOU WOULD GET RID OF THOSE WOPS WHO BOUGHT OUR HOUSE AND LET US MOVE BACK IN. OR JUST ME.

BUT I'LL BET YOU WON'T, YOU ASSHOLE. I HOPE YOU DIE. SOMEONE SHOULD KILL YOU.

The letter was signed Wesley Sperry.

"Wesley Sperry," I said. "Why does that sound so familiar?"

It took a few more seconds, but I finally got it.

Wesley Sperry was Geneva Merrill's dead son.

"Oh, jeez," I uttered.

"Don't tell me you know who this Wesley Sperry is," Karen said.

"I know who he is," I replied.

I told you not to tell me that! the voice of Don Adams said inside my head before I could stop him.

Those wops, I read again.

"Do you think that was the Baroni family?"

"Read the attached note," she said.

Flipping the page I found a handwritten note on lined paper. It read:

5/9/82

Talked with Freddy today –

His legal opinion is that we are under no obligation of any kind. The house on Oak View Drive was properly obtained in a government auction having been seized in a civil forfeiture, no matter what the Sperry kid thinks. Freddy believes there is no reason to trouble the Baroni family with any of this and feels it will all blow over once the kid comes down from his high.

"Is this Tony's handwriting?" I asked.

Karen nodded. "What do you make of it?"

"You don't even have to read between the lines to see that Wesley Sperry was a drug dealer. He virtually confesses it. The government has the authority to seize any property on which drugs are being made, or cultivated, and trafficked. It's called asset forfeiture. Your grandfather bought the house at auction and sold it to the Baronis, who probably had no idea of its history. But the loss of the house seems to have torn the family apart. No wonder Geneva hates drugs so much. Having something like this in your background was sure to leave a scar."

"Who's Geneva?"

"Geneva Merrill, an old MGM dancer. She was also at the Hollywood Celebrity Expo. She was the mother of Wesley Sperry."

"Was?"

"Wesley died of an overdose in 1984 and Geneva became an anti-drug activist."

"Since everything is folding back in on itself, do you think this business with Wesley Sperry and the house is why Michael Baroni was contacting grandfather?"

"Possibly, though why he continued to hide behind his Boris Verdugo identity and didn't present himself as Baroni to Tony is rather puzzling. It's almost like he had some secret that he was trying to protect, and—"

My words stopped, though my mouth was still open.

I felt suddenly chilled.

"Are you all right?" Karen asked.

"Yeah, yeah, I just thought of...oh, *jeez*!"

"What's wrong?"

Karen, you're up on the Valley Slasher case. When were the Baronis killed?"

"Right around the first of June nineteen-eighty-two. Why?"

I glanced at the bitter, angry note from Wesley Sperry, in which he begged Tony Marsh to "get rid of those wops" and return the house to his family. It was not dated, but Tony's follow-up note was: *May 9, 1982.*

"And when did the killings stop?" I asked.

"Nineteen-eighty-four."

Wesley Sperry died in 1984.

"Oh, dear god," I moaned.

"Dave, if you don't tell me what you think you've figured out, I might throw a box at you."

"A minute ago you asked me what I made of these letters."

"I did."

I looked her in the eye, all but daring her to laugh at me and call me an idiot when I said: "These letters make a pretty good case that Wesley Sperry might have been the Valley Slasher."

23.

"Jesus fuck," Karen whispered.

Cecil B. DeMille might not have approved, but I mentally agreed with her.

"Do you think Granddad knew that?"

"Well, we don't know it for a fact," I said. "Whether he suspected as much, I can't say. I have to think that if he did, he would probably have wanted to talk to someone with more authority than me, like the police. But I wonder if Michael Baroni suspected, and that's why he wanted to talk to your grandfather."

"Jesus."

"What I don't know is whether Geneva Merrill suspected her son might be the serial killer."

Which is why it was no longer simply important that I talk to Geneva Merrill again, but imperative.

"Dave, do you think my grandfather was killed because he knew too much about this?"

"I don't know, Karen."

"What has the cosmetic surgeon to do with all of this?"

"Well, that's the really creepy part. The doctor, Jerome Torgesson, is currently married to Geneva Merrill."

"So you think Torgesson is killing anyone he thinks might suspect that his son was the Valley Slasher?"

"Wesley wasn't his son," I said. "I doubt he ever met the kid. Geneva's first husband was Wesley's father, and he's dead, too. But it is possible that Torgesson is killing people who might suspect that Wesley was the Slasher in order to protect Geneva's foundation. She apparently rakes in millions and millions of dollars each year for her anti-drug cause, and if news broke that her son was not simply the unfortunate victim of drug abuse, but the Valley Slasher, I doubt it would help her cause. It would probably result in a litigation nightmare, too, as prominent people and organizations who have donated would demand that their money be returned."

It would, in short, be the personal and professional end of Geneva Merrill.

"But if her husband knows the secret," Karen went on, "she would have to know it, too, wouldn't she? I mean, how else would he have found out?"

"Maybe Torgesson figured it out on his own. I did, after all."

I was waiting for Robert Mitchum to chime in with some variation of *And if you could, any idiot could*, but he didn't.

"I won't know what, if anything, she knew until I talk to her again," I went on.

"You've talked to her once already?"

"Yes, on a pretense to make sure she was still alive, because I suspected this case was about her husband, Torgesson, wanting to kill her, but also killing some other old actors as a way of throwing the hounds off the scent as to his culpability. But now things don't seem quite that cut-and-dried. I'd appreciate it if I could take all of these papers with me."

"Go ahead."

"Thanks. You know, Karen, you hired me in the first place to find out who killed your grandfather, and I think I might have. But it doesn't make me feel good."

"Do you need more money?"

"No, no, not at all. I mean, thanks, but from now on I'm working for Tony. I'll let you know what I find out."

I turned to leave and she stopped me.

"Dave, wait. What I said a while back, the dumb hair color joke––"

"It's all right, Karen. Don't worry about it."

"What I want to say is that going through this divorce has left me feeling a little battered. More than a little, actually. I look in the mirror and I see all these bruises, and I know they're not really there, but I still see them. I feel them, too. So maybe what I wanted, more than dragging you to bed, was affirmation that someone still thinks I'm attractive. A younger man who thought so would be even better."

"You are a very attractive woman, Karen," I told her. "Two weeks ago I well might have taken you up on your offer. But it so happens that I've just started a relationship with someone and it's good. I don't want to screw that up, no matter how attractive the offer. Or the offerer."

She examined my face as though searching for a lie, but there was none there.

"Wow," she said, finally, "there are still guys out there who aren't total jerks. You've given me hope."

"She also knows how to render me unconscious with a pinch on my neck, like Mr. Spock. So I know better than to cheat on her, even if I wanted to."

Karen laughed. "I hope she appreciates you. But you are going to call me when you have something, right?"

"I promise."

Karen went back to trying to organize the boxes of paperwork.

You handled the doll pretty well, Bogie said in my head.

Yeah, well, not calling her a *doll* probably contributed.

As I strode back to my car, I tried to think of what to do next.

The smartest thing was probably to call Dane Colfax and tell him what I'd deduced, but I already had one unanswered call into him. Besides, keeping him up to speed might expose my little officer-impersonation stunt with Terry Brucker.

So that left talking to Geneva Merrill.

From my cell I decided to try calling her house.

As anticipated, Jeffries answered.

"Hi, this is Carl's son, the detective who was over there earlier today," I began, acutely aware that the sound in my ears was that of ice thinning. "It's important I speak with Ms. Merrill as soon as possible."

"She is not here," the butler replied. "She is having her hair done, after which she was going to stop by the Farmers Market. I dare say she will not be home for hours."

"Let me give you my number and please ask her to call it."

I rattled off my cell number.

Jeffries read it back to me and then said: "How interesting that a West Los Angeles public servant should have a San Fernando Valley area code."

Whose the detective, you or me? the raspy voice of Charles Mc-Graw demanded in my head.

"It's a personal phone," I replied, "and even though I work here, I can't afford to live there. Have her call me, please."

I had no guarantee that Geneva Merrill would get the message, or call back if she did. So I decided to take a chance.

It took the better part of an hour to get to the Los Angeles Farmers Market, a rare still-living legend that since the 1930s had hosted fresh produce, fish, and meat stalls, surrounded by open-air restaurants and, increasingly, stuff stores. Next to it once rose Gilmore Stadium, another on a long list of city landmarks that now existed only in photos, having been torn down decades ago to make room for Television City, an enormous TV studio that was the production home of CBS. While the Farmers Market itself had managed to resist major changes, it was now an adjunct to a high-end shopping mall and housing development that was created by one of those billionaire developers who gobbled up neighborhoods like Pac-Man, only to resculpt them into their own urban-values image.

In the past I'd gone to Farmers Market just to hang out for a while, have a calzone at a place Sinatra used to patronize, and try to imagine that it was really 1946 or 1956, when some of the celebrity photos that hang on the walls of the eateries were newly framed.

Maybe if the Hollywood Celebrity Expo were to be held here instead of some sterile hotel conference hall it wouldn't seem so depressing.

Today, though, I was not looking for a nostalgia fix.

I was looking for Geneva Merrill.

After about a half-hour of walking around, without success, I went for the calzone, since the taste for one was now implanted in my mouth, and settled down at one of the small tables that were jigsawed into the footprint of the market.

I was on the last bite of it when I saw her.

Geneva Merrill's hair was perfectly coifed and a little more golden than before. She wore sunglasses and a simple blouse and slacks, and was carrying a cloth tote that appeared to already be weighed down with produce. She had stopped in front of a candle shop and was looking at the samples in the window.

Leaving my plate on the table, I got up and went to her.

"Excuse me, Ms. Merrill?" I said. "We met earlier."

She turned to face me. "We did?"

"Yes, I came to your house to talk about the burglaries."

"Oh, right, yes, of course you did. I'm sorry, but I cannot recall your name."

"I'm Carl's son."

"Yes, of course. So are you following me now, detective?"

I thought about denying it, but then reconsidered.

"Well, let's say I'm keeping watch over you."

"What on earth for?"

"May we sit down, somewhere?"

"Oh, really, is this going to take that long?"

"Please, ma'am."

I walked her to the first available table and we sat.

"I've already told you we haven't been burgled," she said. "Nothing has changed since then."

"Right, but I'd rather talk about Palmer Hanley?"

"Palmer...oh, you mean that religious nut who started the horrible phony church?"

"No, I mean the man who wanted to marry you right after the war."

She became so still I wondered if she might have been stricken with something.

"Back then you were known as Ginny Castle, and you and Palmer were talking about eloping until your parents prevented you," I went on.

"Nobody knows that," she whispered.

"Palmer knew it, but Palmer's dead now."

"Palmer's dead?"

"It's been in the news."

"I pay little attention to the news. It has become so depressing."

"So has the fact that several other actors from that Celebrity Expo you attended have been killed."

"What is it you want from me, detective?"

I took a deep breath. "This is not easy or pleasant for me to ask, ma'am, but I want to know if you are aware that your late son Wesley committed a string of murders in the 1980s attributed to the Valley Slasher. I also want to know if you are aware that your husband, Dr. Jerome Torgesson, may be committing a string of murders in very bizarre ways today."

For the second time in as many minutes, Geneva Merrill froze in place, like a statue. Finally she said: "Detective Carlson, are you insane?"

Hard to say, the polls haven't closed yet, Robert Mitchum said cheerfully in my head.

"I know this must sound like a shocking proposition—"

"No, it is preposterous. Libelous, even. You have taken leave of your senses."

"Ms. Merrill, I have evidence linking—"

"I don't care. I won't listen."

"It's possible your life is in danger."

"By my own husband? You must be demented! I have no time for this."

She started to get up.

"I know about your losing the house on Oak View Drive," I blurted out. "I know how upset Wesley was about that."

She stopped and turned to glare at me. Then she slowly sat down once more.

"I ask you again, detective," she said. "What is it you want from me? Are you attempting to blackmail me?"

"No, of course not. I want you to go to the police and tell them everything you know."

"I thought you were the police."

"Well, not exactly. I am a detective, but a private one. My name is Dave Beauchamp—"

"*You are not with the police?*" she screeched. People at tables around us stopped talking and turned to look.

"No, but—"

"Then I *will* go to the police, you lying, slanderous psychopath! I will go so I can file a complaint against you!"

With that she, grabbed her bag, rose and stormed away.

"I know, Bogie, I know," I sighed before he had the chance to comment. "That doll I didn't handle so well."

As Geneva Merrill disappeared into the milling crowd of the Farmers Market, I tried to think of what to do next. As far as I was concerned, the door had just closed on my investigation. The only thing I could do now was turn everything I had over to Dane Colfax and hope I didn't get my license yanked for impersonating an officer.

I headed back to my car and fought my way out of the Farmers Market parking lot. It was now nearing four o'clock, and I hadn't even checked into the office yet today, so I decided to swing by before heading back home.

As the crow flies, my office wasn't that far away from the Fairfax district of L.A., but I wasn't travelling by crow.

Eating a little, perhaps, but not traveling by it.

It took about forty-five hot, smoggy minutes to drive over the mountains that separated the L.A. basin from the Valley, and then another twenty to get to my building.

I went up to the office and saw a flashing light on my phone machine.

It was a call from Louie.

Dave, you wanted me to research Dr. Jerome Torgesson, her recorded voice said. *Well, newspaper files turned up only two items of interest. One, for what it's worth, he's a lot younger than his wife... she's eighty-five, he's sixty-eight...and two, he seems to have gotten into a bit of trouble in 1981 during a routine nose job when the patient had a severe reaction to the sunlamp Torgesson was using in the procedure. It turns out the patient had an allergy to extreme sunlight. I did a little database snooping and found the records of the case. The patient survived, but the fact that the surgery had to be stopped mid-way through in order to treat the reaction meant that the nose job was compromised. The patient filed suit and had to have a subsequent surgery...a lot of them, actually...to fix what he felt Torgesson had done to him. Now, wait till you hear the patient's name...*

"Whoa," was all I could utter when I heard her recorded voice say:

Michael Jackson.

Her message continued: *Remember he used to carry umbrellas around all the time? He had some kind of skin condition and couldn't take the sun. Look, I gotta run now. Adios.*

I sat at my desk in silence after the message had finished.

Finally, to the empty office, I said: "Louie, you're good."

Aside from potentially solving the mystery of the late singer's obsession with altering his face, something I couldn't believe had never been brought to light, Louie laid out the motivation for a cosmetic surgeon to go out of his way to make certain that any future patients disclosed every known allergy, so nothing of the kind would happen again.

Whether Geneva wanted to believe it or not, the evidence against her husband was stacking up taller than the Watts Towers.

I had to get Colfax involved now.

I punched in his work number and waited as it rang.

"RHD," a voice answered.

"Is this Detective Lopez?" I asked.

"Yes it is."

"This is Dave Beauchamp again, and I really need to talk to Dane. I mean, Detective Colfax."

"Hey, Beauchamp. I passed along your suggestion about the botulinum toxin, and they're checking."

"Great. But is Colfax there?"

"No, he's in a meeting. Want me to have him call you?"

"Please."

After taking my number again, Lopez hung up.

There was not much for me to do until Colfax called back except watch a movie on my laptop. I checked the Webfilm sites to see if there were any newly-added movies that I hadn't seen, or at least hadn't over-seen, but the pickings were slim. There was a plethora of brand-new thrillers and horror films starring no one I'd ever heard of, most with one-and-one-half star user ratings, meaning even by modern standards they were trash. Who continues to make this stuff? And why?

After poking around I finally found a British *noir* from the late fifties starring Kenneth More that I hadn't seen, and downloaded it.

The music and photography were all right, though the performances were too elegant to be believably hard-boiled. This was particularly true of the leading lady, an actress named Siobhan Justice, who came off more like she was appearing in a Noel Coward play than a gritty crime drama.

By the end of the film Colfax still had not called back. It was almost six now, and despite the earlier calzone, I was getting a little hungry. It was time to pack it up and go home.

Colfax could always call me there.

I already had the lights turned out when the phone rang.

"Great timing, Dane," I said to the empty room. "Beauchamp Investigations," I answered.

It was not Dane Colfax.

"Mr. Beauchamp, this is Geneva Merrill."

"Hello, Ms. Merrill," I said.

Was she calling to tell me to expect a lawsuit?

"Mr. Beauchamp, I think I'm in trouble."

"What's the problem?"

"I...I'm afraid...oh, god, how do I even say this?"

There was a long pause before she continued:

"I'm afraid you were right."

"About your husband?"

"This is his club night, so he won't be home until late. I have to confess that I thought you were crazy earlier today, but even so, I came home from the Farmers Market and went into his private study and did a little snooping. I've found something."

"What did you find?"

"I'd really rather you see it."

"Are you at your house?"

"Yes. Can you come over?"

"I can be there within the hour, traffic permitting."

"Good. My god, I'm so...please come, Mr. Beauchamp. I...I may be in danger. Please hurry."

The line cut off.

I was out the door and down to the car in no time. As I buckled in, I called Hannah to tell her something had come up, and I might not be home for a while.

"But I have a roast all ready to go in, Dave," she said.

"I'm sorry, honey, but this is important. Go ahead and cook the roast, and I'll have some when I get back."

Reluctantly, she agreed.

It was twilight when I arrived at Geneva Merrill's Holmby Hills estate. Rather than park and walk to the gate, I drove up, and the harp-shaped doors opened immediately.

Pulling up in front of the mansion, I went to the door and rang the bell. It was opened not by Jeffries, but by Geneva herself.

"Thank god," she said, practically pulling me in. "Thank you for coming. It is our butler's day off, and I didn't know who else to call."

"That's fine, ma'am," I said. "Now, what did you find?"

"Come this way."

She led me to the door of a side room and opened it.

It was a smallish, but airy office with a large mahogany desk at the center of the room, upon which sat a computer monitor and a Tiffany lamp. A portable bar was to one side, and filled bookshelves lined nearly every wall. Behind the desk was a leather executive chair, and an expensive rug covered the floor. There were no windows in the room, and the overhead light, which Geneva switched on at the wall, offered warm, if subtle illumination.

Now *this* was an office.

"Jerry leaves his desk unlocked because he never expects anyone to come in here," she said, going to the desk and opening a drawer. "I still can't believe it."

I took a step toward her when suddenly she snapped up her head.

"What was that?" she asked, breathlessly.

"What?"

"I heard a noise. Mr. Beauchamp, are you armed?"

"No."

"Not a gun? Not even a knife?"

"No, I'm afraid not."

"Oh, that's good," she said. "That's very good."

"Why is that good?"

She pulled a revolver from the desk drawer and pointed it at me.

"Because you won't be able to defend yourself."

24.

So this is where we started, with me feeling the cold, metallic press of the gun against my head, held by a killer whose identity I had not even considered, while the events of the past week had just flashed before my eyes.

Inside my mind I heard the voice of Moe Howard, the leader of the Three Stooges, bark: *Why don't you drill a hole in your head and let the sap run out?*

It was now looking like I didn't have to go to all that effort. I was going to have a hole in my head soon enough.

All I could do now was try to stall.

"Would you mind telling me why you killed Palmer and Tony and Wilbur and all the others?" I asked. "You did kill them all, right?"

Geneva Merrill sighed and nodded.

"It's really a long story. I don't know that we have the time."

"Look, Geneva, you've been so clever up to this point but a bullet isn't very clever. It's traceable."

"Only if one is stupid enough to get caught," she replied. "I'm not stupid."

"You have proven that," I went on. "You fooled me. But the police will know the bullet came from your gun. And then there's the inconvenient fact of my body being inside your house."

"And why do you suppose that would be?"

"You asked me in."

"Did I? Or have you been stalking me, following me on a shopping trip to the Farmers Market and confronting me with crazy accusations, and then biding your time until you knew I would be here alone in the house before you made your move? I am confident Jeffries will be able to identify your body as the man who illicitly gained entry into my home by pretending to be a police officer. I am equally confident that the real police will be able to produce some witnesses from the Farmers Market who overheard you threatening me."

"I was not threatening you."

"As far as I am concerned, you were, and I'm quite confident I can convince the police that after confronting me in public, you broke into my home while I was here alone and threatened me physically. I had no recourse but to draw a gun and shoot you. After all, I am a woman of advanced years, while you look, what? Twenty, and strong?"

"I'm thirty-three," I told her.

"Really? Are you a patient of my husband's?"

"No, just good genes. But there's a flaw in your theory, Geneva."

"Oh? And what would that be?"

"I have a friend in Robbery-Homicide who knows I've been investigating your husband in regards to the murders."

Her face hardened, as best it could, having had so much work done to it.

"That is rather unfortunate," she said. "I'm confident I can work around that, somehow, but it does rather throw the stalker story into doubt. Unless I didn't know you were a private detective and thought you were a burglar. Without my contact lenses, I could have mistaken you for anyone. Would you mind if I sit down while I think this out?"

"Hey, take as much time as you need. I don't mind."

"Oh, you're very cute. But don't get cocky, Mr. Beauchamp. You have bought yourself a small extension of life, not a long-term one."

Keeping the gun raised, she walked backwards to the desk, and opened another drawer, pulling out yet another weapon.

"Come over here," she said, keeping both guns trained on me.

I did as she said.

Geneva Merrill sat in the chair behind the desk.

"Sit on the floor, beside me," she ordered.

I dropped to the floor. She put the new weapon up against my temple.

"Do you know what I'm holding?" she asked.

"My guess is it's a stun gun."

"Quite right. Have you ever been tased?"

"No."

"I'm told it's not fun, particularly when fired directly into bare skin. Would you care to find out?"

"No."

"Then I advise you not to do anything stupid, because I really have no compunction about turning your brain into jelly should you try. Are you comfortable down there?"

"No."

"Well, that hardly matters. But while I try to figure out what to do with you, why don't you tell me what you know, or think you know."

Stretch it out, dear boy, the voice of John Barrymore said inside my head. *Make ev-er-rie syl-la-bull coun-tah.*

"Well, let's see, what do I know? At first I had assumed that it was your husband who had killed the other actors, because they all died from unusual but virulent allergic reactions, and he was in a position to know what they were most allergic to, having performed cosmetic surgery on each of them. At least, that was my conjecture. I further surmised that there was really only one intended victim, which I thought was Tony Marsh, because Tony had some evidence that appeared to link your son Wesley to the Valley Slasher killings of the 1980s. The other murders, with the possible exception of the man you knew as Boris Verdugo, who was the first one to suspect the truth, I thought must have been misdirection. Innocent people being killed so Tony wouldn't be singled out by the police and a motive for his death investigated. All very Agatha Christie. Up until you pulled out the pistol and the stun gun, I assumed that your husband was doing it to protect you. But now I have to amend my suspicions, based on your admission that you had killed them all yourself, to say that he simply abetted you by providing you with information. How am I doing?"

"Surprisingly well," she responded. "Not a hundred percent, but certainly on the right track. Your biggest misstep is the assumption that Jerry had anything to do with any of this. He knows nothing."

"Really?"

"Really. I had access to his files, particularly the ones that contained the information about the allergies. So I knew that Verdugo was allergic to rubber, that Marsh was allergic to peanuts, that Constable was diabetic, that the bubble-headed girl from that comedy show has had deadly reactions to bee stings, and that Prescott had a fish intolerance."

"Fish intolerance?"

"I visited him one night," she said. "He used to have me as a guest on his radio show. I made the martinis that night, extra dry, but with a tincture of fish oil. He went into anaphylactic shock."

"So it really *was* you Brucker saw outside Prescott's house."

"Who's Brucker?"

"The police officer who was with me when I visited your house."

She frowned, and then said, "Oh, good heavens, *that's* why I recognized that oaf. He came out to harass me as I was leaving. Am I being followed by the police?"

"He's not really a policeman."

"I see. Like you."

"I may not be a policeman, but I am a detective," I told her. "More to the point, I was a friend of Palmer Hanley's. Why did he have to die?"

"For the same reason the others did," Geneva replied, as though it was the most obvious thing in the world. "Though he did present quite the challenge, being allergic to horses."

"You killed the man you once wanted to marry?"

She glared at me in silence for a moment, then said: "I still don't know how on earth you discovered that."

"I told you, I'm a detective. How could you do it? You loved him once."

"Oh, please! What would my life with Palmer have been? Stuck in New York doing trade shows or maybe a touring company, until he decided to cash in by starting his own religion? No, Mr. Beauchamp, if I ever regretted my parents splitting us up, I have long forgotten it."

Knowing how he felt about her so many years later, I was glad he never lived to hear this.

"Besides," she continued, "when I saw Palmer at that show, he was such an old, old man. Of course, he didn't recognize me. I doubt he could have recognized himself in the mirror."

"You'd be surprised," I said. "He was sharp until the end, as well as a pretty decent guy."

"Oh, yes, a pretty decent guy who ruined the lives of thousands with that phony church of his. But it makes no difference now. I already have a pretty decent guy in my life, one who is sixty-eight years old but looks forty-eight. As arm candy goes, my Jerry is addictively sweet. But that's neither here nor there. The problem is how to dispose of you?"

I'd been given an opening to try and stretch the conversation out even further and decided to take it.

"You know, Geneva, hearing you talk about addiction is a bit ironic," I said.

"What does that mean?"

"Your foundation, built on the body of your son. How many addictions did he have? Heroin? Cocaine?"

"Oh, he had his addictions, all right. Including what is perhaps the most seductive of all addictions. For the right person, murder becomes addictive."

It took me a few seconds to absorb that.

"So the Valley Slasher was simply a murder junkie," I said.

"Yes," Geneva admitted. "Why do you think I killed the miserable bastard?"

"You...killed your own son?"

"He murdered those people who bought our house, the Baroni family. He was high on something, and actually came home and confessed. I told him he must never mention it again to anyone, ever. But then he couldn't stop. He had to kill again...and then again. He became addicted to killing. And with each subsequent murder, he got a little more careless. I realized that before long, he would give himself away and then that would be the end of him. The end of us. The end of me. So I decided to take matters into my own hands. He was already a hopeless user, so I gave him a little extra one night."

"My god," I uttered.

"My husband at the time, Edmund, Wesley's father, suspected what I had done, so I had to take care of him, too. I drugged his drink before he went out driving."

"You've raised millions for anti-drug causes, and yet you murdered your husband and your own son with drugs," I marveled.

"You don't understand. Had Wesley never gotten hooked on drugs, we would not have lost the house and he would not have committed that first gateway murder. I would not have had to kill Edmund, because there would have been nothing requiring silencing. Besides, had I simply looked the other way, how many others might Wesley have murdered? What are the lives of two miserably unhappy people compared to all of those I may have saved by taking matters into my own hands? How many countless others have been spared by never becoming addicted in the first place?"

"And you couldn't simply have turned your son over to the police?"

"And be known from then on as Geneva Merrill, mother of a mass murderer? Do you really think being the mother of a teenaged killer enhanced Lana Turner's reputation and career?"

Lana Turner's daughter Cheryl Crane had knifed Turner's boyfriend, mobster Johnny Stompanato, in the late fifties. While it did not end Turner's career, she acted under shadows and whispers for the rest of her life.

"If Wesley had killed only one person, I might have survived it, like Lana did," Geneva went on. "But a serial killer...in this business you are only as good as your last performance, and I did not want my last performance to be the one I gave on a witness stand. Instead I have been honored in Congress for my good work fighting on the front lines of the war on drugs. But then some months ago I received a letter from the Baroni son, telling me that he suspected Wesley was the Slasher. He said he believed information from the man who sold our house would confirm it. Well, that could only mean Tony Marsh. I could not allow him to destroy everything I had worked for."

"Did you know that Michael Baroni and Boris Verdugo were the same person?" I asked.

"Oh, yes. I had handwritten letters, you see. He had this way of drawing a little squiggle as the dot over the i, both in 'Baroni' and 'Boris.' The Bs were the same, too. So yes, I figured it out, but I didn't let on to him that I knew, even when I went to his home. He was caught totally unawares. I arrived with a large bag containing my stun gun and that rubber mask. I knew of his allergy because of Jerry's files. When I arrived he was wearing a bathrobe with very little on underneath, God spare my eyes. He started to go to his bedroom to get properly dressed for me when I tased him, stripped off the robe, put on the mask, and managed to drag him out to the pool."

"It must have been a challenge," I said. "Boris...Michael was not a small man."

"Do you have any idea how strong you must be to be a dancer?"

"Okay, fine. You're strong. What about Tony?"

"That was so easy. I replaced the water bottles at his table during the autograph show with ones whose necks I had coated with peanut oil. Even if he detected a slight taste, his natural reaction would be to drink more water to counteract it."

"So Boris and Tony knew, or at least suspected Wesley, but that still does not explain all the others," I said. "Why kill all these innocent people who didn't have the connection with you and your son?"

Her eyes took on a faraway look.

"Have you not been listening, Mr. Beauchamp?" she asked. "For the excitement. For the thrill. For the tingle of danger. Will I get caught? Not if I'm smart, I won't. Then comes the euphoria of having gotten away with it, but that quickly subsides, so the process must start over again. I discovered Wesley had been *right*. Murder *is* the ultimate turn-on. It *is* addictive! It offers the most natural high there is, particularly if the murder is creative, not simply the result of a common bullet or a knife blade. Done right, murder is an art. My murders were masterpieces, like completing the perfect grand *jeté*."

"You're insane," I moaned.

"I'm an artist. Unfortunately, killing you will be one of those mundane quick fixes, with no artistry. It was the same with that idiot Leach. I had to get rid of him or be exposed. It wasn't like a pure, exciting murder."

"How was Leach going to expose you?" I asked, hoping to buy at least another minute.

"I had dispatched him to find some kind of horse part—hair, or a tail, or something—and what does he come back with? The entire head! I couldn't believe it at first, but I came to like the idea. I told him it was a joke for an old friend, and made him deliver it. But then when Palmer died Jay started to put two-and-two together, so I had to silence him. It was simple poison, I'm afraid, nothing clever like the allergy murders. You might not know it, Mr. Beauchamp, but some substances used in the cosmetic surgery and implant field are quite toxic."

"What did you hold over Leach to force him into compliance with you?"

"You're sweating, Mr. Beauchamp. I can see it. You are getting nervous, trying to prolong this conversation as long as possible in hopes you can escape. Well, I'm afraid you can't. But watching you suffer is appealing, so I will tell you about Mr. Jay Leach. For years he talked to me about doing an autograph show for him, for which he was supposed to pay me but he never did. Later he became a problem. You see, Mr. Beauchamp, in addition to being an alcoholic, Jay Leach was a gambler. He came to me begging for help because he had gotten into debt with some rather disreputable moneylenders. I've been told the term 'Shylock' is now politically incorrect, so I won't use it, but they were very nasty people to whom he owed quite a bit of money. I covered his losses, foolishly, perhaps, but it prevented him from being killed. Since he had no way of paying me back, I struck a deal by which he would work off the debt to me by running errands."

"Like obtaining a horse's head and delivering it to Palmer Hanley's apartment."

"Legal paperwork, picking up the dry cleaning, obtaining horse parts, yes, whatever I required. No questions asked. But then he made the mistake of asking questions. An even bigger mistake was the idea that he could actually blackmail me."

"The police already know Botox was the substance that killed him," I said. "That will lead them here eventually."

"And if it does, I will counter with my suspicions that Jay Leach was the one behind all the killings, and that after I confronted him and threatened to expose him he stole the poison and used it to commit suicide."

"You think you'll get away with that?"

"Quite a number of us signed contracts with Leach for his autograph show that never came about. He made promises he could not keep and owed money he could not pay. I believe I could make a compelling case that, in his alcohol-addled condition, he decided killing the parties of the second part was the only way to escape being sued, or worse."

"And if you kill anyone else, they'll know it wasn't really Leach at all, because a dead man can't murder."

A momentary expression of concern flashed across her face, then faded away. "I'll adopt a different *modus operandi*, then," she said. "I may have gone through all the people with unusual allergies anyway."

"Look, Geneva—"

"Mr. Beauchamp, I am becoming bored with all this talk. I have also concluded what I should do with you. Stand up, please."

She kept the stun gun pressed against my temple as I managed to rise to my feet. Then she put the barrel of the revolver against my head, too, and slowly lowered the stun gun and stuck it against my back.

"Walk to the door," she said.

Pointing one weapon at my temple and holding another against the small of my back while keeping in step behind me would have made for an awkward position for anyone but a skilled dancer.

We made our way out of the office and through the living room, to the front door.

"Where are we going?" I asked.

"Outside," Geneva replied. "Then we're going to get into my car and drive up to the top of Mulholland Drive. It is quite a challenging drive, particularly at twilight. Have you ever driven a Jaguar?"

"No."

"I think you'll like it. Of course, I will drive back alone, you understand."

The Jag was parked beside the house.

It was silver.

Not that I needed confirmation at this point, but if I ever saw Terry Brucker again, I could tell him that his memory of the color of the car driven by Gayne Prescott's "sister" was accurate.

Who was I kidding? My chances of ever seeing "Officer Brucker" again were probably zip to zilch.

Geneva told me to get behind the wheel of the Jag.

"You're not really going to shoot me if I don't," I said, hoping I sounded confident.

She turned the barrel of the revolver out and pushed her hand against my head, then fired.

I was not hit; she had not intended to hit me. The bullet went straight in front of me. But the combination of the shock wave and the deafening sound convinced me that she would if she had to.

I got behind the wheel.

She got into the back seat and held the revolver against the back of my head.

"Um…there's no key," I told her, talking louder than usual because I couldn't hear very well after the gun went off.

A moment later a set of car keys landed on the passenger seat. I slowly took them and started the car up. Then I buckled myself in.

Safety first, after all.

"You're going to have to give me directions to Mulholland," I said.

"Turn right out of the gate," she replied. "And put the lights on. Otherwise you might drive us both over the edge."

I felt a tear escape my eye. While I had been held at gunpoint before during my checkered career as a private investigator, I had never been in a situation quite so hopeless.

I was going to die.

I didn't want to die.

I wanted life.

I wanted to live with Hannah.

Was that really too freaking much to ask?

More tears clouded my eyes as I pulled through the gate onto the street, and I struggled to suppress a sob. If I had to die tonight, I didn't want to do it crying like a baby.

I fumbled around until I found the headlight lever, pulled away, and turned right onto the street as directed.

"Give it gas," Geneva ordered.

I accelerated.

The Jag had incredible pick-up; so much so that I found myself unable to stop it in time as another car zoomed toward us in the opposite direction.

The sudden, violent stop caused by two fenders meeting each other propelled me forward, though the seatbelt prevented me from hitting the steering wheel. But it also propelled Geneva Merrill forward and into the back of my seat. I heard her scream and felt the revolver fly past my head, grazing my ear, having been wrenched out of her grip by the impact.

I reached for the gun, which had landed on the floorboard, but the seatbelt was now preventing me from reaching it!

Behind me, along with the angry cries of Geneva Merrill, I heard an electric spark.

She had fired the stun gun into the car headrest, missing me.

I could not rely on being missed a second time.

Frantically unbuckling the seatbelt, I reached for the gun and opened the car door with the other, and then dived headlong onto the pavement, landing painfully on my right shoulder.

The driver of the car that hit us was now out and examining the damage.

"Get back in your car!" I yelled at her.

Then I heard the shout: "*YOU*!"

Shaking my head to clear my vision, which had been clouded by the darkness, the pain, the fear, and the moisture, I got a good look at the other driver.

It was Miranda Love.

29.

"What are you?" Miranda demanded. "Some kind of demon sent from the depths of hell to torment me?"

"Miranda, get back in your car!" I yelled."

Now Geneva Merrill was out of the Jaguar, the stun gun in her hand.

"Look what you've done to my Jag!" she screamed at Miranda, and in a move that would have taxed a dancer one-third of her age, Geneva hand-sprung over the conjoined fenders of both cars, landed gracefully in front of Miranda, shoved the stun gun into her chest and fired.

Miranda did some pretty fancy dancing of her own before finally falling down onto the pavement.

"Geneva, it's over," I said, pointing the revolver at her. "The last thing I want to do is shoot you, but if I have to, I will."

"God…damn…god…damn…god," she cried over and over again, before collapsing onto the hood of Miranda's car.

The stun gun slid from her grip onto the street. I didn't pick it up; I merely kicked it out of her reach. I wanted to make sure her fingerprints were preserved on it.

Pretty smart, kid, Bogie said to me.

"How come you're never around when the shooting starts?" I asked aloud.

With the dangers of being tased or shot now removed, I transferred the revolver to my left hand and pulled my cell phone from my pocket. I tried to punch in 911, but my hand was shaking so badly that it took three tries.

As soon as I hit *send* a new car drove up. It was the neighborhood security patrol, I cried out for joy, at least until the driver jumped out, drew his weapon and assumed firing stance.

"Drop it!" he shouted at me.

"Nine-one-one, what is your emergency?" the operator said over the phone.

"I said drop it!"

"My phone or the gun?" I asked the guy.

"Both!" the guard shouted back.

"Nine-one-one, what is your emergency?" the operator repeated, more slowly this time.

"Sorry, I'll have to call you back," I told her.

Miranda Love now started to moan. It was a low, eerie sound.

To the security guard I said: "All right, I'm lowering both, just take it easy."

I removed my left finger from the trigger of the revolver and very carefully placed the cell and the gun on the hood of the Jaguar.

"That's Mrs. Torgesson's car," the rent-a-cop said, slowly approaching. "What have you done with her?"

"Nothing. She's right there. She tried to kill me and then she tased that woman lying on the ground."

"You're crazy."

"Probably, but she still tried to kill me, and she still tased Miranda Love. The stun gun's over there. I really think you should call for an ambulance."

"Who are you, anyway?" the guard asked.

"Someone who just escaped death," I said. "Would you mind if I sat down?"

Suddenly dizzy, I sank down to the pavement.

"Put your hands on your head, where I can see them," the rent-a-cop ordered, and I did.

Lowering his gun only a little, he walked over to the accident site. "Mrs. Torgesson, are you all right?" he asked.

"What?" Geneva sobbed. Then seeing the guard, she sprung up like a jack-in-the-box puppet and lunged for the guard. "Give me that gun!" she screamed. "I need to kill someone in self-defense."

It took the guard nearly a minute to subdue and handcuff her, a tribute to both Geneva's physical fitness and the guard's refusal to believe she could actually be a menace, at least until her angry right hook split both his lips.

After pushing Geneva face down on the hood of her Jag, her hands cuffed behind her, the guard retrieved the stun gun and the revolver and tossed both into his patrol car, then called for police backup and an ambulance. Then he came back to me.

"You can lower your hands now, I'm not going to cuff you," the guard said, through swollen lips. "I can't. I only had one pair. But Mrs. Torgesson...she was always so nice to me." He shook his head. "You think you know someone."

Sprawled across the car hood, her legs flailing futilely, Geneva screamed that all of us would pay dearly for this. She was still screaming when the sound of the first siren was heard.

It was an ambulance.

Miranda was moaning louder than ever, and had begun to regain a little bit of control over her body, but not enough to stand up. It was impossible to tell if she was seriously hurt, though her hair was standing out in all directions, like a fright wig, due to the electric shock.

The paramedics lifted Miranda onto the gurney and wheeled her toward the ambulance. The last thing I heard before they shut the doors was her voice shouting: "Call Channel Four! Tell them to send that Akoti woman to meet me at the hospital!"

By the time the first of the police vehicles arrived, Geneva Merrill had cried and screamed herself out. As she was being led to a police car, all traces of the lithe and graceful dancer had evaporated. She shuffled lifelessly like an extra from *Zombie Castle*.

I was taken to the nearest police station as well, though before being loaded into the back, I was cuffed with zip-ties. The young policewoman who fastened them on said: "Sorry to do this to you, sir, but we have to take precautions."

"I don't care, officer," I told her. "I'm alive. That's all that matters."

The ties were removed at the stationhouse, where it took more than an hour to complete my statement, with two detectives listening in.

"The Valley Slasher case?" one of them said, incredulously. "Are you sure you're okay?"

"I'm still alive. I'll see Hannah again."

"Whatever you say," the detective replied.

As I was signing the statement, Dane Colfax walked in.

"A stun gun this time!" he said. "What is it with you and women, Beauchamp?"

"Oh, jeez, Dane, do I have to go through all this again for you?"

"Eventually, maybe. I've been spending some time with Geneva Merrill. She started off by claiming you were stalking her, and that you broke into her house and threatened her, and she had to defend herself with the gun."

"I was lured to her house by Geneva herself. If you examine her phone records, I'm sure you'll find that she placed a call to me this afternoon. Speaking of her gun, did she happen to admit firing it next to my head?"

"Yes, in self-defense."

"Then why am I still alive, Dane? If I was really threatening her, why didn't she actually shoot me? Why just hold the gun up to the side of my head?"

"You'll be happy to know that I asked her that myself. She said she wasn't sure how the gun worked."

I lowered my head and laughed grimly.

"So that's her explanation for holding me at gunpoint in her car," I said. "She was forcing me to drive her to the nearest gun shop for lessons. Hey, wait, a minute. Why don't you ask her why she simply didn't tase me, if I was so threatening, and then call the police?"

The detective smiled.

"You're learning," Colfax said. "I asked that precisely, and again, she claimed she didn't know how the taser worked, either."

"She knew how it worked well enough to stun Miranda. She tried for me in the car, but missed. Then she dove for that security guard's gun."

"I heard about that, though the Merrill woman denies it. She said it was Miranda Love who dove for the guy's gun."

"Jeez, Dane, she's shining you up like Aladdin's lamp."

"Look, Beauchamp, I didn't say I believe her. Her story's got more holes in it than a screen door. But I've interrogated some gang-bangers who weren't as tough as that old broad."

"Language, Dane," I cautioned. "She's going to have a good lawyer. I'd hate to see the case thrown out because you called her an old broad."

"I'll change the subject then. Do you have any idea why Miranda Love was even there at the scene?"

That old broad? Bette Davis said inside my head.

"I haven't the slightest idea. You'll have to ask her. All I can tell you is that I am probably the only person alive who was actually happy to see Miranda Love show up suddenly."

After a few more questions, I was released and driven home, since my car was still parked in front of the Torgesson mansion. I would have to ask Hannah to take me up there the next day to retrieve it, if the police hadn't already impounded it by then.

It was now completely dark. I had failed to show up for dinner, which made Hannah nervous enough. Then watching a police cruiser pull up in front of the apartment and seeing me unloaded from the back caused her more panic. But when Hannah found out how close I had come to dying, she nearly killed me herself by hugging the breath out of me as she sobbed on my shoulder.

"It's okay, it's okay," I gasped. "I survived."

"This time," she replied, tearfully. "But what about the next time? Now that I've found you, I can't lose you! And we'll have money, Dave, from Mr. Hanley's estate, so you won't have to work anymore."

"Well, talk about it later, okay? But Hannah...you're crimping my lungs!"

EPILOGUE

The last two months have been eventful, but not dangerous, unless one wants to consider talking about marriage dangerous.

Geneva Merrill pled not guilty to each of nine counts of murder in the first degree at her arraignment. Due to her age, she had not been remanded, but due to the severity of the charges, she remained on house arrest in her mansion.

The ankle monitor must have made it difficult to do grand *jetés*.

Dr. Torgesson, who believed in his wife's innocence one-hundred-percent, was footing the bill for the assemblage of hotshot attorneys, who were offering the theory that Jay Leach had been the real killer. Under that scenario Geneva, fearing she would be the next victim, was only defending herself with that revolver and taser. Even though I knew the truth, from a legal standpoint that version of events might raise enough reasonable doubt within a jury to get Geneva acquitted.

Team Hotshot was also working overtime digging up deflective dirt on each of the victims. For some, it was easy to find. Edie Gogos had a history of drug abuse, as did, surprisingly, Gayne Prescott—a revelation that provoked a string of angry, denial letters to newspapers from Terry Brucker. The best the lawyers could unearth for Tony Marsh, though, was an old lawsuit brought by a home buyer who felt Tony had cheated him. Similarly, all Wilbur Constable could be smeared with was an attempt to help out an old friend, a comedian who had become so down-on-his-luck that he turned to pimping to get by.

Palmer Hanley provided the biggest target. He was being portrayed by Team Hotshot as a career criminal who created a phony religion to dupe and harm the public. That, however, was challenged by lawyers for what was left of the Temple of Theotologics who fought back, not on Palmer's behalf, but their own.

The question of why Miranda Love had suddenly appeared in front of Geneva's house that night proved to have a simple explanation. The photo of her that had been taken by that fan at the Hollywood Celebrity Expo, the fan she'd chewed a new one into, had been posted online, and it was terrible. The picture was so unflattering that it forced Miranda to reassess her low opinion of facelifts. Calling Dr. Torgesson for an appointment and finding him out of the office, she bullied his home address out of the receptionist and showed up at his home just in time to crash into Geneva's Jaguar.

The irony was that she did not even know Geneva was Mrs. Torgesson.

Miranda wasted little time in trying to capitalize on her participation in the sensational case, announcing that she was working with a writer and composer on a Broadway musical based on her life. In attempting to express her prediction that the show would "bring down the house," she instead told the press "the house will fall on me," which generated endless Wicked Witch of the East jokes in the social media.

Every now and then I feel sorry for Miranda.

The player in this grim drama who was far more deserving of pity was Michael Baroni. The discovery of a diary written by him revealed that on the night of his parents' murders, he had been on a sleepover at a friend's house. What seemed on the surface like an incredible, lifesaving stroke of luck came at a cost: the stepfather of his friend had taken the opportunity to molest young Michael in the shower the next morning. The boy had become so traumatized from his rape and his parents' murders on the same night that he eventually retreated into an entirely new personality, Boris Verdugo. That name, he wrote, was chosen because his avenue of escape when reality became too unbearable was re-watching his favorite old Universal horror movie *House of Frankenstein*, which starred Boris Karloff and Elena Verdugo.

Jeez, I should have been able to figure that out.

Only when Boris began to suspect Wesley Sperry of being the Valley Slasher did he come forth as Michael Baroni.

When the story of Michael's past had been published by the L.A. *Weekly*, Amber Holmes called me in tears, desperate to talk to someone, and distraught that she had not been nicer to him when she had the chance.

Since Hannah and I are just about to come into our inheritances, she is after me almost every day to give up the PI racket. It is something of a moot point, since over the last month I've turned down all but one case. That one came from Karen Robinson, who felt she was being stalked by someone. It turned out she was correct: a friend of her ex-husband's had been paid by him to frighten her.

The truth was, I was not sure what I wanted to do from now on. I had never felt entirely comfortable or secure as a private detective, but neither could I deny that, somehow, I got results for my clients. Some of them, anyway.

"What do you think, Palmer?" I asked the decorative urn that contained his ashes, which rested peacefully on a small corner table in our apartment.

There was no reply.

Yeah, sure; the only old actor who doesn't speak to me inside my head is the one I'd actually gotten to know.

Life's a bitch, kid, Bogart commented inside my head.

Jury selection for the trial of Geneva Merrill was barely underway when the phone rang at home one night and Hannah answered it. The tone of Hannah's voice as she said, "Just a minute," told me I was going to receive another update about the case from Louie Sandoval, who had been covering it for the L.A. *Times.* It was probably a good one, since Louie usually left messages for me at the office (where I still checked in, even if I wasn't actively accepting cases).

"Dave, you're not going to believe this," Louie said, a note of excitement in her voice. "It turns out that Torgesson had a hidden security camera in his office. One of the videos contained a long conversation between you and Geneva Merrill, during which she has either a pistol or a stun gun pointed at your head."

"Whoa. Did the audio record?"

"It sure did. Her entire confession, motives and all, is on the tape. It blows her self-defense theory straight to hell."

"And the D.A. has this?"

"Torgesson personally delivered it to him. He had the system installed after he found that his files had been rifled. He assumed the butler had been doing something in his office, but it was really Geneva, looking through his paperwork for information about her prey."

When will people accept that the butler never *does it*? the fluty voice of Eric Blore, Hollywood's butler supreme, said in my head.

"Torgesson discovered the tape only a few days ago," Louie went on, "and now he's thrown Geneva under the bus. He's refusing to pay for further legal fees, which means the dream team of attorneys is falling apart faster than a Tijuana high-rise. The D.A.'s hammering Geneva to cop a plea, and it looks like she might. She doesn't have a lot of other options."

"Jeez."

"But you're a hero all over again, Dave."

"What do you mean?"

"The way you come off on that tape. You've got a Smith-and-fucking-Wesson *and* a stun gun both positioned within an inch of your brain, and you're playing out the situation like a goddamn network news anchor! Shit, *querido*, I'm getting moist just thinking about the danger you were in."

I knew from experience that Louie Sandoval had an unusual, if pretty darned enjoyable, Pavlovian response to danger.

"I don't suppose you and I could, you know...for old time's sake?" she asked.

Jeez, where were all these women when I was in college?

"I don't think so, Louie. Thanks anyway."

"You haven't married Pippi yet, have you?"

"No. Not yet."

"So you're not obligated—"

"Sorry, Louie."

I heard her sigh. "Will I at least be invited to the wedding?"

"Um...well, I'd have to ask—"

"Oh, shit, Beauchamp! You can face down a serial killer with firepower in both hands, but you can't stand up to your squeeze?"

"She pinches, you know," I said, hoping Hannah wouldn't hear.

Louie laughed and said, "All right. Call me sometime."

Then she hung up.

"What was that about?" Hannah asked.

"Well, it turns out I'm playing a co-starring role in a video with Geneva that's going to send her away for the rest of her life."

"Better not be one of those naked videos."

Now that made me laugh.

I took her in my arms. "You really need to trust me more, you know that?"

Then the phone rang.

"It's probably *her* again. Don't answer it, Dave."

"It might be important."

"The machine can get it."

"You're right."

I let it go through to the machine. But after a few words, I recognized the voice of the caller.

Going to the phone I listened to the rest of the message.

It was Vince Mazetta.

"Did he really say what I think he said?" I asked Hannah, who closed her eyes and nodded.

"He said someone's out to kill him, and he needs that return favor from you," she replied. Then after a pause she sighed, "Go ahead and call him."

"That's why I love you," I said, replaying the message to get the phone number Mazetta had left.

As I punched in the number I heard the voice of Edward G. Robinson say inside my head, *I just hope you know what you're doing.*

So do I, I replied.

AUTHOR'S NOTE

As readers we have become accustomed to seeing the disclaimer, "The characters in this book are fictitious; any similarity to real persons, living or dead, is coincidental and intended by the author." Obviously there are characters in this book—more accurately, the ghosts of their personas—that are recreations of actual Golden Age Hollywood celebrities. I employ this particular conceit with utmost respect for and appreciation of these legendary actors, respect that comes from being a lifelong film buff.

One person whose name does not appear in these pages but who I must thank is Carol Sperling, proofreader and editorial eye extraordinaire. If there is a mistake in this paragraph it's because Carol did not proof it.

I also wish to thank John Betancourt and Mary Burgess at Wildside Press, two fine people who truly care about books; my son Brendan, who has the unenviable task of gauging which of my jokes or puns is too excruciating to retain; and my wife Helen, who for decades has put up with my rushing away from the dinner table, or elsewhere, because I had an idea that had to be written down.

And, of course, to you, the reader. As Bogie once said, *Here's lookin' at you, kid.*

ABOUT THE AUTHOR

Michael Mallory is the author of the "Amelia Watson" Edwardian mystery series, the "Dave Beauchamp" Hollywood mystery series (published by Wildside Press), the horror novel "The Mural" (also published by Wildside), and more than 125 short stories. A recognized film historian who has written eight nonfiction books on pop culture subjects, and some 600 magazine and newspaper articles, he also occasionally acts on television (*Mad Men, Vegas, Mob City*). Mike lives and works in the Los Angeles area.